USING LIES
AS ALIBI'S

SILK

SJM Books are published by:

SJM Publishing
P.O. Box 92757
Washington, DC 20090

ISBN: 978-0-9844477-0-1
LCCN: 2010903021
First Printing, January 2011
Second Printing, January 2014
Printed in the United States of America

Using Lies As Alibi's

NOW STOP!!!

Go to Datpiff.com and download

"Three Year Engagement"

By

William Casanova

for free!

Hey SJM Family,

I dedicate this book to anyone who continues to say **I CAN** when it comes to pursuing you're dreams and everything around you says you can't. Keep on pushing forward! We, SJM, believe that you **can**!

Silk

1

Okay ….Okay! Damn it! I'm up! I know my hatred for alarm clocks has to be very obvious; especially since you're watching me beat this snooze button into submission. I already hate getting up this early in the damn morning; then top it off; I was up until 3 am partying with William Casanova at Townsend University! Yes, I'm hung over and beyond twisted but hopefully by the end of the day, I'll be sitting on top of the world. This is the first day of my future. I've just finished nursing school, graduated at the top of my class, thank you! It's Friday August 7th. Today, I embark on my new life. This is the point in my life where, it's time to either shit or get off the pot! Shit just got real!

As you can see it's 6:30 a.m. and I'm up so called trying to get ready for my interview. It's just so damn hot in this mini matchbox sized one bedroom apartment, I can't focus. This heat/ hangover combo has my head spinning; even the roaches are sitting in front of the fan! I can't wait to get some money and move out of this little ass place. Let me stop tripping! I'm lucky to have a home. It's just that this joint is so small that if I paint it pink, it can pass for a Barbie playhouse. No joke! I can run a bath, cook, wash dishes and answer the front door at the same time. Speaking of water let me jump my behind in the shower. I'm sweating like an N.B.A. player who just finds out that he's gotten some random stripper pregnant on Twitter or from Kid Fury and Crissle on *'The Read"*.

I have a good feeling about today. I can feel it! I've got this job in the bag. Now, I just have to get there and convince them to hire my black tail. A sister was a breath away from robbing banks. Shiiitt! I was! But, I'm too scared of jail, don't have a man to play Clyde to my Bonnie, and I damn sure can't use my car for a quick getaway. While singing *"Three Year Engagement"* reminiscing over last night's performance, I began glancing over the clothes in my closet searching for something to wear. The only thing, I'm sure of is that I want to make a lasting impression. After much deliberation; I decided on a royal blue YSL pants suit. I know it's not exactly what you call professional but it looks so damn good and I look so damn good in it. Ha man! Besides, I have to get one mo' wear out of it before I give it back to Lexie. Child, we're not even gonna talk about the fact that I borrowed it from her eight months ago. What? Shut up! You know you've borrowed something before; probably what you're wearing right now. I continued to sing; for once in my life I'm truly happy.

"This is....the three year...engagement...if your girl is loose you better watch your back, if you haven't heard about me, I'm the girlfriend stealer."

While dressing, I practiced answering questions for the interview again and again in my mind. I've got to be on top of my game. No mistakes allowed. They say breakfast is the most important meal of the day and since I need all the help I can get I better prepare myself a damn good one. See, I play too much. Walking toward the kitchen, the closer I get, the more I realize that I'm fooling myself. There's nothing in here but two hot dogs with no bread, a half carton of spoiled milk and two eggs. What a feast! I'm glad that this is not a reality show and there is not a camera on my crazy butt right now. At least, only you can see me opening and closing cabinets like food will magically appear. You and I know damn well, I don't have any magicians in my family. Not an uncle, cousin, nothing. Child please! Watch this, abracadabra. Nothing! Let me boil these eggs. Let me ask you something, I have a half bottle of 5 hour energy, if I drink the half bottle will it last for at least two and half hours? Whatever!

The steam erupting from the pot where the eggs are boiling broke my chain of thought. Damn, it's already 7:30!

I better put some pep in my step before my unemployed ass misses the bus. I can't be late for this interview. This job is a game changer; it's going to make my life easier. Let me stop running my mouth and get out of here. I've got to be on that next bus in 18 minutes. I wouldn't even have to catch the bus if the raggedy piece of shit I call a car would run for longer than a week without breaking. Yeah, I got a bucket so what! Anyway, I grabbed my purse and went flying outside. I almost broke my neck and ankles coming down the stairs. The bus is coming. I can see it. It's a block away.

As I was running for the bus, the only thing I was thinking about was the fact that I couldn't miss it. I glanced over my shoulder to see how far the bus was behind me; I should've been looking ahead. Next thing I know, I ran straight into this dude. I hit him so hard that his $8.00 coffee flew up in the air, while he fell to the ground, with me landing on top of him. Coffee went flying everywhere; splashing little caffeine drops all over my suit. Shit! Now you know a bitch is heated! I haven't had this damn suit on for five minutes and already something has stained it! I don't have time to go back and change. How am I supposed to go to an interview looking like this? Shit! What a way to start the day, wouldn't you say so? Not to mention, I'm straddling some stranger at 7:40 in the morning with my ass touted to the sun and a bus full of people staring and laughing at me. I feel like a white person who just used the N word at a Jay Z concert; all eyes on me. I'm going to just play this shit off. I got up, fixed my clothes daring them to say something and looked at everyone like they were crazy for staring at me. I yelled my apologies at the dude as I boarded the bus. Made it! Barely! Whew! This is definitely a woosah moment! That was a crazy! I hope that this is not a sign of things to come. Damn, I broke my nail. I quickly got to a window and looked out at the man I'd knocked down. He's propping himself up with a silver BMW 745iL, holding his head. I crashed into him so hard I swear it feels like I chipped a tooth. Sike! I wonder if he's hurt. I hit him like Orakpo! I wonder if that's his car. Oh well! If he is, there's nothing that I can do for him now. He sure is fine though. I wouldn't mind being his reason for coming home. I've got to find a way to get these damn coffee stains out. I can't believe this.

Today's starting out on a rough note and now it's getting worse. It's only 7:50 and already it's about 95 degrees outside. But on this bus it's about 130. There are no seats. I'm standing up, packed in like a sardine with a bunch of strangers. Some who've never heard of soap and water? Others who don't believe in toothpaste and deodorant! Rush hour Gumbo! All kinds of smells; say what you want but funk and perfume don't mix. If that wasn't bad enough, I have someone's perverted ass grandfather trying to grab a handful of my butt cheeks on the sly. For real! I'm telling you, next time he's going to get introduced to the back of my hand. He tried again, and I tried to slap the skin off his face and gave him the stare of death! My stop! There is a God! Let me get off this bus before I end up on YouTube for whipping the ass of a senior citizen.

The subway is a little better. I found a seat and began mentally preparing for my interview. For some reason I felt the need to pinch myself. Why, I don't know but I did. I guess it's some type of reality check. I'm actually making some moves for myself and I'm handling my business very well, if I must say so. I spent so many years messing my life up, running the streets dealing with hustlers looking for an easy way out. Now, I'm older and understand what life is about, there's no such thing as a free ride. Everything is going to be alright! I feel confident that things are changing for the better. Can you pass me that newspaper on the seat beside you? Thank you. I began to read. After glancing over a couple of headlines I stopped. Nothing but crime and murder! People doing crazy shit to kids! Too depressing! It's never any good news in the news. It's entirely too early in the morning to be in that frame of mind. As the train is approaching my stop, I'm beginning to feel butterflies in my stomach. Then again it might be gas, since I haven't eaten anything except those eggs and that half of 5 hour energy drink this morning. That was so dumb of me! Why didn't you stop me? Everyone knows, eggs give you gas. I don't think that was a very good combination choice! I just hope that I don't get the runs or something. Oh, that would be too embarrassing.

This is it! Showtime! Here I am standing in front of Hobson University Hospital a ball of nerves; ready to change my life. Here goes nothing! Time to put on my game face! This is one of the biggest hospitals in Washington, D.C. They pay good money and have great benefits. I've got to get this job. Tilting my head back so that it was properly positioned showing an air of confidence, I strolled through those doors like I was floating on air; oozing confidence. They better get ready cause' here I come. Room 232? Where is it? It's been about five minutes that I've been wandering around trying not to ask anyone for directions. You know how it is when you go for an interview and get lost? You always seem to ask that evil, overworked, underpaid motherfucker where the office is and then they come out of their mouth with some real foul shit. Knowing that your first reaction is to cuss them out, you bite your tongue because they usually end of being your boss or shift supervisor. Fuck it, I'm just going to ask this nurse right here.

"Excuse me, can you please tell me how to get to room 232. I have an interview with your HR Department."

"Catch the D bank elevators to the second floor. Turn left and HR is the last office on the right hand side of the hallway. It's the one with the BIG RED LETTERS that say HR."

What? I know that you saw that shit! Did she just give me attitude? I uttered thanks through gritted teeth, handed her Simone's' business card from CHOW, and made a mental note of the name on her tag. Robin. See, what did I tell you was going to happen? I told you! Shade begets shade! If I ever see that sarcastic bitch again, I'm going to knock them dusty ass matted tracks out of her head. Focus! Okay, I'm back. Let's go this way; I see the sign for the D bank elevators down that hall. Here it is. Wait a minute, let me push the button. Since I've been waiting five people have joined me; a woman and her son, a white doctor and 2 nurses who are heading for the cafeteria. We all boarded the elevator. I pressed 2.

"Oh shit! This is not happening." My mind screamed or did I say it out loud.

Do you think that they heard me? You are not going to believe this! Here I am in the elevator with all of these people and my stomach is doing monkey flips. I'm about to cut loose something funky and real unladylike at any minute. I held my breath and squeezed my butt cheeks together. I'm talking super-duper squeeze. I don't know what holding my breath will do but I'm down to try anything right now. *Elevators please hurry up!* I can feel it coming. Oh no! I slammed my purse onto the floor trying to cover the sound as the fart escaped. I don't think anyone heard it but they're damn sure are going to smell it. I grabbed my purse from the elevator floor, the doors opened, and I hauled tail out of there. The little boy still inside the elevator yelled out, *"Mommy, what's that smell?"* I pretended not to hear him and kept walking; never looking back. I finally found the office; good thing the bathroom is one the way. I better run into the bathroom and make a pit stop first. You know, make sure the smell isn't still lingering. Freshen up! Its 8:45 let me hurry up. Lord, please don't let that happen while I'm in this interview.

"Hello, I'm Rhonda Washington. I have a 9:00 appointment." I stated introducing myself.

"Oh yes, you can wait in that office right there. Mr. Hughes is running a little late but he should be here shortly."

"Okay. Thank you."

"Ump Humph."

Why so much attitude this morning? What the heck happened to common courtesy? Everybody got their faces all bawled up. I know it's rough out here but damn! Smile! I strutted my way through the office with a walk that would make a seeing eye dog bark to the blind man to give him five. With all of the sharp looks, gritting and mumbling that's going on, might as well give them something to talk about. It's entirely too early in the morning for haters. While waiting in the interviewers' office curiosity began to get the best of me. My eyes began to wonder. First, I checked out the pictures and plaques on the wall, you know basically casing the joint out, hoping to get a feel for the man that would be interviewing me.

My attention is drawn to a stack of applications that are sitting atop this beautiful mahogany desk; less than a foot away from me. My tunnel vision locked in and I can't stop staring. I began to fidget in my chair; squirming anxiously. I need to go through those applications to see if there's someone more qualified for the position than me so badly its killing me. That wouldn't be right; would it? What do you think I should do? Okay, watch my back! I eased a little closer, a little closer and just as my hand was about a half inch away from the stack, my concentration was broken by the sensual smell of Versace. Why didn't you tell me someone was coming? You are one sorry excuse for a lookout! You're fired!

I looked up to find this gorgeous specimen of a man, in a six foot two frame with caramel colored skin. Trying to maintain my composure, I took the hand that I had been reaching with, and ran it through my hair; you know, trying to play it off. Slowly surveying this masterpiece standing before me, I'm beginning to feel a warm tingling feeling below my waist. He has eyes that you could get lost in, lips that make you moist and a body that made you want to sin. Have mercy! Instantly, I began to get embarrassed. Not so much because I'm getting aroused. Mostly because, I just realized that the ebony prince that's causing the heated heartbeat in my VS panties is the same man I'd knocked over this morning while running for the bus. It's him! Lord, I hope he doesn't remember me. I was moving so fast I don't think he got a good look at me. He's staring at me like I look familiar. I don't know what to do. On the real, I want to break out running instead I just eased back down into my seat!

"So we meet again?"

Damn! He remembers. From sheer embarrassment I nodded yes.

"Are you okay?" I asked.

"You didn't stay to find out."

He flashed this *I've been to the dentist my entire life smile* that made me shift positions in my chair. This man is fine as hell. I love a man with pretty teeth. I'll be damned if I let someone put a messy mouth on me; have me douching with Listerine. Yuck! No thank you! I'll pass!

"I'm so, so sorry. I was rushing to get here. Please forgive me" I pleaded.

By now, I'm at the point where I'm saying forget the interview. What's up with dude? Don't laugh, I'm serious! I mean, there are plenty of hospitals and nursing homes. If push comes to shove, I can just do private duty cases. Can you feel me? This brother makes me want to show him all of my qualifications and I don't mean nursing either. See, that's my problem. Let me stay focused!

"Shall we begin?"

I laughed to myself because I know that he's not talking

about what I'm thinking about. Part of me wishes he was.
"Sure." I answered.
Barely maintaining my composure I survived the interview. I couldn't stay focused for shit! I tried! I really did but my mind kept drifting off. *"Sex on the late"* kept playing in my mind. I'm trying to picture how his father must look. He must be a helluva man to help create this.
"Ump...Ump...Ump!" I muttered under my breath.
"Excuse me. Did you say something?"
"I said thank you for your time." I quickly answered, realizing that he'd heard me uttering groans of approval. I can't fake, the thirst is real.
As he stood up from behind that desk, my eyes are glued to his waist. It's like I'm in a trance or something. I'm trying to move them but I can't. I need to get myself together with the quickness. *"Snap out of it Rhonda, you came here to get a job not a man. Stay focused!"* Yet, I can't help wondering if what's behind that zipper is as well structured as the rest of this package. Please give me strength. I've got to get away from this man before I jump on him. He looks like he's toting something nice. I rose from my seat and began to exit.
"It's nice meeting you **again**." He extended to shake my hand.
"I'd like to apologize again for this morning. I am really so sorry!"
Taking his hand we began to shake. He stopped without releasing my hand.
"Maybe you can make it up to me?"
"How could I possibly do that?"
"Let me take you out to dinner."
Knowing that each and every part of me was screaming, yes! Yes! Oh hell yes! I replied:
"Sorry... but I don't mix business with pleasure...however, if the circumstances were different, the answer would be yes."

"Let's pretend they are different... now will you go out with me?"

"Maybe another time... another place." I flirtingly whispered.

I know he's watching so I put on my super sexy strut. Pausing for a second at the door, I said:

"Goodbye, Mr. Hughes."

Child, I gave him one of my sexiest looks. I am feeling myself and him. I know they say that you don't get your honey, where you get your money. That's the rule; baby rules are meant to be broken. I'm going to put my name all over that! Mr. Rodney Hughes will be mines. Leaving the hospital my face was overpowered by a smile. A smile that would make you think I'd just hit the Powerball for $100 million. For some reason, I feel like I have; right now I feel like a schoolgirl with her first crush.

All the way home I was totally oblivious to everything around me. I'm caught up in the rapture of my imagination; thinking about wild shit like how our children would look. Who would be my bridesmaids? What he'd be like in bed? What would his mouth feel like against my special place? I know that's a bit much, the man had only asked me to dinner, so what! This is my story and my life. Now I have to begin plotting on how I'm going to pull it off. I've got to have that man! Okay! If, no, when I get the job, the first thing to do is to find out what our work relationship will be. If he's my boss, or supervisor, it's simply out of the question. I don't care how fine he is! I'm not going there. If I don't get the job I won't call his black ass at all. However, when I do get the job and I find out that he has nothing to do with my daily duties, I'll just call him and take him up on his offer. Watch me! Which reminds me, I've got to program his phone number into my iPhone. I want to be able to pull it up and call that ass ASAP. Damn! Missed my stop! See, running my mouth with you! I started ringing the bell frantically.

The driver snapped that he'd heard me the first five times as he pulled the bus over to stop. Normally, I would give him a piece of my mind. Not today! I'm too busy day dreaming about Rodney to even reply. I refuse to let anyone spoil my moment. I just put back on my Beats headphones and tuned back into Teia Hill *"The Date Whisperer"*, exited the bus and began my journey home. By missing my stop I've added six blocks to my walk. Why walk them with an attitude, right? Besides, I'm right in front of Levi's, so I might as well get something to eat. We both know that my refrigerator is on E for empty. The roaches are even beefing with me about grocery shopping. They keep leaving me post-it notes with the word *food* spelled in crumbs and shit but I'm doing the best I can. I don't remember inviting them over my house anyway! They act like they can't understand that it's a recession and they're chipping in on the rent or something. The only thing that can be even considered luxurious in my house is cable and that's bootlegged. What? You act like I'm the only one! I'm going to start paying as soon as I get out of the hole. You better not tell on me either. It's rough out here! I stopped by the Literary Joint Book Lounge and copped a copy of *"Charde's Destiny"*. I've been hearing so much about the book and they say the girl sleighed the soundtrack.

Soon as I hit the door, I took off all of my clothes, put on some boxers and a t-shirt and flopped across the sofa. Then I turned both of the fans I had sitting on the coffee table towards me. This is as close as I get to a/c. Don't judge me! If I do a little digging I know you have some secrets as well. Where is that remote? Oh here it is. After finding the remote control, I started flicking channels, finally tuning in to watch Maury. Maury is baby mama central; the place where everyone is a million percent sure; knowing that they've slept with half of the city. I should watch *"The Haves and Have Not's"* that I recorded. Tyler and Oprah did that! Yes honey, Ms. Candice is everything! Naw, fuck that! That show makes me mad. The dogs are living better than me. Yeah, I'm hating and what? Between eating my fish sandwich and one of favorite shows *Paternity Court*, I fell asleep. Awakened to my preset recording of *Queen Latifah*, by my soon to be cut-off telephone.

"Hello."

"Hello. May I speak to Rhonda Washington?"

"Who's calling?" I asked disguising my voice; thinking it might be a bill collector.

"This is Mrs. Willis, from Hobson University Hospital."

"Yes, this is she!" I replied chipper as hell; trying to sound awake.

"Hi, Ms. Washington…how are you this afternoon?"

"Fine thanks for asking…and yourself?" I asked trying to sound both awake and professional at the same time.

"I'm blessed thanks for asking. I also have something to say that I hope you will find to be great. We'd like to offer you a position with our hospital. Would you be interested?" Mrs. Willis replied.

"Yes!"

"Will you be able to attend an orientation this Friday at 10 a.m.? You will be receiving a formal offer letter and other forms in the mail probably by tomorrow. If you have computer access, I would recommend that you complete the forms and watch online orientation video before arriving however if you can't just arrive at least one hour early. Also, you are required to watch our orientation video and update your shots because you have to work so closely with the patients."

"Yes ma'am, I'll take care of everything and I will be there. Excuse me, how much did you say this position pays again?"

"It pays $20.25 per hour, 80 hours, and includes possible overtime and a full benefits package. You will be required to work every other weekend and holiday, is that okay?"

"Yes ma'am! I will be there with bells on."

"Congratulations. See you then."

"Have a great day!"

$20.25 an hour! Did you hear that? She said $20.25! That's the most money I've ever made on a job in my life! I'm rich! I'm rich! Oh yeah! I got some benefits! I got some benefits! What's my name? Wiping at the tears forming in the wells of my eyes, I kissed the receiver before hanging up the phone. I jumped up and down on the couch for about five minutes giving thanks for the blessing. Immediately, I picked the phone up again and called my mother to tell her the news. I want her to tell all those old nosey ass busy bodies that said I would be pregnant by fifteen, to kiss my well you know the rest. I'm working for one of the greatest hospitals in D.C. Thank you! Also, tell those old bitches that they are paying for me to go back to school in the fall to become a RN. I'm running this! I turned on MTV Jams and my joint was on! I turned up Seven Streeter and Chris Brown *"Won't Stop"* and danced around my matchbox.

The rest of the week I ran around getting ready; preparing myself mentally and physically for work. I bought uniforms, got all of my required shots, completed my paperwork, worked on a budget, and learned to sleep at night instead of all day. You know, how it is when you have no place to go. I hadn't realized how lazy I've gotten. Unemployment brought all of the trifling ways up outta of me. Uh huh! See! I know damn well that ain't what I think it is! You see this shit? Chicken bones! I have chicken wing bones under my sofa. Now you know that makes no damn sense! I have to get back to reality, quick! This ten-month period of unemployment has made me lose my God given common sense. I've done more in three days, than I have in the last five months.

Finally, it's Friday. I'm sitting in the Human Resources office waiting to be called for orientation, I'm extremely excited. Maybe I'm a little too damn excited. I can't tell if it's the job or Rodney. Nervously, I adjusted my form-fitting hunter green Betty Johnson dress. Suddenly, my heartbeat began to accelerate. It's him! It's Rodney. He's standing no less than ten feet away from me and coming closer. I thought that I would be prepared for this. This man is so fine, my mind is blank.

"Congratulations. I see you got the job?"

"Yes." I nervously replied as I smoothed down the back of my hair.

A lot of people tell me that I look like a chocolate Rihanna, the singer. I even cut my hair like hers. I wonder does he think so.

"Nice suit."

"Thank you…but it could never look as good as that dress you're wearing today…
I began to blush.
… Rhonda…?"
Ooh! He remembers my name.

"Yes?" I purred.

"Have you thought about my offer?"
A loud voice rang out across the office just in time to interrupt our conversation. Thank you Jesus!

"Rhonda Washington!"
Saved in the nick of time I thought as I stood to leave.

"Maybe I'll see you soon."

"You will, sooner than you think."

What is that supposed to mean? I swear my knees are so weak I just know that at any moment they're going to buckle right under me. This man turns me the hell on; you hear me! He's made my panties moist again!

Orientation went well. We learned our way through the hospital, got our first schedules, and enjoyed a banging complimentary lunch. We were free to go by one o'clock. I'm on the morning shift so my schedule will be 7 a.m. to 3 p.m., Tuesday through Saturday this week. I really want to see Rodney before I leave. I know it's crazy but I have to see him again. I've got to think of an excuse to go to Human Resources. I got it! My employee badge! Rushing to the office I thought of several ways to accept Rodney's' offer. I mean why not? He has nothing to do with my job. Right? Good men are hard to find especially fine ones with a BMW, a job, and a 401k. Where's that office? My internal GPS lead me to the HR office like I've been working here for years. Here it is! The office was completely empty with the exception of the receptionist. The receptionist acknowledged my presence with a slight head nod. She appears to be about forty or forty-one. She put her Subway sandwich down and took a sip of Pepsi.

"Barbara... hold on for a second please...
She covered the receiver.

...Miss, they've all gone to lunch and won't be back until then. Can you come back after two please? They've all gone to lunch? Barb, are you still there?" She asked placing the receiver back to her ear.

"Thank you."

Snapping my fingers, I thought of how I'd just missed my future husband. I will see him again. You can bet your last dollar on that. This game of cat and mouse is intriguing every ounce of my being. It has the same effect as waiting to open presents on Christmas. Why is it that you always want something even more when it's not yours? I really want to get to know this man but everything inside of me is screaming *No! Don't do it!* I can't lie, I'm a little apprehensive about dating someone I work with; I've never dated a coworker before. He is just so damn fine and my body is definitely calling for him. What's a girl to do?

2

Once again it's on! It's my world. I'm the main shit stain in the Hanes, or in this case the Versace silk boxers. What do you see when you look into the mirror? When I look into the mirror I see an ebony masterpiece of a man that God has given to women, ME! I'm one fine mother fucker, if I don't say so myself! I'm blessed with a thick mustache, thick eyebrows that accent my light brown eyes, one dimple in my right cheek, a long tongue and a big toy for the ladies to play with. I rock nothing but the finest gear and make eighty plus thousand a year. No kids! No begging baby mama's! Driving a convertible BMW 750iL! Any woman would be lucky to have me. Yes, you heard me correctly! You know that y'all females nowadays are into sharing! Shit, this is the age of butt shots, strippers and jump offs! I love me a proud jump off! Fortunately, there **is** more than enough of me to go around.

When I finally made an appearance outside, everyone was sweating me. I don't know why, well yeah, and then again I do. Big Daddy has that kind of effect on them! All women love me and I can't get mad at them. I'd want me too! Women do anything for me. Especially if they give me a chance to knock the bottom out! First, I eat it up, and then I beat it up. I don't have a problem with getting an entrée before a meal. That ain't for everybody though; I ain't going like that. It's a lot of lonely women in need of some stress relieving strokes so they call on Big Daddy. I always show up for work! Shit, I get busy with mines! Ha! Ha! Ha! I'm only twenty- five years old, living like the king I am. Hell no, I ain't no drug dealer. Stop thinking every black man that has something of value is a hustler. You're right to a certain extent, I am a hustler; just not the type you think. I'm America's nightmare. I'm an educated young black man with money, a big love stick and the ability to stop a motherfucker from getting a job anytime I feel like it. I know you're probably saying, "He's is a conceited motherfucker!" You know what? You're right! I have enough reasons to be one! Don't hate the playa!

While pushing the button to turn off my car alarm, I noticed that some bird shit had stained my whip. I unlocked the car, started the engine Tyga's *"Young Kobe"* blared from the Bose system that the joint I was rocking last night on the way in. It finished and I popped in my man Jay. As he spit verse after verse from the, *"Magna Carta"* joint, I wiped down my rims until I could see my reflection. Damn, what a reflection it is! I couldn't help but smile as I started thinking about Rhonda. You remember her? Yeah, the one that knocked me over that morning. I walked into my office and there she was; I knew that was a sign. For real! That girl is fine with an ass like an income tax return! Her ass is like 2 Nerf basketballs. Every time I see her she reminds me of Gabby Moe's, *"Twerk Something"*. Speaking of Gabby Moe that *"Lately"* joint with him and Raheem DeVaughn was the shit! I wonder did she get some of those ass shots. What do you think? She got some nice tig-ol-bitties too. I can already see myself sucking those joints. And, she comes across as if she at least has a bit of common sense. She's trying to do something with her life.

I really could care less about her nursing skills; I'm more interested in her bedroom skills. Throughout the interview, I didn't hear a mother fucking word she said. I was memorized by that body. I couldn't help but wonder if she could throw that thang like a pro. The way I see it, I give her a job, she gives me some head. Sounds fair to me! It's a win/win situation. She is so fine she got me out here on some sexual harassment steeze. I ain't never done nothing like this, well maybe once or twice but I'm trying to make a hobby of it. I'm not trying to be her man, baby father, a step-father, or none of that shit. I'm looking for a re-occurring one-night stand. I just want to bang her out, put my clothes on and ROLL. I'll take a shower at home. No spending nights. No breakfast! Sunlight will never catch me still in a chicks' house; you know what I'm saying? There's not a woman out here that can say "she had breakfast with me"! Maybe in ten or fifteen years or so, not now or anytime in the near future!

I want some recyclable stress free sex! Straight karma sutra style work that's it! I'm just trying to stick and move. I can't fake with you, I am digging her a little bit but she looks like one of them high maintenance chicks. You know the kind that only fucks with hustlers and ball players. The use what you got to get what you want money chasers! Keeping it 100, wit' a body like that, she can get a little of mines. A very little! A brother has rules! Maybe she can get some gas money or something but I ain't paying no bills, getting no hairdos or buying shit from any mall. Not going to happen!

Do you think I should call first and ask if I can come and see her? Oh yeah? Well, I'm not! I think a surprise visit would be best. Besides, I already told her that she'd see me sooner than she thinks! Suppose she has some bamma ass dude over there when I get there; that would be fucked up. That would be some *"Love and Hip Hop"* type of drama. The way her eyes were glued to my pole, I doubt she has a man. She didn't think I saw her watching me but I did. She was dickmatized! I could tell that she wanted me to knock her off right there in my office. Ain't no way she has a man. If she does; he definitely ain't smashing her right! What do you think? Man, fuck that! I'm going over there anyway. I put on Casanova *"We Both Grown"*. I turned it up and cruised through the city. The girl he's singing about is the girl for me. Grown! I need her to be independent too though. Later for them label princesses! It cost enough as it is to keep me dressed. I can't dress her and me! Give me a plain Jane that's a freak and I'm alright. My money is only long enough to keep me fly. Don't judge me! I'm just keeping it real!

See, when I want something I go get it. Right now

Rhonda is what I want. If she plays her cards right I might even keep her. Shit, she'd be lucky to have a fly young businessman on the rise like myself. I know my worth! I know how hard it is to find a man nowadays! Let me break it down for you; I have it all looks, my own crib, stability, no kids, money, and ten and a half reasons for her to adore the section below my waist. I know its 10.5 reasons because I actually measured it. I got that life changing meat. Not to mention the fact, it's been mentioned that the ratio of women to men is like 13:1 ration. I'm just seizing the moment. I'm a young man and I love to feel a woman's legs tremble as their wrapped around me. Oh yeah. Have ya' climbing the walls. Three more songs played as I drove. I be doing some wild ass shit. You feel me, just enjoying life. The more you get to know me you'll see what I mean. I just hope she can handle it?

We're here! Showtime! She lives in N.E. Man Greg and I had some fun around here back in the day. Matter of fact, after I hit her off, please remind me to go over his house and get my clippers. Gotta keep the shape up fresh! What is that? Who would drive this piece of shit? You see this lil' tacky ass ride parked in front of me. Damn, I thought they been stop making those. You remember what Cole from Martin used to drive? What where they called again? Yeah, that's it! I understand why it's parked though. What year is this piece of shit, "82"? A ride like this can be hazardous to your image and health. Whoever owns this shit needs Exhibit to come back on TV and *"Pimp My Ride"* ASAP.

I made my way to her building door. Time to see what the sugar walls are like! My heartbeat quickened as I waited for her to answer. I'm getting nervous. This is unusual for me. I've done this move at least 40 times. What's wrong with me? I hit the breath spray, doorbell, and within a few seconds someone was coming down the stairs. No female has ever made me nervous before. She smiled seeing me through the window as she snatched open the building door.

"What are you doing over here? I don't believe you. Come on in."

We made our way up the stairs to her second floor apartment. Damn, she looks good! Watching that ass jiggle and bounce as she ran up the stairs confirms that at this second there's no place else I'd rather be! I swear it seemed as if she was twerking without even trying. I wonder can she stand the pressure of this pipe.

"I hope that I didn't catch you at a bad time."

"Excuse my appearance. I was cleaning up and I wasn't expecting any company. Would you give me a second to change?"

"That's alright…You don't need to change…You look good to me. I like it! Natural beauty!"

"Sure ya right!"

I studied this beautiful black woman. She's wearing an RGIII jersey wit' no bra. Gold stretch pants or leggings, whatever you call that shit, which is so tight that the camel toe has me mesmerized. I know she's not wearing any draws; not with a print like that. She was walking on the back of some white sneakers. No make-up on whatsoever and she's still fine. Looking like Rihanna's sister! Knowing that I was lying I said:

"I didn't mean to interrupt. I can come back another time."

"That's okay…. Would you like something to drink or something?"

"Something!" I replied.

"Oh yeah…like what?" she asked.

I wanted to say, *"I want you to kill that roach crawling up the wall behind you"*. But since I didn't want to fuck up the moment and can shake my clothes out before I leave I said:

"You…why do you think I'm here?"

"I don't know. You could be taking a census or something."

We both laughed. At this very moment I can tell that she isn't gonna be like the rest. After only 5 minutes of conversation, I can tell she knows who she is and what she wants. She definitely ain't looking for love or, thirsty for a relationship. Is she for real?

"So you're trying to tell me that you don't want a relationship?"

"No... right now. I'm just trying to take care of myself. I can't be an asset to anyone until I'm together. I really need a car, some new furniture, and a lot more. And no, I'm not looking for a prince to come on a white horse and give it to me. I'm going to get it myself. So when he rolls out, all he'll have to take with him are his clothes." She said.

"That's what all women say then two months later they start throwing wedding ring hints." I joked.

"Not me... I don't need a man to be happy."

"What are you a lesbian or something?"

"Why do I have to be a lesbian... because I said I don't need a man?"

"I'm just asking...don't shoot me. I think lesbians are sexy and I'd be willing to join in!"

"You play too much! Not that it makes a difference but no I'm not gay. I just don't need a man to determine my worth."

"Why are you so cold? What's wrong with a brother helping you out here and there?"

"As soon as you allow a man to do for you financially he thinks that he owns you or, that's all you wanted in the first place. It makes things too complicated."

When I said that all men aren't like that, Rhonda gave me one of those looks like, yeah right. She passed part one of the test; she's sure 'nuff independent. She's right though, she does need some new furniture. This fake-ass discount leather sofa is making my shirt stick to my back. She also needs an air conditioner. It's so hot in here, my nut's think we're at the beach. I asked if she would like to go get something to eat. When she asked me to stop past a money mover machine, she was awarded an A on part one of my test. My girl! Of course, I offered to pay for lunch if she'd pay for dinner.

"How much of my time do you plan on using up? How do you know that I don't have something planned?" She questioned.

"As much as you allow me...besides whatever you have planned can't hardly compare to what I have planned for you." I grinned in my mac mood.

"Oh really?"

"Really!"

"Let me go and change...put on something more presentable."

"Alright! I see you're watching *"Being Mary Jane"* joint. Do you mind if I change the channel while I wait?"

"Help yourself...I'm just going to jump in the shower real quick I won't be long."

As she disappeared into the back, I glanced at the photo's she has displayed. She has a lot of books. Every shelf is full except, these three particular shelves? Only two have books by two authors Zane and Wahida Clark and the third is empty.

"Rhonda, why on these two particular shelves do you only have a couple of books?"

"Those are Zane and Wahidas' shelves. They will be filled only with their books. The third is going to be filled with my cousin Karen. She's an author and that's where I will keep her books. She just signed a book deal." She screamed over the running shower water.

Um humph! I got one of them chicks. I know who Zane is! She got that Cinemax show. My mind began to picture that water caressing her body breaking my chain of thought. I sat back on the couch, flipped through some channels until I found MTV Jams and Ciara's *"Body Party"* video. She got her man on that joint. I'm about to have Rhonda singing that shit to me! I'd show her little ass something! I turned it up and must've forgotten where I was because, I started singing wit' her. Got loud too! Then Will, came on with that, *"Don't Start None"* joint. That joint be rocking like shit. Time to get this party started. I plan on having Rhonda; working like she's in a video.

"Don't quit your day job! Sike! You not Willi Will or Juvi Oso but you got a lil' flow wit' you. Maybe one day you'll give me a private show." Rhonda said interrupting my private party.

"Anytime...anyplace." I replied quickly trying to maintain my composure.

This chick is smoother than me. Almost! She looks so mouthwatering standing there in that lil' robe! It must be one of them Victoria Secrets' joints. I wonder what's under it. I licked my lips thinking how I would love to un-wrap her like a Christmas present.

"I've just gotta put on my outfit and I'll be ready."

"Bet." I really wanted to say **no you don't**. I just didn't want to seem pressed or pushy.

After about ten to fifteen minutes, she came out wearing some skintight jeans, wit' this YSL shirt tied up. Her bellybutton's pierced. She has a tattoo of a scorpion on her left breast, pretty feet and smells like a fruit basket. Damn, she's sexy! Now, we all know that skintight gear ain't made for everybody but it's sure made for Rhonda. Thank God she's not one of them bamma ass chicks. Oh yeah, she passed part two; the dress code. You'll never catch me out in public wit' a low budget, ratchet hood rat. Rodney Wayne Hughes must have a top flight chick in public. Never ever will you will ride up on me and catch me with some chicken head bitch. I admit I'm vain! Only official dimes ride in the 750. Ha man! Now, behind closed doors is something else. I'll fuck one but I won't be seen with one.

Now let's tally up her points. Pretty caramel brown skin; check! Healthy body! Her own apartment! Fly! Independent! Smooth! Good company! And, she's as arrogant as me. She's eight for eight. If she can cook and throw that thing she'll be a perfect ten. 'Cause man I'm telling you I can't stand those stiff pretty broads. The kind that don't want to mess up their hair or, should I say the horses' hair! I certainly don't have to worry about that hair stuff with Rhonda; she ain't got but that much. That's one problem out of the way. I hate a pretty, warm blooded corpse. You know, the one's that talk all of that shit but for real they're scared to rock the mic.

Then they have the nerve to be moaning like they're actually putting in some work. I call them back breakers, 'cause you damn near have to break your back just to get a nut, while they lay there hollering. Talking 'bout some whose is this? In my mind I want to say, "**Not yours**". Didn't your momma teach you that sex is a participation sport? It's like fucking a human like blow up doll. And another thing, whoever started that lie about *how you dance is how you screw* needs to be shot. I believed that shit! I've had some broads that can dutty wine and all those other nasty erotic dances in the club but once I put this pole up in them, they couldn't do none of that shit.

We went to Dave & Buster's up in Arundel Mills for lunch. We talked and she kept me laughing. Man, Shorty is cool! Before I knew it, I had put my pimping on pause. For some reason she relaxes me. I don't feel like she wants something from me. It feels strange but I like it. You know what I'm saying'? Rhonda told me all about her upbringing. How she struggled to put herself through nursing school. She's real tight with her mother and dreams of one day opening a restaurant with her. Point nine. She must be able to cook. I suggested we have a couple drinks and go play some games.

"Rodney you so crazy!" She said leaning over to take a shot on the video game.

"Crazy about you! Hold the gun like this." I instructed while stroking her arm and pressing my manhood against the softness of her voluptuous body simultaneously.

"Look Rodney, I know you've got this whole seduction thing happening' but don't try to sice me up. You don't have to fake with me. I know you're not tripping off me like that. It wasn't love at first sight. We are not about to dash off into the sunset and get married. That's okay though, because I'm not tripping off of you either. But...I do like you and enjoy your company." She said throwing a major curve in my mac game.

"So what are you saying?" I asked leaning back into my chair."

"I'm just saying don't sell me any dreams or empty promises. Keep it real with me and everything will be fine. I'm a big girl, I can handle it. No games."

"What makes you think I'm running game on you?"

"Men think that **all** women confuse sex with love, I don't. I know the difference between I'm cumming and I love you."

"Sex...we're not even having sex." I said sounding like a punk.

"Not yet."

Man, oh man! I can't believe she just said that. She's got me fucked up! I hate to admit it but she's got me a lil' intimidated. I see now that I'm going to have to find a new approach for her. I've got to switch my game up! She's got some shit with her so my work's cut out for me. I shall not be defeated. I've got to regain control of this evening.

Since we were already in the mall, after window shopping we decided to see a movie. I want to see, "*Ride*

Along". She wants to see, *"About Last Night"*. Like she'd been doing all day, once again she got her way with me; without much effort I might add. It was a good choice. That shit was hilarious!

For some reason, I want to know what makes this woman tick. She's intriguing the hell out of me. Why does she feel the way she does? She's independent without putting brothers down. I've been with her for almost five hours and she has yet to say anything bad about all brothers. You know, the way some women do? They never individualize always generalize. Even though she's been dogged by some paper thug named Patrick, she says one man shouldn't have to pay for another man's actions. To only be twenty-four, this little cutie is kinda deep. I better stay on my P's and Q's. Another thing I love is the fact she ain't got no rug rats. No Kids! No baby daddy's! No baby mama drama!

Even though initially I didn't want to see it, I must admit that I really enjoyed the flick. That joint has me feeling some type of way. It was funny as hell but felt long as shit; especially when you're trying to get to the crib and get into some freaky positions. Shit my soldier's been saluting all day long! I probably got blue balls. I gotta release this! When we get back, I'm gon' try my hand. I know that thang is probably so good, wet! I wonder what kind of panties she has on. She probably has on a G-string? I'm gon' tear her lil' pretty ass up. Man, let me get something else on my mind.

To have grown up in "The Gardens," she has a lot of class. If you don't know what "The Gardens" are, let's just say it gives the word ghetto a whole new meaning. I've dated some hood rats in my day. NO morals! NO class! The ones with no class were rich too, don't get me wrong. I now understand what it means when they say, it ain't where you from its where you at; where your mindset is at. If you think ghetto, you'll stay ghetto! As the course of the day went on surprisingly, my main objective was no longer getting into her draws. It's getting into her mind. Damn! What's wrong with me? She's totally thrown off my game plan.

"Boo, I've been with you since eleven o'clock this morning...how long before I get the dinner you owe me?"

"I'm sorry...are you hungry?"

"Damn skippy!"

"What do you want to eat...

I looked at her, then looked down to that special place below her belly button and smiled. Licking my lips.

"... Rodney for real! What do you want? I'm going to cook for you."

"I don't care. Surprise me. I think its sweet that you wanna slave in a hot kitchen for me."

"Don't break your arm patting yourself on the back, sexy. I don't want to spend sixty dollars on a meal that I can easily make for twenty... although; you are worth the sixty and then some."

"You're not making spaghetti are you?"

"No and I don't need voodoo to get you sprung!"

"What am I gon' do wit' you?"

"I don't know. What are you capable of?"

"Everything!" I bragged.

"Yeah, that's what your mouth says."

We both agreed that since her crib is so hot, we would have to invite the devil to join us, and her little brown buddies, it would probably be better if she cooked at my crib. We stopped at the grocery store for a few things for her secret recipe and headed to my house. She came in and went right to work. Reclining in my white leather chair, I watched Rhonda cook for me and I feel comfortable. No pressure! I'm not feeling like tomorrow morning when I wake up there'll be a moving truck outside, moving her shit in. I'm on cloud nine.

While eating I can't hold up my end of the

conversation. I'm too busy getting my grub on. Damn! She fixed some Jack Daniels salmon, garlic mashed potatoes, and asparagus tips. This food is hitting. She definitely needs to open a restaurant. I've got a couple dollars to invest. Point number nine is engraved in stone. I began to battle with myself. I can't put my finger on what she's doing to me but I like it. I'm also scared of it. To tell the truth, I'm almost scared to bang her. If it's as good as I think, I might want to keep her around for a minute or two. I know that she doesn't want a relationship and I thought I didn't. What's happening to me? I need some air. After deciding to go for a ride, we cruised through the city with the convertible top down. She's not even complaining about the wind messing up her hair. She changed to radio station trying to find some sounds.

"Do you have any CDs?"

"Black case on the back seat."

Out of the corner of my eye I watched her move with the grace of a panther as she moved around the car. Man oh man, she's turning me on. It wasn't supposed to be like this.

"What you looking at?" She asked with a smile on her face like she knew the answer.

"You! What kind of music do you like?"

"All kinds."

"Well, Ms. DJ… let me see your work."

She put on the remake of all remakes, *"Can I Come Over"*. I fucks wit that! Fatz killed that remake! One extra credit point! Parking on the cutoff by National Airport we sat on the hood of my car and talked. I feel like I can tell her everything. I practically did. I told her all my business. Well not everything! The scenery is fly. Mellow. I poured us a couple glasses of Moet. This is certainly not the way I'd planned it. Real talk! According to my calculations I should've had the draws five hours ago and been gone to pick up Kenya. Oh shit! I forgot about Kenya. Oh well, fuck her! She's nerve wrecking as hell anyway. Besides, I told her it was over the last time we slept together; we need to create some distance immediately. I wouldn't fuck her with somebody else's dick. That is one crazy ass broad. I'm done with her!

"It's getting kinda late and thanks to you, sexy, I didn't get a chance to finish cleaning up my apartment."

"Yeah okay! I'll take you home but it's gonna cost you."

"Oh really?" She inquired.

"Really!"

"Cost me what?"

"How 'bout you lay them pretty wet lips on me." I suggested.

"Which pair? Sike… I'm just playing but I was hoping the prices are a lil' more expensive." She replied.

She's throwing some shit in the game. Have you noticed that she calls me Sexy, not Rodney? I kinda like that shit. I've been so wrapped up into trying to regain control of the evening; it didn't dawn on me that we were back at her house. My heart's beating fast. My hands are sweaty and my throat has gotten dry. What's wrong with me? I wonder if she is one of them witchcraft women. Did she put some voodoo on me or what? Is that voodoo shit real? I shouldn't have eaten that food! We chilled a lil more then I drove her home. I didn't want to come off as thirsty.

Luck was on my side! She invited me in and we spent the night making the mattress scream. *Real Sex Episode 1.*This woman took me to another level. Baby girl, got some porn star tendencies. She's a freak with it! I tried everything I could think of but she wouldn't give me **no** head to save my life. I used every trick I knew, short of slamming her head down there but it didn't work. She put it on me, wore my ass out. Just as I began to drift off to sleep, she woke me up and asked me to leave. Fucked my head up! I couldn't help but laugh to myself. She hit me with my own move. I'm usually the one showing someone to the door. The one time I ever really wanted to stay. I was even going to break my rule! Can you believe this? I kissed her goodnight and walked off laughing while singing "*We Both Grown*" to myself.

3

Yeah, I fooled Mr. Loverman! He thought he was gonna lay up in here all night, not. This ain't the Do Drop Inn. He got some sex because I wanted him to have it; I also wanted him to have some door. Hello! I don't know why people think that because you have sex then you automatically get shack up rights. If we're gonna play house it's gonna be in ours. Not his! Not mine! Ours! Although, I must say that the sex was bomb. I sure could use a refill this morning. I swear I'm having an Elle Varner moment like a mug! My body is still tingling from his touch.

I went across the hall to my neighbor and best girlfriend Simone's' house. I had to almost beat a hole in the door for her to hear over that loud music. She's blasting *"I Love It Baby"* as she snatches open the door. That's her workout music. Child, she put that song on every damn morning and does some type of homemade workout. You can't tell her that she ain't killing it. This is pure comedy! Ghetto aerobics at its finest! The stereo is beyond loud. There's no way to explain why the bass hasn't knocked the pictures off the wall. You can't tell me Casanova ain't standing in the living room performing a concert with her. Pausing in the door entryway with her hands on her hips and a cigarette hanging out of her mouth, she waves me in. Ump, she looks like some shit.

This is very unusual for Simone. I've got to give credit where credit's due, this is one fly bitch. I call her a lil' diva! She's only five foot four and can dress her tail off. Baby girl walks the streets everyday like she's on the runway. We're not even gonna talk about the hairdos. Simone was and still is the official hair queen. Being a hairdresser, she's sported everything from dreads to being a bleached blonde. Yes, her entire outfit must be brand new every day. Head to toe! I swear I have never seen her wear the same thing twice. She says it cost to be beautiful 24/7.

So her rule for men is, no dough, you gotta go. Ha man! Not only do you have to have money, you must be very generous with it. She's going to be in your pockets like a lining. Believe it!

"What's up Miss Thang?"

"What's up good girlfriend."

"Simone girl, you lookin' kinda rough. I expected to see you in your workout gear. You must've had a long night?"

"Girl, rough ain't the word. What's up?" She asked.

"Can you do my hair? I need a hot oil treatment and a shape up. I got big plans for tonight!"

"I've got you covered sis! When do you want to get it done?"

"Now works!" I pleaded.

"Alright. Let's get it over wit'. I've got things to do. People's money to spend." she laughs.

"I hear you."

Simone's good peoples! She's saved my ass in many ways on many days. It's just some of the things she does that I don't agree with. I'm the type of person that respects other people's choices in life as long as it doesn't interfere with me. You know, judge not lest ye be judged. Simone is just cut-throat and ruthless as hell. Sometimes I feel so bad for the guys that she fucks wit'. One of her favorite sayings is, I keep my house packed with men *'cause, love don't live here anymore*, so I've got plenty of room. Now, that I can understand!

What I don't like is the fact that she's not straight up about it. She pretends to be in love with them. If I must say so, she can beat any man at games of the heart. If it was a contest I would put my money on her. She's a pro! She can cry at the drop of a hat. And, every one of them nigga's thinks she is so in love with them. It's funny as hell but it really scares me. I can't help but think that as crazy as people are today, she's gonna break somebody's heart and they're gonna hurt her or, kill her. Every day, I watch the news praying that she's not on it; found dead in the alley somewhere. Nigga's ain't playing about their money. The game has changed. You know what I'm saying? Now please don't get it twisted, I can say that about her but you can't! She can be as wrong as two left shoes and I'm going to be right there by her side. Thick or thin, until the end!

"Girl, I know I look worked-out." Big Man came over here last night. I manhandled his fat ass. Money started flowing like a slot machine! I fucked him so good that I had him chanting, Nam myoho renge kyo."

"Girl, you sick. How long are you gonna keep him around?"

"He's gonna be around for a while. Money runs outta his pockets like water from a faucet. Then again it all depends on how long I can stomach his fat, little dick ass. Fucking him is like masturbating with my pinky. Thanks to *Bedroom Kandi* I can tolerate him a little longer. He makes me sick! Those dead president's sure help me with recovery though."

"Are you ever gonna settle down? Fall in love? Get married? Don't you want that?" I inquired.

"What? Love? Marriage? The fairy tale? Honey, let me tell you something. From seventeen to twenty-two I had sex for love. I didn't get anything but a broken heart, rug burns, yeast infections and a daughter. From twenty-two to twenty-four I didn't do it all 'cause my heart was broken. I was too busy trying to figure out where I was going to live and how I would support my child alone. From now on, I spread eagle strictly for pleasure and money. In my book money is pleasure! No loot, no loving. Can I get a witness?"

"Witness!" I agreed.

We both laughed. As the warm water flowed, she began to massage the shampoo into my scalp and I drifted into thought. I guess she's right. Life is survival of the fittest. She's twenty-six. Has a seven-year-old daughter name Minyon. Minyons' father, Marvin, is locked up for attempted murder. Not to mention that she just lost her job at CHOW. Too much of her personal business was coming into the salon and the owner was not having it. The only family she has is her mother Boodie; and she's a bigger mess than Simone. That's my girl though, I call her Ma. Now she's an O.G! She got pro game! Her name speaks for itself. I know for a fact that's where she gets it from. She idolizes the ground her mother walks on. All you hear is how Boodie worked some rich hustler out of this and that. I can't fake; Boodie is a bad bitch for her age, no joke! She's like 48 but she looks 28 and her body is ridiculous. Ms. Boodie is a beast! She turns them out! I see their bond; they have been all each other had from day one; talking about the apple and the tree. Simone has to live and love doesn't pay the rent. I understand the logic, I just couldn't do it. To me it still seems like prostitution. The geography and method are just different. Right or wrong, I'm still right here helping her spend it. I really need to stop bumping my gums, it didn't bother me how she got the money when she helped me pay my rent. Sista kept me with food and from getting evicted those seven months that I was unemployed. That little unemployment check I was receiving wasn't cutting it. Falling off of my high horse snapped me back into reality quick. She's proven to be a ride or die friend to me and that's all that matters.

After she finished my hair we laughed, talked and tore into some Patron margaritas. Bottom's up! OK! After emptying the bottle, and 2 blunt's later, and we are feeling no pain. Of course Will's, *"Don't Start None"* is on repeat. You can't tell us we ain't at the Ibizu or Lotus. I'm fucked up; for real! Ooh, Simone is pissy drunk. This is so not cute! Oh oh, here comes the drama! All of a sudden, this bitch decides that this is a good time to burst out crying. Didn't the bitch read the bottle, it says *drink responsibly!*

She's started mumbling some bullshit about Marvin that makes no sense whatsoever. I can't stand a crying drunk. She's drunk and I'm drunk. She's going to blow my high. I am most definitely not feeling this! What can I do? Before I knew it, my dumb ass was crying too. For what, I have no earthly idea. We look like the ghetto version of "Pete and Repeat." I managed to drag her to the couch where she fell asleep. To be so small, her little ass is heavy. I'm gasping like an overweight asthmatic. I'm sweating and shit! Let me carry my drunken ass home! After tussling with her, I have no energy left; so I literally crawled across the hall to my house. I'm crawling because, every time I try to stand up, I fall down. My legs feel like spaghetti noodles. It's obvious that the ground is the best place for me. Whew! I made it! I fumbled with my key forever until the door had pity on me and finally opened. End of story. That's all I remember.

Next thing I know, its eight o'clock at night and Rodney's standing at my door. He said that I'd called him crying and left a message on his machine. Immediately, I became embarrassed. What did I say? I can't remember, do you? How did he get into the building? Fortunately for me, the only thing that he could make out on the message was Rhonda, house, alone and come. He picked me up off of the floor, gave me coffee, Tylenol, and put me into bed. He's cracking up. For some reason he finds this shit very amusing. I, on the other hand, can't find anything funny. I feel sick. Ugh! Ugh! Before I could make it to the toilet in the bathroom, I threw up everything inside of me all over the floor. There's a path from the bed to the bathroom, coffee included. Oh, this is so embarrassing. I know I will never see him again after this. I tried to straighten up and get my sexy back, to no avail because I spit up again. He bathed me, put on my PJ's, and laid me down. Then he cleaned up my mess, showered and joined me in bed. As I lay in his arms and tried to fall asleep, I began thinking that

I could get used to this safe feeling. He must like me, 'cause I'll be damned if I would clean up somebody's spit up. That shit would be there until they got their selves together. I might cover it up with a towel or something. I guess I'm not that mature! Would you do it?

It's been three weeks now. Everything seems to be all right. I love my job. Everybody is great except this power hungry charge nurse, Robin Green. I guess she is really trying to be all that she can, old bitch! What did I tell you? Remember the smart ass that gave me directions to HR when I came for my interview? Yeah, the one that talked to me like I was slow? That's her! She's this broken down lonely wanna-be diva in dire need of some dick and an attitude adjustment. She's mad at the world because she going to die surrounded by cats and dick-less. I hate that chick with a passion! Her daily goal is to get me fired! That's why she's an old maid in training. She keeps on checking behind me constantly like I going to steal something or kill a patient. From what I hear, supposedly she has a thing for Rodney. They went on a date once. I guess he fucked her and dumped her. I can't say I blame her. But if she puts one finger on him, I'm promise I'll chop it off. That's my man! Trust! Maybe, she suspects that I'm dating him and that's why she's sweating me like the Feds! She can act simple if she wants to! I'm two minutes off of her big forehead ass and time is ticking.

At work Rodney and I don't really see each other unless we bump into each other in the halls or cafeteria. When we do we act as though we're only co-workers. We speak and keep it moving; no long conversations. That's how I want it. I like to keep my private life private. Besides you get more information that way. Everything is falling into place. I've ordered some new furniture, got an air conditioner, and finally got that piece of car towed to a garage. Rodney cracked up when he found out it was mine. He asked me did I have a death wish. I told him that he'd better stop talking 'bout my "Benz". He just laughed. I love my car. Especially, on those cold winter mornings. At least it has heat and I'm not at the bus stop.

These three weeks have been pure heaven, as far as I'm concerned. This man has wined and dined me. Not to mention the fact that he's licked and sucked every part of my body from head to toe. Alright! Tonight we're going to see Jill Scott. I'm going to fuck his brains out when we get back. I've got my mind made up; tonight I'm pulling out all tricks. Rodney is going to lose his mind when he sees me. I'm wearing this black Gucci halter dress. It's clingy in all the right places and reaches all the way down to my ankles. I have these beat ass Manolo stiletto sandals as the perfect accent. Who's the bitch! These joints cost $1,200.00! I didn't eat for 2 months saving up for these joints.

I'm gonna get locked up tonight! The way I'm gonna be strutting in this dress has got to be a moving violation. Trust! Okay? Okay! I dashed over Simone's' house so she could put some finishing touches on my hair and do my make-up. Yes, my hair is snatched and my face is beat! It, my hair, looks as if I'm wearing a black mink hat. It has so much shine that you can see your reflection. We both went back to my apartment.

While I finished getting dressed Simone, being the music freak that she is, found her way into my CD library. Next thing I know, my house is filled with the soulful sounds of Raheem DeVaughn. He's singing songs from, "*A Place Called Loveland*". Ooh! Sing it! I love me some Raheem! Talk about mood music. I'm manicured, douched and waxed, ready for a freaky night relaxing with my baby. I'm hitting on all cylinders! Ump! Ump! Ump! That's one gorgeous man. Simone says that she's sick of hearing about Rodney; she wants so badly to see him. She better look with her eyes and not her thirsty snatch. I really would hate to have to beat her ass! I'm just kidding. Humph! No I'm not! Simone is a free agent in every sense of the word!

She'll screw anything and will play any position available from wifey to jump-off. I kept her away for a reason. The truth is what it is, if she catches me slipping best friend or not, she'll get it in. I hope this nympho doesn't make me have to kill her. I really like him.

"How did you meet him anyway?"

"I never told you?"

"No. I'm just asking because I like to hear the story. Of course you didn't."

"I knocked him down running for the bus on the way to my job interview."

"You bullshitting?"

"For real! Then to top it off, he was the one who interviewed me for the job."

"It could only happen to you."

We were interrupted by a knock at the door. Casanova's, *"Carin's Interlude"*, had just come on as I opened the door. Rodney's' eyes almost jumped out of his head. Oh, that's right! I just remembered that he's never seen me in my serious drag. Honey, if his bottom lip was any closer to the ground, he could spit shine his shoes.

"Hey Sexy." I purred.

"Damn Baby, you look so good! Turn around for Daddy; let me look at you. How you get all that up in that dress? I can't wait to get you out of it!"

We began to passionately kiss. For that moment, I forgot Simone, Jill Scott, and everybody else. It wasn't until Simone turned the music down and loudly cleared her throat that I even noticed someone was with Rodney. I think Rodney forgot about him too. Once inside, Rodney introduced his cousin Greg to Simone and me. Simone instantly became more interested in Greg once she learned he was a very successful real estate broker. Apparently, he's got the real estate game on lock.

Greg appears to be very nice. He's an average looking guy. Not ugly and not cute. He's just average.

He's kinda pudgy in a five foot ten frame with some spots on his face; like he used to have acne and he's shaven off his beard. However, he does have a pretty smile and a nice bulge in his leather pants. Brother looks like he's working with something nice. Ooh, I hope Rodney didn't see me looking. I can't help it! Let me get myself together. Greg had an extra ticket so he invited Simone to join us. Apparently his date fell through. I thought that poor Simone would go into convulsions. She wants to go so badly but can't get a baby-sitter in time, so we left. Her trifling ass would've left Minyon home alone in a heartbeat if she thought she could get away with it. Her mother used to dump her off on anybody she could, so that she could run after a man. Simone is the same way. That's just between you and me. We got into Rodney's car and started on our journey to party with Jilly from Philly. That's my girl!

"Rhonda, I've heard a lot about you." Greg said.

"I hope that it was all good."

"It was!"

"Well, that's good." I responded.

"What school did you go to?"

"What with the third degree?" Rodney interrupted.

"Just making conversation." Greg replied.

"I went to Woodson and you?" I questioned.

"Rodney and I went to Dunbar…that black and red Crimson Tide baby!"

"That's the school that they just remodeled. It's been on the news all week. Oh, so that's how you know each other?"

"No! That's my cousin." Rodney explained.

"Put some Chuck on, so we can get ready to throw down."

Rodney put in the Chuck Brown CD and we were in route to the Verizon Center. I can't lie; I got sad for a minute. I miss me some Chuck Brown, he was our

Godfather! The entire ride thus far, Rodney can't keep his free hand off of me. He's rubbing my legs, and stroking the back of my neck. At every light he wants to kiss me. I can't tell if I'm just that irresistible or, if he's just trying to claim his territory. I'm starting to feel like property in the middle of a pissing war. Do you think he saw me staring at Greg's' bulge? Ooh! I can't help myself. I have an addiction, I'm a crotch watcher! This is gonna be a wild night.

Greg and Rodney snuck some Ciroc into the show. When Rodney offered me a drink he sarcastically asked, *"Are you sure you want some?"* We both laughed. I know he's referring to the night he found me drunk on my living room floor. The show was great; we partied, and sang with Jill until we were hoarse. On the way out we stopped to take some pictures. Rodney and I took one then we all took one together. I won the coin toss and got to keep all of them. My baby bought me some roses. I'm having a great time! He really knows how to make a woman feel special. I feel like there's no other female here tonight. All of his attention is on me and that's just how I like it.

Since Rodney's too twisted to drive, Greg drove us back to Rodney's' house and got into his car. Well, well, well! Is that a black 2014 Porsche Panamera? Apparently, Greg's love for luxury must be as bad as his need for speed! Nice! Play on playa! I ain't mad at you! Now, back to business, I've already decided that tonight would be the night that Rodney gets the full treatment. Tonight has been so perfect, it seems as though it can't get any better but it will. I promise you that! I guarantee you Rodney will shed tears tonight. Watch me work. Rodney has the ultimate bachelor pad. Complete with fireplace, candles in the bathroom, a king-sized bed with mirrored canopy top, and sheer curtains surrounding it. I wonder how many women have been in this bed. He's freeing himself from his Legna E'curb sweat suit. I licked my lips with anticipation while admiring his sculptured chest. This mother fucker is fine as hell! I slipped into the bathroom, changed my outfit, lit some candles, drew a bubble bath in his oversized tub, turned on the jets to keep it warm, and loaded up the CD player. I had all of my fella's with me Luther, Teddy, the Isley Brothers, Whispers, and Charlie Wilson. When I went back into the bedroom, Rodney was already in bed and has the nerve to be drifting off to sleep. Ooh, no you don't! Wake that ass up!

"Sexy." I purred into his ear.

"Yeah baby?"

"I got something for you." I moaned kissing on his neck.

"Oh yeah? Well, give it to me then!" He said as he rose to prop himself up on his elbows.

Hitting the remote, *"Nasty You Out"*, jumped out of the speakers as I climbed atop the marble top dresser and began to do a serious striptease for him. I had on my lil lab coat, stethoscope, and glasses. This performance is about to be Caliente' and Stadium worthy! I'm about to give my own version of Beyoncé's *"Partition"* video up in here! His eyes popped open. By the time I'd slithered out of my lab coat, Rodney was out of the bed and on his feet. I stood before him in only VS "Pure Seduction" lotion and high-heeled sandals. The poor man appears to be in a trance. I have that effect on men. It's a curse! Don't hate!

Round one consisted of a body massage. I wore only my birthday suit as I rubbed him down with warm oil; our bodies shared the oils as our hands explored each other. In case you're taking notes. The Whispers were singing, *"Say Yes"*. It's time to show how this sista' works! I oiled every part of him except for his manhood. I have something else planned for that. After putting a decent amount of ice cream into my mouth, I took him in until I felt the tip of his penis massaging my tonsils as I massaged his shaft like a pepper grinder. His body jumped, he gripped the mattress, and his eyes popped wide open.

That's right, watch me! Watch this pretty bitch work! Some women don't like for you to watch them give head. Not me! Watch me! I look amazing while I give mouth hugs! While the taste of butter pecan tickled my tonsils, I took him in and out of the warmth of my mouth. I continued softly twisting and stroking the shaft while playing with his balls with my free hand. This nigga is freaking out! When I knew that he was about to cum, I deep throated his manhood and using my jaws for suction slowly pulled from the shaft up. Once it was completely out of my mouth, I blew softly across the tip. And what! His body erupted so quickly, I barrage of milky missiles came my way. Ding. Ding. Round two is over. After he stopped shaking like he was having a seizure it was time to go back to work again. To the bathroom we go. Did I swallow or spit? You a lil nosey ain't you? What do you think I did?

I had it setup so that Teddy's, *"Turn off the Lights"* would come on when I hit the bathroom switch. He bathed me. I bathed him. My body tingled with joy as I felt his manhood slide into my wetness. I rode him like a bull until my body jerked with pleasure. My back arched into a perfect semi-circle as he gripped my ass and teased my nipples with his tongue; we made waves, waves, and mo' waves. Surfboard! What! The floor was soaked. As the water drained from the tub so did the juices from our pleasure. Round three was complete.

Sometime during these last couple of weeks I've fallen hard for Rodney. I want him to know how it feels to be loved by me. Really loved by me! That's why I haven't given him any head before; everything ain't for everybody. I don't believe in putting strange dicks in my mouth; you know what I'm sayin'? I know damn well he ain't going to sleep! Oh no, ain't gon' be none of that! I stared into the mirror overhead as the Isley Brothers sang, *"Between the Sheets"*. On all fours I went, my plump wet backside inviting him in. I know that I was asking for a lot but he was up to the challenge. He gently took hold to my waist pulling me closer. He began to enter me. I looked back at him with a mischievous grin and shook my head no. Wrong hole! I'm going to give you some ass, literally. This mother fucker is scared as shit. Let me find out! I can tell he's never done this before. He's fumbling with the rubber. Poor baby! I guided him in and softly swung my hips with the grace of a belly dancer. We moaned together with pleasure from every stroke. I keep continuously squeezing and releasing my muscles as he travels in and out of my wetness; like I was doing anal kegel exercises. With every stroke my intention is to drive him crazy. His eyes are rolling up in his head. He looks as if he's going to faint. Lord, don't let this boy die on me! I would hate for the brother to die from a pussy overdose, or in this case ass overdose! How can I explain that to his mother? Maybe I'm moving too fast? I really care about this man! I know I'm alive but I swear heaven must be like this. How did I let this happen? I'm falling in love with him and I know he doesn't feel the same. I don't want to get hurt. Rodney's too damn fine and sexy to be faithful. I've gotta stop this before it's too late. After tonight, I'm going to start pulling away. I have to end this before he breaks my heart. However, I fully plan to carve my name in his heart and mind tonight! He'll never forget me or tonight!

Laying in his arms with my back to him, for some reason, a steady flow of tears began to stream down my face. Shit! Flashes of past relationships blinded me with pain. Patrick dogged me then, kicked me to the curb, and the fear that Rodney will do the same is overwhelming. I think I've made a mistake. I have to end this! It's as if the CD player was reading my mind here comes *"Somebody To Love"* Fats putting in work. Either way, I'm ending this. I fucked up! Tonight will be the last night for us. That's when he whispered, *"I love you"*, and pulled me closer placing kisses upon my neck. He's holding me so closely that I can feel his heart beating against my bare skin. His heartbeat matches mines. It's like he knew what I was thinking. Nothing can compare to this moment. He wiped the tears from my eyes. How did he even know that I was crying? I feel complete. Safe! Secure! Loved! I know I said earlier that I'm not into shacking, I changed my mind! Shut up! He asked me to move in and tomorrow, I'm moving in with him until we find a new place. What? I know you have something to say, so get it off your chest?

4

Girl, what is your name? It's a good thing that I took that half of Viagra. Yeah, young dudes use them too! Don't act like I'm the only one. I planned on turning her out but she flipped the script. No woman has ever whipped it on me like that. She was insatiable. Well, that's probably because with them it was just sex. When you add feelings to it, making love is some powerful shit. I can't lie; I was in denial about my feelings for her. I knew I liked her; I just refused to accept the fact that I was falling in love with her. But, last night she broke me down like a widow at a funeral. I couldn't hold that shit back. I had to tell her. You'd be surprised what some crucial head will make you want to confess. Before I knew what happened, I'd blurted out, "I love you". It was all over after that! I ain't ever had a back shot in my life! Real talk! 25 years! It wasn't for lack of effort; the chicks just backed out at the last minute. That shit brought me to tears. Between me and you, I was scared as shit! I didn't know what to expect. I thought I was going to rip something and she'd be shitting forever. Or, we'd end up stuck like dogs and the ambulance would have to come and get us. Eventually, I man'd up, and I'm here to tell you, ain't nothing like it. Shit, my body is still jerking. That's one secret she'll never know and you better not tell her either! I've been thinking about settling down anyway. I think I've found my perfect ten. No female out here can top that performance or her. I'm still tripping off of what she did. I knew she was a freak! I told you! I've got my own little Heather Hunter. Looking down at my baby as she slept, I know there's nothing I can't accomplish with this woman by my side.

I know that her living with me is a big step, but I need 24 hours of Rhonda. I practically broke my neck and back trying to pack her stuff up. Even though I'm helping move her shit, I still can't believe that I even asked. She won't give up her old apartment though. She says, *"If I ever start to feel crowded"*, she'll always be able to give me space. Space? Who the hell wants space when you're hurting a mattress like that? Not me! After packing, we took her bucket to the shop. I'm surprised that piece of shit even started. The mechanic told her to junk it. I agree with him but she says it's a classic and refused, so we drove to another shop.

"Baby, let me help you get a car. You don't have to continue to drive that piece of shit."
Did I just say that shit out loud? It's only been a couple of weeks and I'm already moving her in and offering to help her buy a car. Damn! I'm sprung!

"Why are you joanin' on my Benz?"
"Your what?"
"My Benz! It's a bucket to you but a Benz to me."
'"You need to get that hazardous piece of shit off of the road."
"That ain't all I need."
"Oh yeah? What else do you need?"
"I need you. Not your money."
"No...what you need is some AARP for that old ass car!"

She began to kiss me. I'm really glad she didn't call my bluff and take me up on my offer. I can't afford to help her get a car anyway. It just seemed like the right thing to say. I was pump faking like shit! When the mechanic finally came back outside, he said it would be ready in a couple of days and the bill would be six hundred and fifty dollars. For what? The whole car is not worth that much. She's determined to keep that piece of shit. It got her through school and will get her through school again when she returns. She wants to get her R.N. status.

We decided to go see Greg; he'd just sent me a text message. I haven't really seen much of him since the Jill Scott show. He's been boo'd up with Rhonda's' friend Simone. They'd exchanged numbers and have been seeing each other ever since. To tell you the truth, I really didn't like him talking to Rhonda. That was strange for me because I've never felt this way before. I know how easy she is to get attached to, and after only five minutes of conversation, she had Greg wrapped around her little finger. Jealousy was eating me up that night. That man is like a brother to me; but that night I couldn't shake the feeling that he wanted Rhonda. I know he would never cross that line but I couldn't control my jealousy.

When we got to Greg's' house Simone answered the door. She's here with her daughter, Minyon. Minyon is sitting in the middle of the floor playing a Bratz game on the PlayStation 4, Greg had just bought for her. That joint cost 400 bones. I just hope Simone ain't trying to work my partner for his loot. She better not try to take his kindness for a weakness. That's my dawg! He's one of those dedicated type of brother's; you know what I'm saying? He's a good dude. Never ever, will I let her play my partner! Now I ain't saying she's a gold-digger... you know the rest.

"Hey wassup?"

"Wassup champ? How you doin' Simone?" I asked.

"Hey everybody."

"Hi, Simone." Rhonda added.

"Hey girlfriend...girl... I hardly see you anymore. Come into the kitchen. Let's talk." Simone said.

"Simone, don't disappear with my baby."

"I'll bring her back, Rodney, I promise."

I need to holler at Greg about the situation with Simone. From what Rhonda tells me, she still has some type of relationship with Marvin, her baby's father. Supposedly, he's getting out of jail this year. I have to warn my boy. I decided it would be best to chill until Greg and I are one on one, then I'll give him the scoop. We talked about sports for a while. I got my clippers, asked to borrow his Belly of the Beast, "*Total Annihilation*" CD, and Rhonda and I rolled out.

I had to leave. Simone is getting on my mother fucking nerves. I hate the way she talks; you know wit' that project twang. She's always smacking her lips and moving her neck. She's got some shit wit' her, and something about her irritates the hell out of me. I don't trust her! I've decided to take Rhonda over to meet my mom's. This will be the first time they'll meet. She's talked with her a couple of times on the phone, yet still has never seen her. Can you believe it? Me, Romeo Rodney, taking a woman home to my mom's? Mom's still can't get over the fact that she's living with me. Me either! Shit, I still don't believe it! When my mom talks about Rhonda she says things like, "She must be a helluva woman." She is! I know my mom's is really gonna like her. She knows that I have good taste. They're a lot alike.

"Where are we going?" Rhonda asked.

"I'm taking you to meet somebody."

"Who?"

"You'll see...Just chill out...Enjoy the ride." I said.

"Well excuse me."

"You're excused."

Rhonda smacked me in the back of my neck and laughed. Then she burst out singing the Casanova, "*I Like It*". I took that as a hint that she wanted some music so, I put on latest CD by the Backyard Band. We partied with Big G, Weensey, and the BYB family for the rest of the ride to my mom's house.

When we arrived at my mother's house, we found her and Ma Wheeler sitting on the porch. They were playing cards and grooving to Earth, Wind, and Fire off of an oldies CD. Now, I know where I got my love for music. Come to think of it, there was a radio on in every room of our house all day and night. My mother's genuinely surprised to see us. She had no idea we were coming over. I think she's also shocked by Rhonda. Before Rhonda, all of my female friends were light-skinned with long hair. Or, should I say long weaves. That would be a more accurate description. It wasn't that they were all I would date, it just happened like that. Rhonda is the exact opposite, brown skin with short hair. She's a chocolate beauty. I hugged my mother and Ma Wheeler as I introduced Rhonda. In case I didn't tell you, Ma Wheeler is Greg's mother. Excusing herself, my mother pulled me aside to whisper to me that Kenya's in the house sleeping. Apparently, she'd come to my mother crying; claiming that she's pregnant by me! Say what? That bitch is lying. I'll kill her! I've got to get Rhonda out of here.

"Rhonda baby...."

"Yes ma'am?"

"Would you mind giving me and Betty a ride out to Rod and Reel? There are some things that I need Juice to stay here and take care of." My mom requested.

"Juice?" Rhonda questioned with laughter.

"Yeah honey. When Rodney was a baby he was so tiny with this big head his Daddy used to say that his head looked like a jug of juice. That's what we nicknamed him."

Everyone laughed except me. I'm having a hard time finding my sense of humor. Especially, since Kenya is inside talking 'bout she's carrying my child. I don't believe this shit. I don't want a baby with this bitch! Everything bad that ever happened to me was because of her. The last time I was with her she raped me. Yeah, I said she raped me! She gave me a whole bottle of Moet to myself and started sucking me off; after I was drunk. I didn't want to have sex with her and I damn sure don't want a baby by her. Matter of fact, how does she know where my mother lives anyway? I ain't never brought her ass over here. I can't wait til' they leave. I'm gon' kill this bitch and bury her skank ass out back! Watch me! Bet you in be on the next episode of "*CSI*".

"What's wrong Juice? You look like you've just

got some bad news or something." Rhonda inquired with concern.

"Naw baby. I'm just thinking about how much I'm gonna miss you."

"Aw! Betty ain't that sweet?" Mom's said.

"Gave me a cavity. Young love, I remember it well." Ma Wheeler joked.

"I don't know how…you ain't never been young or, in love." Mom's teased.

"Now, Sandra girl, you know I got that snapper. I've had Otis sprung for forty years. Might be some snow on the roof but there's sure as hell is a scorching hot flame in this furnace." Ms. Betty boasted with pride as they laughed and give each other five.

"Ready Ms. Hughes and Ms. Wheeler?" Rhonda asked.

"Baby, just call me Sandra or Ma."

"Yeah baby…and just call me Ma Wheeler everybody does." Greg's mom replied.

"Let's go. I'm anxious to learn all about the young lady who managed to get my Juices' nose wide open." My mom teased.

"Yeah...and I wanna know about your friend Simone, that's been practically living with my son Greg."

"I will be back as quickly as I can Rodney."

"Take your time….enjoy yourself. I will see you when you get back." I yelled.

As they pulled out of the driveway I felt like a weight had been lifted off of my shoulders. Moms be covering for me like shit! I love her! Briefly I thought about Ma and Ma Wheeler. They've been friends for forty years; since junior high. Ma Wheeler was the first friend that my mother made after moving to northwest, from down south. Mom's is still a country woman at heart. That woman likes everybody. That's why I can understand her telling Rhonda to call her Ma, and Kenya being in our house.

Opening the screen door, it feels like I'm opening the door to my future. If she does have a baby my quality of life will never be the same. Everything will change. Not to mention, I don't want a baby with this crazy ass bitch! I'm powerless in this situation, and the only way to stop her is to kill her! I can feel my anger level rising. With each step I climb, I'm getting madder. Who does she think she is, telling my mother some fake shit like this? She ain't pregnant! Every time I hit that I was strapped up; sometimes I even doubled up. I'm not saying she's not pregnant; I'm just saying that it ain't mines. Ain't no mother-fucking way! I always knew she was a lil' off. You see, this is what I get for dealing with a nut. A fatal attraction! I'm going to put an end to this shit right now! I began to sprint up the remaining steps to get to her faster.

Kenya's this chick I met at the go-go one night. The dude she used to deal with had threw a drink in her face, smacked the taste out of her mouth and left her there because, she'd let another bamma dude buy her a drink or at least that was the reason she gave me. The bamma she was with didn't actually leave, security tossed his ass out. If I had any sense I would've followed his lead and left her ass there too. But no, I had to stick my nose in other folks business. She was fine and her ass was fat so on went my Captain Save-A- Ho outfit. Everything that looks good ain't good for you. She's a dime! Believe me! Light-skinned, naturally long hair, no weave and she has these bow legs, Man, I'm telling you, the girl looks like she's been riding horses all her life. It was sad, she was crying and holding her bleeding mouth so I offered her a tissue and before long a ride home. It's been nothing but drama ever since. This is one stressful ass female to be dealing with!

She's also the one who introduced me to smoking woolies; joints of weed laced with crack cocaine. I was at her house one night lounging, drinking some Moet. She was smoking a white boy and led me to believe it was just a joint of weed. I've smoked many joints with her before but this one was different; it smelled sweet. She told me it was some red devil gunja. I never saw her roll it, so I just took her word for it. Man, I got caught slipping. Fucked around and got hooked on crack; ended up in a rehab. Just thinking about it makes me want to go to a meeting. I'm just getting on my feet. I've been clean for almost three years. She seems determined to destroy me. Once she even told me that, if she can't have me, nobody will. I thought she was joking! I see she wasn't! Why me?

As I stood in the doorway of my old bedroom watching her sleep; a lot of shit is running through my mind real quick. I don't know what to do! It's literally taking everything inside of me for me not to pick up this lamp and burst her mother fuckin' head wide open. I know I should've left her ass alone when I came home from rehab. But no, I had to tap them skins one mo' time. One led to two and you know the rest. I can't lie the sex is bomb. But it ain't worth all the drama that comes with it. This is what I get! I should've left her and her drugged up body alone. She's always blowing up my cell phone threatening to kill herself. She cut my tires. Hide in the hallway of my old apartment building til' I'd leave then she would break in my house to sleep in my bed while I was at work. That's why I hurried up and got that townhouse. Now this! How am I gonna tell Rhonda? Well, I have about one hour to figure it out. That's how long it's gonna take Rhonda to get back. I shouted:

"Kenya! Wake your ass up! Get the fuck up! Kenya! I know you hear me! You're mother fucking ass ain't sleep!"

I continuously kicked the bed until it began to rock. She turned towards me rubbing her eyes as she awakened. Then she smiled. What the fuck is she so happy about? I must've interrupted a dream or something? She's still grinning. I know in real life she can't possibly think I'm happy about this? Did she really think that I'd be ready to play Daddy? Smoking cigars and throwing a party? She needs to give me some of what she's been smoking!

"Why did you lie to my mother? You ain't pregnant! If you are it ain't mines!"

"I ain't lying! I am pregnant! I'm three months and it's yours!"

"Fuck if it is! Either you think you real slick or that I'm real dumb! I flushed all my swimmers. How are you gon' be pregnant when I used protection?"

"The last time we were together before I put the rubber on you I put a hole in it. I told you I wanted to have your baby; and now I am! So, don't tell me I ain't slick! And there ain't shit you can do about it." Kenya snapped with perched lips and the **nigga what** look of confidence.

"Oh hell no! You did what?" I asked bewildered.

"Mother fucker you can hear! You heard me Daddy!"

She leaped from the bed and spat in my face. Next thing I know, I had my hands around her throat, trying to choke her ass out! I began to slam her from wall to wall. She's swinging wildly and clawing at me trying to break my grip; fighting for her life. I can feel her windpipe crushing underneath my fist. I see her gasping for breath but I can't let go; instead I squeezed harder. Her eyes are bulging. It's like I'm having some type of out of body experience. This bitch is going to die, right here, and right now! If my little brother Coco hadn't stopped me, I probably would be facing murder charges. I know God's watching because I don't know where Coco came from. He appeared out of nowhere. He grabbed my neck from behind; chokehold style freeing her. She slid down the wall collapsing onto the floor. My hand print was etched into her skin like a tattoo. She's coughing like a chain smoker and gasping for air. At this moment I don't care about jail or anything else. How could she do this to me? As he pulled me backwards away, I took my right foot and attempted to punt her head like a football but I missed. I was trying to kick a mother fucking field goal with her head. I've never wanted to hurt anyone so badly in my life; especially a woman. I've never laid a hand on any woman in my life! This is not happening! It's a nightmare. A bad dream! Before I could stop myself, I was going after her again, this time I tried to turn over the dresser on top of her limp body as it lay motionless on the floor. Coco tackled me from behind and knocked me onto the floor. Kenya got her wind back just in time to jump up and ran out of the room.

"I'm gon' kill you bitch! I'm gon' kill you!"

I shouted as Kenya dashed out of the front door like a gold medalist. Coco read me the riot act before leaving. I went to the Mom's living room bar, grabbed some Remy, and took it straight to the head. When Rhonda returned, she found me in the living room drunk as hell sitting in a reclining chair; listening to some throwback music, Lyfe's, "*We Cry*". Crying like a bitch! I lied and told her I was upset because I'd been thinking about my father. Rhonda knew that my father had died three years ago, of prostate cancer. She didn't give it a second thought. I learned long ago, a lie is a good alibi if you tell it right. Just as expected, she went right to work comforting me. I refuse to lose her over this shit! Rhonda took me in her arms and rocked me. I cried even harder. I broke down just like a lil' bitch! This situation got me feeling some type of way. I know if that baby ends up being mines, she'll never hold me like this again. She is not going to put up with Kenya's shit and definitely won't believe that she put a hole in the rubber! Shit! Rhonda assured me that everything will be okay. If she only knew the truth! The entire ride home I didn't say a word. I want to tell her but

my lips won't move. I can't bring myself to tell Rhonda
that less than 20 minutes earlier, I had my hands around a
"supposedly" pregnant female's throat. I almost killed a
woman claiming to be carrying my child. This shit is
fucked up! I need a joint!

By the time we got home, my mind was warped to
say the least. I'm emotionally drained. Not to mention that
my ego is severely bruised due to the fact I let Rhonda see
me cry. Men don't cry! What can I do? I can't erase it. I
can't tell Kenya what to do with her body; as if she'd listen
anyway. Women's rights are some bullshit! What about
the man? What about my rights? Aren't I allowed some
mother fucking rights? I should call the police and have her
ass locked up for hijacking my sperm! Can I do that? This
whole thing is depressing the hell out of me. I took another
drink of Remy straight and eventually said fuck it!

I've decided not to tell Rhonda; I'll just wait it out.
Anything can happen! Right? Maybe Kenya will get hit by
a bus, have a miscarriage, or something. I don't care what
she says; the one thing I do know is that's not my baby!
How she just gon' make me a father? This is some bullshit!
I don't know what to do or what to think. I'm just getting
my life back on track. I've got a good woman and a good
job. I've also got this fruitcake that can't and won't let go.
You need to understand that every low point and negative
thing that happened to me, Kenya had something to do with
it. Between me and you, I didn't think I would *ever* get off
of that shit. I was gone! My father had just died, not that
that's an excuse, and I really didn't give a fuck anymore.
Drugs dulled the pain. I was a crack head in every sense of
the word. I didn't believe that I would bounce back from
that shit the way I did; but I did and now my life is good.
Just when things are looking up, here she comes with her
scandalous ass to fuck my life up again. It's my fault; I
broke one of the most important rules of sobriety; you just
don't leave the drugs alone, you leave the people alone.

5

Every since that day at his mother's house, Rodney's been acting strange as hell. He has become very protective of me; never wanting me to leave his side. Very moody! He's lost his appetite. He no longer has the desire to remind me of how fine he is, or how good his sex is; he's completely different. I don't know this man! I'm beginning to feel like a prisoner of love. He can keep saying it's about his father but I know that it's more than that; I'm not dumb by a long shot! If he wants to keep it secret and deal with it alone, then so be it. I refuse to strain my brain. He'll talk when he gets ready, and I'll be ready to listen; until then life goes on.

It's been two months and nothing's changed. Well, I take that back, something has changed, me! I'll be damn, if he's going to make me a hostage. All I've been doing is going to work and coming home. I'm tired of this home girl housewife shit. My uncle's having a cabaret tonight and Simone and I will be up in there! I'm going to get turned up! Since we're going out tonight, we went to Tyson's Corner to get some new gear earlier today. I needed a shopping pick me up anyway! Like Rodney the weather has also changed, and I was definitely in need of some new winter fly shit. I haven't treated myself since God knows when.

I really don't know how Rodney and I hit this speed bump in our relationship; but I'll be glad when it's over. He's so cold and distant now. It's getting so bad between us I'm planning my exit. Shit, the money he's been giving me to shop with I've been saving, using it to pay the rent at my old apartment, and storage fees on my furniture. As shady as he's acting, I might be back there sooner than I think. Even though I love him; mama didn't raise no fools. I'm not giving up my apartment. Oh no! I thought that once we'd moved into our new townhouse my feelings would change, they haven't. He sold his old one so that we could have a fresh start together in a home that belonged to both of us. My feelings probably won't change until we say, "I do"; if we say, "I do". Especially if it keeps going like this; I wish I knew what was wrong so I could try to fix it but I'm tired of wrecking my brain.

    Simone's here to pick me up. As I was leaving, I stopped to kiss Rodney, who was lounging in his favorite white leather reclining chair watching the game. I caught a glimpse of myself in the mirror. Damn, I look good! I'm hooked, wearing a Christian Dior hunter green leather skirt set. The skirt falls perfectly over my purple boots. And you know I'm toting the purple Celine bag that I got from Lexie. What! Fierce! I knew I couldn't afford the CD suit when I bought it but it's so fly I had to have it. If I pull a few double shifts next week and a lot of overtime, I'll break even. The suit's was too bad to pass by. The double-breasted jacket is cut so low that on me it shows much cleavage and my tattoo. Yes, I have on a good bra; girls looking perky as hell! I knew that Lexie would loan me the bag so I went for it. I'm out to get noticed tonight. With all the fine brothers that come to my uncles' cabaret, I can't look tacky. I have to be in rare form. I don't want any of them but I sure want them to want me. Simone's outside blowing the horn like she's crazy. I leaned in for the kiss.

    "Bye sexy."

    "Where are you going?" Rodney asked.

    "To my uncles' cabaret remember?"

    "I know you're gon' put a shirt on first…right?!"

    "What?" I replied.

    "You heard me… you look like you're going tricking or something! Put some more clothes on or sit your ass down somewhere…you ain't going out looking like that without me there!"

    "You must be out of your got damn mind!"

    "Naw baby, you must be out **your** mother fucking mind! You're my woman. I ain't going to have you with your titties hanging out like that in public without me."

"Yes, you call me your woman but not your property! You don't own me! You didn't give birth to me and you damn sure didn't raise me. I'm my own woman! You're just reaping the benefits."

"Rhonda, stop fucking around with me before I hurt you...go put on some clothes."

"Before you what? Hurt who? Wait on it!"

Out the door I stomped! I tried to slam the door behind me so hard it would come off of the hinges or, at least shatter the little glass window squares in the door. I can still hear Rodney calling my name; he must've lost his mother fucking mind. Who does he think he is? Better yet, who does he think I am? I ain't one of those booger bear bitches that he's used to. I'm from a rare breed; I'm from the ***Bitch Who Ain't Having It*** tribe! He ain't my father and the last time I checked, I'm a grown ass woman! I stomped my way to Simone's waiting silver CLK350. I can feel her "Nosey Heifer" senses tingling. She can sense that something is wrong. As soon as I got into her car I slam the door, and I asked for a cigarette; I don't even smoke! She's looking at me like I'm crazy. She begins to laugh and shake her head showing that she's obviously entertained by my relationship pothole. This only irritates me more! Now I understand why she uses men. After some sex, a couple of days, and a few dollars, they think they own you. He ain't bought the cookie; he's just leasing it with an option. I should have never bought a house with him. He's not my husband, that shit was so dumb. Simone can't hold back any longer, curiosity has gotten the best of her so here comes the questions.

"Girl what's wrong with you? Is your g-string riding up in your butt or something? Face all twisted up...Oh, I know...first fight. What was it money? You going out tonight? Or, was it about that outfit you're wearing with your girls hanging out? My guess is number three."

"Rodney is tripping. And why are you all up in my business? You better be keeping track of the tricks you're turning and hope that Greg doesn't find out." I snapped.

"Well excuse the hell out of me! Worry about your own hot pocket not mines! I got my reasons why I do what I do!"

"Ain't no reason....greed is the only excuse for you."

"Pump your brakes bitch!" Simone warned.

"I learned it all from you." I replied.

We both started laughing and I popped in *"Answering Machine"*. I sang along. If Rodney doesn't straighten up, this is what he will be talking too. After that, I put on TGT's *"I Need"*. I understand now what Simone means when she says "Dude's ain't shit!" I know the difference between a black man and a nigga and Rodney is doing some nigga shit! Now, I'm hopelessly in love with this fool. I know that Simone means well. It's just that I'm not the type of person to discuss my relationship problems with anyone. Especially a chick, be realistic, the closest chick to you is the one who sleeps with your man. As of right now, as far as I'm concerned, I'm single! I refuse to let the argument with Rodney spoil my night. I changed the mood by putting on my Kendrick Lamar CD. Whatever I do tonight, it about to go down! I started singing, *"trick don't kill my vibe"*. Oh yeah!

When we arrived at the grand ballroom, of the Hyatt Regency Washington, the first person I see is Lexie. C'mon with me, you've got to meet her. This is my girl! Look at her rich ass over there looking like she took a bath in a Brinks truck! Ms. Lexie Benjamin in the flesh! Yeah, that's her over there; the one talking to that fine ass dude. Yeah! That's one of her brothers, that's King. I know, he's fine as shit right? Those mother fucking Benjamin's are all of it! I wouldn't mind spending a night with any of her brothers. They all radiate money, sex, and power. King looks like he could fuck the shit out of you too! Ump, wit' his sexy chocolate, bald headed self! If I wasn't with Rodney, I sure wouldn't mind letting him inside my sugar walls. I know their reputation precedes them and you've probably heard a lot of bad things, but they are good people. The Benjamin's are just not to be fucked with; plain and simple! As long as you remember that, everything will be fine. Lexie has been like a big sister to me every since I was about twelve years old. Trust me, I've seen a lot of shit; I know what I'm talking about! C'mon let me introduce you to them. My Uncle DJ is also standing with them. Child, they have on so many diamonds, it's looking like a rap video up in here; it's a bubbler's playground. This is definitely my kind of party. G. Baker Presents sure throws one hell of an event! I'm tired of being around broke struggling ass people. If you hang with nine broke people you will be the tenth. This is my type of crowd. I know you see these thirsty ass bitches trying to catch a bubbler. I can't hate, do what you do; people are trying to make a come up.

    I haven't seen so many fine player's in one place in a long time. Simone keeps elbowing me. I'm about to back hand her ass if she doesn't calm down. She's like a kid in a toy store a week before Christmas. Do you see how she's acting? I swear I should tap her right on her damn chin. You'd think she's never seen a man before. We twist and turned our way through the crowd making our way over to Lexie and them. Lexie immediately pulled me aside and teased me about still having her YSL pantsuit and Celine bag. Yeah, the one I wore for the interview. Honestly, I didn't think she would even remember; her closet is an entire floor, no bullshit! Her damn closet reminds you of a mall inside a home! We cracked up laughing. It's nice to be out with my friends again; instead of cooped up in that damn house with Dr. Strangelove. We partied all night long. I met this gorgeous dude named, Bruce. Even though I was mad at Rodney I'm still loyal. I'm just going to hit you with the highlights and we're gonna keep this thing moving. Ooh, he's so fine! I spent most of the night with him dancing and talking. He wants to see me again so I played the game and yes I flirted but I also know that I'll never see Bruce's fine ass again. But tonight, I'm going to have fun. No matter how mad Rodney makes me, I still love my man! In a way, I think it's kinda cute that Rodney so jealous. By the nights end, I'm feeling very proud of myself, 'cause Bruce was all of it! It was *hard as hell* to watch him walk away. Damn, doing the right thing is hard as a mother fucker!

Simone's hot ass has hooked up with this dude named Chuckie; he's from northeast, over Trinidad area. As sure as you're reading this, she hopped in his car and headed straight for his home or the closest hotel. I drove her car home. On the way home, I ran through what had happened in my mind. Drama! Beyonce's "*Grown Woman*" is playing on my phone. It took me back to "*Irreplaceable*"! To the left! To the mother fucking left! When the song ended, I put on WPGC 95.5. When the first couple of songs finished, I turned off the radio and drove the rest of the way pumping Stiletto's "*Big Girlz*" on repeat cause Shaynna murdered that third verse! I pulled into the driveway, cut the car off and began giving silent prayer, that upon my return, Rodney would be either sleep or at least in a better frame of mind.

Opening the door to our townhouse, a strange odor attacked my nostrils. It's a strange sweet smell. I'm serious! It smells like some type of sugary marijuana. Rodney's still sitting in the same chair. I scanned the room. It looks the same as when I left. It's a little more crowded than when I left though. There are these two other dudes here that I've never seen the entire time that I've dated Rodney. And, they all look strange as hell; almost possessed. He looks like he's high as Cooty Brown but he doesn't smoke? I continued to scan the area where they're sitting but I swear that I don't see anything strange. Nothing out of the ordinary! I see an empty liquor bottle with three full drinking glasses. No roaches, Swishers or blunts! No kind of drug paraphernalia whatsoever! What's the fuck is going on? Rodney rises from the chair and begins to make his way to me. Does his mouth looked twisted to you? I know that I'm a little tipsy but am I fucked up or is he? I know that you can see that something ain't right! Mark my words! He grabbed a hold of my arm so hard I can feel his fingertips pressing against my veins; like he's taking my damn pulse. Next, my arm quickly starts to go numb and I snatch away from his grip.

"What the fuck is wrong with you grabbing on me like that? Don't put your fucking hands on me! Who are these people? What's that damn smell?" I snatched away.

"Why you asking me so many damn questions? None of your mother fucking business! This is my got damn house! You don't want me to ask you about your clothes then don't ask me about my friends." He barked while reaching out for one of the strangers to give him five.

"**Your house**! You must be out of your fucking mind. Oh, you're trying to play big for your little friends huh! Okay! However, last time I checked my name is on the mortgage! You know what…fuck it Rodney… just forget it!" I screamed!

"Yeah forget it then! I ain't gon' have no bitch disrespecting me in **my** mother fucking house."

"I don't have time for this shit!" I said making my way up the stairs leading to the second floor. He yanked me by my arm back down the two steps I'd already climbed. I caught my balance quickly.

No the hell he didn't just put his hands on me! Oh hell no! I sat my purse on the step and got ready to introduce him to the S.E. side. I'm about to body his bitch ass!

"Look bitch...don't walk away when I'm talking to your ass!" He shouted!

"**Bitch**... I got your bitch!...

Before I realized what I was doing, I was in *get in that ass* mode! He got me fucked up! I'm an honorary Benjamin! Lexie, Uncle Smiley, and every one of her brothers made me train to fight and shot all caliber hot balls every day! He should have checked my street resume! I threw a straight jab that snapped his head back and an uppercut that grazed his nose only because he moved just in time! I was trying to pop him right in his fucking mouth! He is in shock! He thought it was sweet; until now! His fists are bawled up like he wants to take this to the next level. This is right up my alley! Bring it! I immediately went into my bag producing a straight razor like it was time for a close up on his neck. I flipped it open and stepped straight to him, daring him to make a move so that we can make the news. He huffed and puffed while I'm posted up ready to work, skirt and all. Then he walked off! Mad as hell! His boys were mesmerized and laughing like they were watching a free pay per view. Little do they know they can get it too! I'm taking all comers! He was beyond humiliated so he kept running his mouth. You can talk but don't touch! I guess he's trying to save face in front of his boys.

....yeah that's what I thought! You better walk off!"

"Look here Rodney, I may be many things; but one thing I'll never be is **your bitch**. If you can't respect me then you don't deserve me. Somebody will pick up my shit tomorrow...Mother had you, mother fuck you and the horse your bamma ass rode in on. And, I wish anyone of your bitch ass bamma friend's say anything! I hate you! Fuck all of y'all!" I screamed as I stormed out slamming the door.

I jumped back into Simone's' car and began driving

around in circles throughout the city crying; I can't think of anywhere to go. Simone's at the hotel or wherever with that Chuckie dude. My old itty bitty apartment's empty; the furniture's in storage. I should buck a U and go back and whip his ass for showing off! I cried until I got into my fuck it mode and put on some Jeezy! Jeezy got my mind right and back focused. I might be from the trap but I damn sure ain't no rat! I'm a queen in every since of the word. I am not a blow up mattress; sleep on the floor kind of chick; so that's out! I sure 'nuff ain't up to dealing with my mother, so I called Lexie. Of course, she said that I was more than welcome to come over; so that's where I'm heading. Matter of fact; let me turn my phone off! I don't even want to hear his bitch ass voice. He can listen to my "*Answering Machine*" like Casanova says. I hate him! Tomorrow, I'll get up, go to work, and as soon as I get off that shit is coming out of storage and I'm moving back into my apartment. Yeah, sounds like a winner to me. At least I had enough sense to keep my crib. See, it's just like I was telling you; you never know when you may have to make a quick escape. I kept my options open so that I could roll out anytime and now seem as good a time as any.

To my surprise King's waiting in the doorway; he opens the door for me. I walked by memorized by the scent of Hugo Boss dancing from his body. He's always been like a big brother to me but I was little then. This is a new day! Focus Rhonda focus! He informed me that Lexie and her boyfriend Chris were already sleeping but still asked if I wanted him to wake her. I told him no because if I wake her and tell the truth Rodney would magically disappear before sunrise. I assured him that I'd be okay. Then it dawned on me, King Benjamin is alone with me. What are the chances of him being here tonight of all nights. He's has about 5 houses of his own? Either this is a blessing in disguise or a really cruel joke. He's standing in front of me with a wife beater clinging to his sculptured chest, silk pajama pants, and Gucci slippers. His body is perfect! Lord, somebody help me! Damn! He's fine, wit' his gangster ass. Right now a sister could use a true thug in my life right about now. He knew that I was staring at him and he just smiled. Lexie's brothers get so much pussy thrown at them it's ridiculous; and he already knows that he damn sure could do whatever he wants with me. Later for that little sister shit!

He took me by the hand leading me down the marble and glass hallway to the great room. I took a seat on the white sofa that sat in front of the fireplace. Aaah, sookie, sookie now! I've jumped out of the frying pan and into the fire sure. For real though, I'm in no mood for anyone trying to seduce me. Especially, somebody as fine and sexy as this! To my surprise, he's more concerned about me being upset than trying to capitalize on my obliviously bad situation.

"You alright little sis? I was here when you called so I decided to stay and see what's wrong with my baby girl. Something you wanna get off your chest....that bitch ass mother fucker ain't put his hands on you did he? It'd be my pleasure to pay him a visit!" King inquired.
I shook my head emphatically no; lying like hell.

Taking his hand began to rub my back. He laid back and I climbed on top of him; straddling his waist and laid my head on his chest. I'm telling you, that little sister title was not on my mind! I don't know where that came from, I just did it. I closed my eyes and began to cry on and he tenderly began to stroke my hair ever so gently; without saying a word. We both fell asleep. Now that's a man! A real man! I was obviously not in the right state of mind and he didn't take advantage of the situation. I wish he had of! I wanted him so bad; my wet dream had a wet dream.

While Lexies' chef prepared breakfast, I turned off the locator on my phone and called Simone from my cell, leaving her a message letting her know that I'd bring her car back when I got off. Before I left, I kissed King on his cheek and thanked him for last night. He said something to me that I'll never forget.

"When you get ready for a man that knows what to do with you let me know. I've been waiting for you to grow up. You were my first crush!"

I want to know if he's serious about what he's saying but I'm not going to ask. Then he began to kiss my neck ever so softly! I feel my toes curling inside of my shoes. His lips made his way to mines and he kissed me like he wanted to devour me. A man had never kissed me like this in my life! I just know I'm going to fall out right here. Off the no bullshit, I think I came on myself! My nipples are so hard I can poke a midget's eye out. All the muscles in my body are limp. I can't believe my panties are wet from a kiss. I need to pour a cup of ice down my panties ASAP! Let me get the hell out of here and away from this man. Ump! Ump! Ump! No lie, my mind is screaming *take your clothes off.* I could just jump on his chocolate ass and fuck all of my problems away. I know he's toting too because every chick in the hood that's had some Benjamin man meat brags about it. He's right here and I'm right here; all I have to do is throw caution to the wind. Yeah, it will be a gun under the pillow but so what. I'd ride for him in a heartbeat, and I ain't even about that life. Well, okay I am, but not on their level.

I finally managed to free myself from King's spell. I made it to work on time. I have been pretty much kept to myself all morning. A few people know that I'm with Rodney so I'm making sure to keep up my game face. I hate that these nosey ass people all in my business but in a hospital everybody knows everything. I'm going to be cordial, smile, do my job, and move my ass back home. Of course, the first person I see when I leave the locker room is none other than the wannabe charge nurse, Robin. This

bitch better lay low and stay out my way today. I don't
have time for anyone working my nerves! I have too much
on my mind to be verbally sparing with her miserable ass.
On everything, today will be the day; I'll pop her ass and
get fired. I spent the remainder of the day keeping very
busy and to myself. I played the game like a pro. I laughed
and mingled just enough for my drama to go unnoticed. My
shift is over! Free at last. I know my next actions will
change the course of my life.

Walking the winding hallways to the locker room
my spirits are slowly beginning to rise. Yeah I'm sad, but
I'm also excited about what's waiting for me around the
next corner. Who knows, it may even be King Benjamin. I
mean he's not my brother really! I'm leaving Rodney and
that's that. Fuck him! It's over! Can you see that? Over
there! What's that noise? What is that in the distance? It
looks like some sort of decorations in the area by my
locker. The closer I get, I realize the balloons read: *I love
you*! *I miss you! Rhonda & Rodney!* I stood in awe of the,
"Please Come Home" banner, choked up. I know MDH
work anywhere! He went and got my cousin Moe to design
this. My baby came around the corner walking on his
knees; carrying an armful of roses, a box of goodies from
Kyndall TyRelle' Edible Décor, an Exquisite Wristcandy
bracelet box, and begging for forgiveness with "*The Little
Things*" playing in the background. This fool is in the girl's
locker room. I forgave him mostly because I felt bad about
rocking his dome in front of his friends. I hurriedly got him
the hell out of there before we both got fired. Then I
realized that we'd left the banner. I tossed Rodney my roses
and went back in to get it. I'm glad that I did because we'd
also forgotten the balloons.

6

I've been sitting here for twenty minutes waiting on this woman. She knows she should've been ready at six o'clock; this is ridiculous! Simone's entirely too slow. Rhonda and Rodney are meeting us for dinner at seven o'clock at The Cheesecake Factory. Here it is 6:30 and she still ain't ready. She knows that it's going to take us at least thirty minutes to get there. I swear if her ass wasn't so fat; I'd leave her. Minyon has already gone to spend the night at her grandmother's. This is supposed to be our time together, and I'm spending it waiting on her to get dressed.

` "I'm ready Greg, baby. Sorry, I took so long. Gotta keep it tight and present it right for you boo. You like?"

"Is water wet? Now c'mon."

"I'll make it up to you."

"You got that right!"

"Are you gon' drive? My car is acting up."

"What's wrong with it?"

"I need a new one that's what's wrong with it. It's a piece of shit! It's almost 8 years old. I'm getting a new one fast! So, I might as well tell you now that, I'm not gon' be able to see as much of you. I'll have to snatch a lot of scalps to raise that much money. Since my credit score is not that high I'm going to need no less than $5,000.00 for the down payment."

"What kind of car is it?" I asked just playing her game."

"A Range Rover…I want a black one with black interior and my fly black ass pushing it! Let's not talk about it anymore. I want it so bad! I think it's the last step into me finally embracing my new life…anyway let's go eat, boo."

You know, Simone really thinks she's slick. Or, she really thinks that I'm dumb. One or the other! For the last two weeks, she's been throwing hints about getting a new car. Constantly whining about how much she needs a new one. I hate females that constantly ask for things, you know? The way I see it is like this, if I'm supposed to be your man then I know what you need. If I choose to get it, I will. Since we've been together, I've easily spent between ten and fifteen grand on her. For me that's not really a lot except for the fact that we've only been together for a month and a half.

Selling real estate allows me to live a very, very comfortable lifestyle. I'm not trying to brag, I'm just very good at what I do. The money doesn't faze me; it's the principle. Her methods! I ain't no trick! And, she will get what I want her to have, when I want her to have it. Let's see, in 45 days she has accumulated a white 3-piece leather living room set, a ridiculous amount of clothes for her and her daughter, a 73" DLP Plasma TV, and a PlayStation 4. Not to mention, a ridiculous amount of jewelry and cash. I do these things for her because I feel that my woman should have the very best. I know I can physically, financially, and emotionally fulfill all her needs and wants, and I intend to do so. I treat my woman the way my father treats my mother, like a queen. I'm a one woman man. I'm not a wanna-be pimp, or a broke playa. And if that woman loves me the way I love her; I'll do the rest. I'll spoil her rotten. I love the lifestyle my career has provided me. I bust my ass to get here and I believe it's my job to take care of my woman, 100%.

With Simone it seems it's never enough. I can tell she not accustomed to having things because she keeps asking for shit; like it's going to run out. She talks about how she's had so much money; yet she acts so thirsty. One thing about money, if you had it before it doesn't bother you; it's normal. But, if you've never been around it, you can't hide it. You're hands turn into cups and the begging however low key you try to be is relentless. You know, the get it while the getting is good mentality. It's obvious she's never had anyone to treat her like I do. Those other bamma's probably promised her the world; and only gave her some dick. She's going to have to realize I'm not like that! I am man who knows how to get, keep, and raise the value of the things I cherish.

She keeps asking for shit like there will be no tomorrow. I'm really in love with this woman. I just hope that the feelings are mutual. She says she loves me, she cries when I leave, and keeps my sexual thirst quenched. She's perfect! Well except for the begging. She's almost a little too damn perfect; and that's what I'm afraid of. I'm probably making too much out of this, since I'm gonna get her the truck for Christmas anyway. I went to see about one last week. All she has to do is continue to treat me right. It's almost Thanksgiving and the weather's changing. She's got to take Minyon back and forth to school, and get to and from work, I'd give her my Porsche before I'd let my woman freeze; when I know that I'm in a position to help her. You know what I mean? I was thinking about asking her to marry me on Christmas. What do you think? For real? I don't think that it is too soon. Well, I'm looking for the ring right now. Shit, I'm getting too old for this frat boy bachelor lifestyle. I want me a couple of kids and wife, somebody waiting for me to come home. It's too much shit out here that can kill you right now! With every new female it's like playing Russian roulette. I'm not dying over no spoiled kitty! These STD's today are for life! Real talk! What me and Simone have is working! I'm good!

Minyon's my little princess! If Simone and I get married; I'd like to adopt her. Every little girl needs a Daddy to protect her. I plan on being there for her, 300%. Simone says that she won't live with anyone unless she's getting married. She doesn't want to expose her daughter to someone who may be gone tomorrow; you know an unstable environment. The only man she's ever seen her with is her father, and now me. I respect that. Matter of fact, I respect everything about her. I knew she was one of 'dem fly chicks the first time I saw her. She's definitely super high maintenance. The way she put it on, you can tell she's out for attention. Dude's be trying to holla' at her all day; but she had sense enough to choose me. See, I'm not exactly a guy you would see and say, "Ump, he's fine", I know that. Don't get it fucked up; I'm not a mutt either! It just shows that preconceptions are not always right. Simone appeared to be, you know, sneaky and conniving. A hustler's trick! I know that she has a past! I also know who she is when she's with me! She's not like that at all. She's sweet and dedicated. I guess that's why I fell for her and do the things that I do. She said she's through with hustler's which was a smart move for her because I've got more money than about 5 or 6 hustler's put together. I don't know why women think that hustlers are the only ones that can provide for them. Besides, the money train derails when they go to jail; my money keeps going and going!

"'Bout time y'all got here."

"I know. Talk to your friend." Greg said pointing at Simone.

"Girl, you'd be late to your own funeral." Rhonda chirped in.

"Yeah and you better be there when I get there."

"Rhonda, you look nice tonight." I added.

"Thank you, Greg."

"Damn skippy, she looks good. That's my baby. You look nice too Simone." Rodney hurled his half-ass compliment to Simone.

"Tell me something that I don't know."

"Well, alright girlfriend!" Rhonda chirped as they gave each other five.

"Girl… come go with me to the bathroom."

"I've gotta go anyway. We'll be back." Rhonda added.

Rodney seems as though he can't wait for them to leave. As soon as they took two steps he started to spill the beans. In one breath he told me Kenya says she's carrying his baby, and that he doesn't trust Simone. What kind of shit is that? Here he has another woman pregnant, and he's trying to tell me about trust. He can't even spell trust or faithful. Rodney's my boy but he blew me with that! Rhonda has no idea what kind of dog he really is. Now don't get me wrong, I'd give up my life for him in a heartbeat! We grew up from little scrubs together. Yet, we're opposites because he likes to think with his small head first. When it comes to relationships Rodney is in it for Rodney. He's left a trail of broken hearts all over D.C. Now he's the best friend you could ever wish to have; the brother just doesn't have a faithful bone in his body. As sure as I'm sitting here talking to you, that's how sure I am that he's going to break her heart. I just don't want to be around to see it.

I know that I'm with Simone and I love my woman; but I'm still a man! Rhonda is a dime piece! Between me and you, I often wish I would've met her first. She's so beautiful inside and out! I know that she's Rodney's' girl; I respect that to the fullest. She's a good girl and I just don't want to watch him hurt her. It's going to be brutal. I've seen his work. He can destroy the strongest woman! That's why I really haven't seen much of them. Everybody's been doing their own thing. The only reason we hooked up tonight is for dinner and the Sirrah Comedy Jam at DAR Constitution Hall. Which reminds me, we better hurry up and eat so that we can get down there on time. I don't want to miss any of the show and you know somebody will sit in your seat with the quickness.

The food's great and this conversation are probably more comical than the show that we're going to. Rodney and Simone have been going at each other since we sat down at the table.

"That's okay Rodney, you water head son of a bitch! That's why your head is so big your turtlenecks are talking 'bout taking you to court."

"Hey Greg, tell the truth...her pussy so dry it's like peanut butter ain't it? Simone, you so black that you look like dull patent leather." We cracked up.

They are going hard! They remind me of Pam and Martin from Martin's show. It's a good thing that we are all friends. They continued this all the way to Constitution Hall. Rhonda and I are laughing so hard I'm crying. Rhonda keeps hollering that she's going to pee on herself if they don't stop. Man, oh man! Rodney's cutting her up; she should have never started it. I remember when Rodney and I were little; we'd have to fight almost every day. He'd cut on somebody until they got mad, or embarrassed from everyone laughing at them, then the rumble began. It's a good thing that both of us were nice with our hands. As you can see, some things never change; Simone eventually got in her feelings. The straw that broke the camel's back was when Rodney said:

"You so dusty, that your crabs are wearing night vision goggles. Greg you better strap up!"

That did it! Aw Rodney, you didn't have to go there. I know that Simone's mad but I just can't stop laughing. I can see in her face that she wants to kill him and me. I got myself together and came to her defense. It was hard to keep a straight face. She rode the rest of the way to the show with her lips poked out; mad as hell. I spent the rest of the ride trying to hold in my laugh. Simone's' face is priceless. It looks like she's been sucking on lemons all day!

The show was real tight. Funny as hell! Our people have so much talent. I haven't been to a show since Steve Harvey's retirement tour. It's nice to see us doing more than ducking bullets and getting locked up on the news. I hate the way the media portrays us, don't you? Simone was quiet most of the night; until Earthquake came on. I thought she'd fall out of her chair. That brother is funny as shit. Give that brother another comedy special, TV show, or something. Quake is from here also, repping S.E. to the fullest. I really don't care where he's from as long as he keeps telling jokes. First Martin Lawrence, Tommy Davidson, Dave Chappelle, now we have Joe Clair on the radio with Frank Ski and Earthquake taking over everything! Oh, we in the house! I got to support my people! D.C. is such a unique city; you need to have a sense of humor and think quickly on your feet to survive.

When we got home, I wanted to make love to her so bad; I started stripping at the door. I can't wait to get my hands on her little ass; nothing like some good lovemaking to end a perfect evening. Simone is a beast in the bed, she be on some Envious Libra type shit! I was set to move full speed ahead until she burst my bubble. It seems that Mother Nature has totally wiped out my plans. Like my man D calls it "*Shark Week*". I'm down with the towel move. It's not like I've never done it before but it's just not my thing. Instead, I did the next best thing; I gave my baby a hot oil massage until she fell asleep. These hands should be registered. When I was younger, I'm telling you straight up that I wouldn't have done no shit like that; I would've been ghost. Now I'm a grown ass man who understands what a woman needs. The older you get the more you learn. It's not just about pleasing yourself; it's about pleasing your partner.

The alarm woke me at seven a.m. so I can get myself ready to go show a house in Potomac. The guy I'm showing the house to owns some type of an architect firm or something like that. I swear I don't want to get up. This bed is feeling real good. That hawk is out there; it's cold as a motha' outside. Laying up with my woman is where I want to be. Who am I fooling? Let me get my ass up. This is a two million dollar house; nothing feels that good. Good enough to pass up that kind of commission? No kitty in the world is that good. I jumped out of bed like someone had just stuck a pin in me, cranked up my man Wiz Khalifah and prepared myself for the paper chase.

While I showered, Simone fixed me breakfast. She's cooked all of my favorites: cheese eggs, fried potatoes, toast, and turkey bacon. She knows that I don't indulge in pork and she respects that. See, that's what I'm talking 'bout! She got up at seven on a Saturday morning to fix me breakfast when she has nowhere to be until one o'clock. She's always doing stuff like that. That's how a woman is supposed to treat her man; like a king.

Warming up my Porsche, I put on my Fatz "*Just Because It's Wednesday*" and was on my way. I prayed all the way to Potomac that I sell this house. If I do, then I can pay straight out for her truck; without having to touch my bank account. Pulling into the circular driveway a white Bentley Continental awaited my arrival. Damn, that joint is serious! I've got to get me one of those ASAP! They must be already here.

I think he's a white man because his name is Bornstein. What brother do you know with a last name like Bornstein? Surprise! Surprise! He's a brother. This brother's is getting some major paper. He has all three: money, power, and respect. He owns his own architect firm, Bornstein and Associates. They've designed half of the buildings in the state of Maryland. *Main man is getting that bread*, I thought to myself as I read his business card. Now I remember him. I read about him in Black Business and Upscale LIVE magazine about two years ago; I'm surprised that I didn't recognize the name. I make it my business to know the movers and shakers. I'm slipping! If I stick to my plan in three years I'll be him. I already own two 10-unit apartment buildings; by then I'll own two or three apartment complexes and a strip mall.

Strolling through the house, I know I have this deal locked down. His wife wants this house and she has her mind made up. They are a very nice older couple; about

79

fifty-four or fifty-five, something like that. To be her age Mrs. Bornstein is phat to death! She's kept it together well. She's still flexing that coke bottle shape. After twenty-seven years of marriage and four kids she still has it going on. Probably had a little nip/tuck, lipo action but it's all good. Mr. Bornstein is cock diesel strong. He's one of them muscle bound ex-military, former college football star combinations. He became an architect after getting an honorable discharge. He's definitely reminding me that I need to get into the gym. It don't make no sense for an old man to have a better six pack then me.

Since we both played, we started talking football. He's a Dallas fan and I'm a diehard Washingtonian; Redskins all the way. Next year is going to be our year! RGIII is recovered; we going all the way. Mrs. Bornstein's so wrapped in the house that she left us a long time ago. We started talking about the Superbowl. I predict it will be Seattle vs. Denver. It wasn't long before we had a bet on my prediction.

"I hope that your better at selling houses than you are at trying to predict Superbowl teams. There is no way it will be those two teams!"

"I'm very good at both sir."

"You wouldn't want to put your money where your mouth is?" He challenged.

"It wouldn't be right for me to take your money twice." I joked

"Young buck, I'm 'bout to teach you a lesson…how about we bet a $100.00."

"What? Scared money can't make money! You sound a little scared to me? Thought you were so sure?" I began to chuckle.

"5,000.00." He dared.

"Bet! Who's going to hold the money?"

"I trust you. You're good for it. We'll meet and settle up after the game."

"My word is good."

"I know that's not the only thing about you that's good." He mumbled.

I know he didn't say what I think he said. Did you hear that?

"Excuse me, Mr. Bornstein?" I questioned.

"I have something to ask you."

"What?"

"Would you like to join me and the Mrs. on a vacation on our yacht in the south of France? So we can get to know you better? Get away from this cold weather. You can bring your lady and maybe we can do a little' swinging? I'm sure that you have good taste!"

"Hey, ah looka here, Mr. Bornstein. I'm not really sure what you mean by that but I'm only here to show you a house; nothing else. I ain't wit' that freak type shit."

"Don't knock it until you've tried it."

"Yeah! Whatever! What you'll do is your business but if you disrespect me again we're going to have some serious problems, so let's just drop it right here."

"I apologize. You're right, that was very disrespectful. My wife thinks you're very attractive and wanted you to join us! I'm glad it didn't end up in a fight like the last time I extended an invitation."

"Yeah…yeah…whatever! Look here slim…wassup with the house? You going to buy it or what!" All of my professionalism was gone as I replied.

"Oh, there you guys are. Honey, I want this house." Mrs. Bornstein shrieked as she re-entered the room interrupting the conversation and soon to be ass whipping.

"We'll take it." He grinned.

"Let me go and get this contract in order. I'll be in touch later this evening!"

"Wonderful!" Mrs. Bornstein squealed as she jumped up and down before kissing me on the cheek.

I left, leaving them in there. Let me get up out of

here with the quickness! I jumped in my car and began to scrub my cheek so hard; I thought that my skin would come off. I don't know where her lips have been. Ain't that some shit! The only reason I didn't Li' Scrappy his ass and put them paws on him is because I've become immune to it. My cousin Carlton is gay. For years, Rodney and I put up with him and his buddies cracking on us; they were relentless. At least, with them we knew what they were about. They respected us! We respected them! These people don't even know what the sanctity of marriage is about! That's fucked up! I thought about his wife and just shook my head. Poor woman! I bet she ain't really with that type of stuff she's probably just doing it to please him! He looks like an old ass freak type dude! I hope he doesn't bring home something rotten that'll kill both of them. They know that they're too damn old to be acting like that. Maybe, he has enough sense to protect himself and her. What is really going on? Can you believe that shit?

7

For the last three days, Rhonda's been running around here like a chicken with her head cut off. She's about to worry herself to death. She's preparing the Thanksgiving dinner for our newly combined families this year; if my baby doesn't have a nervous breakdown first! She wants everything to be perfect since it's our first one together. She knows that she can cook, and I know that she can cook; what's wit' all the drama? Maybe it's because we're having a house full of people? All I know is that I'll be glad when it's all over; because tonight I'm eating Panda Express. You know that ain't right!

My lil' brother, Coco, came over to watch the game with me. Since our fathers' death, he's changed completely. Coco was attending Dice University on a basketball scholarship. He was the starting point guard; heavily scouted. He stayed on the Dean's list for academic excellence. He was NBA bound! He's the one that was always able to find something positive in any situation. When Pop's died, Coco was only twenty years old. He stopped talking completely for six months and flunked out of school. His game on the court suffered. He went from triple-doubles every game, to missing every shot and riding the bench. Next thing I knew, he'd lost all respect for everyone; he was even beefing with God. He started selling drugs, smoking weed, ripping and running the streets, hanging out all night, and arguing with moms about everything. He just started tripping!

His plan was to distance himself from everyone he cared for; so that when they died it wouldn't hurt as much. Obviously, our Mom's was the first target; we both love her more than life itself. If we'd known our father was sick, maybe it would've been a little easier. We could've been there for him and mom. Our father kept it to himself and we didn't have a clue, never had a chance to prepare ourselves. He wouldn't allow Mom to tell us. He thought that he'd recover and we'd never have to know.

    Unfortunately, it didn't work out like that. Now at twenty-three Coco's one of the biggest drug dealers in D.C. This dude is moving weight like a body builder. Recently, when that stuff went down with Rhonda, I got an eight ball from him. He sold it to me thinking it was for somebody else. That was a lie! Little does he know, I and two people I used to run with sat in here and smoked every crumb!

    Remember the night that Rhonda went to that cabaret with Simone? Yeah that night! That night I lost my mind, sobriety, and almost lost my woman. The next morning, I broke my back trying to get help. I think she knew that I was high but she never said anything about it; neither did I. Now I go to about three or four meetings a week. I just tell Rhonda I'm working late or hanging out with the fellas. I've been clean ever since.

    Coco says he has some good news; he does. Thanks to Kiki, his girlfriend of six months, he's made a 180-degree change; he's re-enrolled in school. He'll be going to G.T.U. in the spring. The coach knew of Coco's game and even got him a tryout for the team. Lil' bro is going pro, I just know it. To top it off, he's become a big brother sponsor to a little boy named Tank, who lives in Shifton Terrace. The Terrace is a drug ridden, low-income housing project; we call it baby Iraq! Now this is the Coco that I know. All through life I've been the fuck up and he's been the bookworm. Now we're both back on the right track.

    Kiki is doing all of these positive things to impact Coco's life without even knowing it. I don't care what anyone says, a good woman can change your life! See, Kiki lives in Shifton Terrace with her little brother Jason, and her so-called mother; when she's there. I say her so called mother because Kiki's mom is a dope fiend/ pipe head. I'm talking about "sell the food out of the refrigerator and turn a trick in the alley" type junkie. Coco was running that strip; that's how he met her, Jason, and Tank. Man that joint used to be a hustler's paradise. Many a dealer got street rich on that block. Kiki basically raised herself and her little brother; because her mom was and still is on it. How old is he? Oh, Jason's six years old. Their mom smoked through her whole pregnancy so he was born addicted! He's a little soldier you should see him! The hospital eventually weaned him off of the drugs. He's okay now just very hyper. He's got ADDH or whatever you call it. ADHD! That's it!

To be only twenty, Kiki's lil' ass is a helluva woman. She's drug-free, educated, hardworking, and fine as hell; with the body of death. She looks like Janelle Monae. Right now she attends Howard University where she has a double major in African History and Business. She and one of her professors Dr. Z are planning on opening a K- 12 school when she graduates. Looking into the kitchen at Rhonda and Kiki; brought a smile to my face. They're very different but their beauty is familiar. They remind me of Moms and Ma Brown when they were younger.

Now, let me school you on Kiki and why I know she's a soldier. I know you heard me mention earlier that she has the body of death; I know many that would give her the world for just a taste. But rather than trick or date a hustler to get paid, since she was sixteen, she's worked at Checkers and part-time at one of those government agencies. She still manages to maintain two jobs every summer, one job during school, and braids hair; that's how she pays for college and takes care of Jason. That's how I know that she's one of a kind. Every woman that I know thinks they're too good to work at Checkers; especially the ones that aren't even half as fine as she is. She's always saying that honest labor keeps you honest. Now, Coco finds creative ways to give her money. She still doesn't know that Coco was a hustler; or she's a damn good actor. He believes that she still thinks that he works with his partner Chris doing construction. He never was flashy and since he's so cheap, it's easy to believe. Greg and I, call him Tommy when she's not around. 'Cause you know he ain't got no job man! I think she knows though!

Being around Kiki has reawakened his love for life. I guess witnessing her struggle, yet continue to progress, had a serious effect on him. She changed him and stopped him from hustling without ever trying. Even though Coco's filthy rich ass definitely has enough money, you and I, both know he doesn't work. He can't put anything in his name, produce a W2, or paycheck stub get it? Since Kiki doesn't make enough to qualify for the hi-rise that Coco wants and he doesn't want her to know he doesn't work; our moms signed for it. Then to top it off, the courts awarded Kiki legal custody of Jason today. The news made me feel so good that I wanted to do a back flip; I did.

"Sexy, what's up with you flipping in the house?" Rhonda inquired.

"Everything's fine baby…finally back to normal."

"Are you sure you're alright?" Coco chimed in.

"Never better! Just celebrating wit' my family! Things are finally back to normal."

"If you're really okay… then come here for a minute baby."

Holding and kissing Rhonda, I know that there ain't a joint in the world that can make me feel like this. No joint has ever got my dick hard! If anything it kept it limp! Rhonda and Kiki, cooked until the early hours of the morning. The crib is filled with the sounds of Tupac, and Biggie; our generation's rap oldies but goodies. Damn, I can't believe all three of them are gone. Rhonda put on Heavy D and the Boyz. Aw! That's my jam.

"The overweight lover's in the house…." Hev flowed.

"Oh, that was the joint?" Rodney added.

"Kick- step." Everyone laughed as Kiki and Coco did the Kid and Play kick step.

"What about the prep and the bus stop." I threw in.

"Naw...I got it the pop." Added Ki-Ki.

"Aw yeah, but if you gon' pop you gotta break." Rodney added. We laughed as he did his Beat Street impression.

"Turn it up....hey... that's the jam. Go see the doctor!" We sang in unison.

Moe D. was getting it in .Man life was so easy back then. I was a young buck without a care in the world. We partied for hours doing every old dance that we could think of. Straight digging in the crates from Rakim and Eric B, Salt and Pepa, Special Ed's "*I Got It Made*" to "*Funky Cold Medina!*" The way we're reminiscing you'd think we are fifty years old. Of course some vintage go-go settled brought it home. As Rare Essence stayed in the pocket, we played cards, drank like fish, and talked about everything; just chilling all night. Today was a good day; can't forget Cube and NWA.

The sweet smelling aroma from the kitchen woke me up on Thanksgiving Day; Simone and Minyon have already arrived. I've apparently slept until 1:30. The rest of the family will be arriving shortly so I better hurry up. I can hear the laughter and greetings coming from downstairs as Lexie and Chris entered. It's a small world! Coco and Chris are running buddies, and Lexie and Rhonda are best friends, yet we never met. Rhonda didn't even know Coco. Then again, the Benjamin's play by their own set of rules. I bet their friends sign a confidentiality agreement or some shit like that. I ain't going to lie, just having them here I don't know whether to be nervous or feel like we are the safest house in DC right now. Neither, Rhonda nor Coco, ever even mentioned that they knew them, that right there should tell you something.

I still have to go pick up Jean; Rhonda's mother.

My Moms and Ma Wheeler must already be on their way; because I'm getting no answer at the house. I showered, dressed, and made my way downstairs. Coco has already picked up the little boy, Tank; he and Chris are watching the game. Minyon, Jason, and Tank are playing video games. Rhonda, Kiki, Lexie, and that broad Simone are all in the kitchen talking. I can't believe Lexie Benjamin is in my mother fucking house. I knew that my brother knew Chris but had no idea that Lexie and Rhonda were that tight. I grabbed my camera and start taking pictures. I only want proof that Lexie is in my house, but I took pics of everyone to play it off. I don't want to come off as a groupie. I turn around just in time to snap a pic of Ma Wheeler and Mom's coming through the door. The only people missing are Greg, Otis, and Jean. I sat the camera down, grabbed my jacket, kissed Rhonda and my mom's, and then excused myself to go get Jean.

Listening to the new T.I. featuring CeeLo song, "*Hello*"; I cruised all the way to Jean's. I can't help but think of all the things that I have to be thankful for. The streets are busy with people moving about; making their way to friends and relatives homes. The air is brisk with a slight chill and the leaves had abandoned the trees. Since I'm a fall/winter person this is my type of weather. Jean was waiting patiently in the doorway when I arrived. I got out and went to assist her with the food she was bringing. When I crossed the doorsill, the smell from the sweet potato pies hit me and instantly I now know where Rhonda learned to cook. I also see where she gets her looks. It seems that every time I see Jean she gets finer; like wine. After two trips to the car, we were finally ready. She's fixed so much food that Rhonda didn't even need to cook. Jean's so excited about finally meeting my mother. I'm telling you, this woman must have diarrhea of the lips, because she talked a hole in my head all the way back. She's a sweetheart though.

When we got to the house, Greg and his father Otis had also arrived. As soon as Jean hit the door, Ma Wheeler and Mom's snatched her up and the card game began. The sounds of Anita Baker, *"Caught Up In The Rapture"*, filled the house. I have to get at least five or ten minutes alone with my baby; she tastes better than turkey any day! I went upstairs and called for Rhonda.

"Rhonda, come here for a minute." I called.

"Okay." She ran up the stairs…yeah sexy…wassup?"

"This."

I pinned her against the bedroom door, lifted her shirt and bra, and began to kiss and lick on her soft beautiful breast.

"Rodney…there are people downstairs. We can't do this now." She purred as her instincts arched her back.

"Shit if we can't! I want me some brown sugar…let Daddy taste your sweet potato pie!" I begged as I pulled off her Juicy sweat pants.

I lifted her unto my shoulders, placing her pleasure against my face, and my tongue began to explore; you know she gave in. Her legs tightened as she unsuccessfully searched for something to grab. Unfortunately, there was no escape; she was too high in the air. I laughed as she bit her hands trying to muffle the screams as her body began to release. I know her legs are too weak to stand, so I carried her to the bed and laid her on her stomach. My manhood quickly found his place in her wet sugary walls; I gripped her waist and began to pound her into ecstasy. After about forty minutes we returned downstairs. As we were walking down the stairs I shouted:

"I'm starving. C'mon let's eat." I shouted.

"I just bet you are." My mother said.

"Looks like he's been fed to me." Jean added.

Jean and Lexie gave each other five and the house erupted in laughter. Damn, Rhonda and her mother rolling with the Benjamin's? This is going to require some additional research! That will have to wait though, my ribs are touching my back! It's time to eat! As loud and festive as they had been, once they started eating, you can hear hair falling out of an old man's scalp. I can't believe I'm in the same place. Its total silence except for an occasional pass this, oomph, or Rhonda girl you can burn. You know what came next: the people that smoked whipped out their cigarettes, the kids went back to the video games, and the fellas grabbed some brews or drinks, and headed for the basement wide screen to watch the game. Chris has some new $1,200.00 bottle gin. I don't even drink gin but I get to say I drank this with the Benjamin's! I was sneaking selfie's and shit! I was on some groupie type maneuvering. I'm officially drunk as hell and need to crash for a second. Everyone else crashed out on couches, chairs, and the floor. By half time everyone was asleep the food got the best of us.

By seven we were back in stride; some people ate, the card game was back on, and Maze was jumping out the stereo speakers. Lexie and Chris were gone. I immediately went searching for the camera. Sure enough, not one photo of her or him. Shit! I plopped down onto the couch. These mofo's even got the selfies out of my phone. I know Coco helped 'cause he's the only one who knows my password. Suddenly, Greg stood up nervously an asked for everyone's attention. Don't ask me! I don't know what's up; I'm just as confused as you are. At Greg's instruction, Jason turned down the stereo system, and we all watched in amazement as Greg went to bended knee.

"Simone, I've been thinking about this for a long time. I'd planned on waiting until Christmas but now seems as good a time as any....
Greg reached into his pocket and pulled out a blue ring box. Simone started to cry.

.... nothing would please me more than to hear you say that you'll be Mrs. Gregory Wheeler...Will you marry me?"

Every neck snapped in Simone's' direction. It looks like one of those television commercials. Simone grabbed her heart like she was having a heart attack. The tears flowed effortlessly from her eyes.

"YES!!!!" she screamed through her tears.

The house went into an uproar; everybody clapping, crying, and hugging. Ma Brown's so touched that she can't stop crying. She really likes Simone for Greg. Can you believe this shit? Me either! I'm beyond shocked. I can tell that Rhonda isn't as happy as she's pretending. I just can't tell if she's jealous, or if she knows something we don't? I pulled Greg aside and asked him if he was sure; he says that he is. Since Greg is my boy, I don't want to spoil his moment; so for right now I'm going to leave it alone.

After a couple of hour's people started to leave; Coco gave Jean a ride home for me. Everyone had pitched in to clean up; so the house is already clean. I went upstairs where Rhonda was sitting on the bed, scanning through cable channels. She looks upset. Now is my time to find out how she feels about this marriage proposal shit that just went down.

"What's wrong Rhonda?"

"Nothing baby...I was just thinking about Greg and Simone."

"I'm happy for them. That is going to be me and you one day." I stated searching for her response.

"That'll never be you and I. I'll never be like Simone!" Rhonda declared emphatically.

"What do you mean? Why did you say that?" The phone rang interrupting our conversation; Rhonda answered. After pausing for a few seconds, she pushed the 1 button on the handset.

" Hello...oh hey Marvin...no she's already left...she only left fifteen minutes ago that's probably why you didn't get an answer at the house...Minyon is with her...Oh, I'm fine....okay...Happy Thanksgiving to you too." She hung up.

"Why the hell is he calling our house? How did he get our number? How did he even know that Simone was here? I thought that she ain't fuck with dude no more? She said they were on "no contact" status. What's up with that?"

"Figure it out."

This chick's still dealing with her baby's father. Rhonda won't give up any info. She says that it's between Greg and Simone; and she don't want anything to do with it. I'm getting the feeling that Simone's playing my boy like a flute. I think I'll just follow Rhonda's lead and stay out of it. If Greg is that strung out over her that means that she has the power to turn him against me. It's not worth losing a twenty-five year friendship over. Maybe, I should turn on my private eye game and find out what the streets have to say about her. I'll set her ass up and get some proof. I know that bitch got some serious skeletons in her closet; you can look at her and tell she's scandalous as hell.

Rhonda's really disturbed about this; she just keeps shaking her head and grunting umph, umph, umph! It appears as though, at any given minute she'll break down and cry. She says she has a headache but I know better. Taking her into my arms, I made it my mission to sex all of her stress away. Time for the *"Stress Reliever"*, I hit the play button and we made love like we'd never made love before. Afterwards, she laid her head upon my chest. I feel her tears falling against my pounding chest. She must've thought I was sleeping. "Rodney, I **really** love you" she whispered. I'll never forget the way she said it. She emphasized the word really. What does she mean by that? Is she suggesting that Simone doesn't really love Greg? Naw…is she?

8

No the hell she didn't! Please tell me she didn't! I can't believe that Simone has agreed to marry Greg. What the hell is wrong with her? Is she crazy? Better yet, what's wrong with him? Well I know this much, I want no parts of this bullshit. As of this minute, I wash my hands of this whole situation. No more! My name is Bennett and I ain't in it! I mean, let's be real here, since day one Simone has been strictly out for his money; she doesn't love him. She can't even say the word without stuttering! Greg has brought her something every day since they've met. He gives her money; she sends the money to Marvin. Simone is in love with Marvin not Greg. I will say this, in the words of Momma Dee, *"And in that order!"*

Deep inside I know she's going back to Marvin and she knows she is too; I don't care what she says. She doesn't love Greg! I don't think she really even likes him. The little tears that she sheds are all an act; she's the official drama queen. The girl cries over Real Housewives of Atlanta, okay! I can't fake though; I got my life on that slumber party episode! They were on one and Kandi's faces are priceless! One minute Christopher Williams was talking, next minute it was the Royal Rumble up in the good 5 star Buckhead hotel! Shit, I thought that Kenya and Nene was about to bring the noise for a minute! Nene has been pacing all the way up to her arrival like she was waiting for some action. Child, they would have turned Bravo's rating out! Anyway, what was I saying? I lost track for a minute. Between, thinking about that and the Migo's *"Versace"* video I got sidetracked. Shit, the diva Donetella is sitting!

Oh yeah, why is Simone playing with him? How can she be so cold? Who does she think she's fooling? This time she's gone too far; she's actually talking about marrying him. This bitch has lost her mind! She's definitely overplaying her hand. This shit is going to come crashing down and I'll be damned if she's taking me down with her.

Rodney's been looking at me strangely ever since the proposal on Thanksgiving. I think he knows that I know something. I do; but I ain't volunteering any information. I plead the fifth! I'm taking all info to the grave with me! I'm so confused; I really don't know what to do. I mean Rodney's my man but Simone's my best friend? The same best friend who fed me and paid my rent; before I knew Rodney or Greg! Well, I tell you this, if Rodney doesn't ask, I'm not telling him shit. Then again, if he does ask; I ain't telling him shit! Maybe, she does love him; I could be wrong. There's one way to find out and that's to hear it from the horse's mouth; I called her.

"Simone wassup ho'? What you doing? I need my hair done. It's screaming for a touch-up."

"Meet me at the house and I'll hook that kitchen up for you."

"Forget you! What time?"

"In 'bout an hour but you have to help me cook. Girl, you know I can't cook like you?"

"Alright."

She made a mistake by asking me to help her cook. The way I feel right now, I just might poison her ass but Greg may eat some. Maybe I'm being a lil' hasty. Maybe she does love him and is really going to marry him. I'll just keep an open mind until I hear it from her mouth. If Simone's using Greg then I'll back up off the friendship. We'll still be cool but I have to save my own ass. If she says that everything is on the up and up, then we can still hang. Just because Simone's on money that's no reason for me to let her bring me down with her! It took me a while to find love and BFF or not, I'm going into CYA mode. I should take her tail right on Judge Mathis and sue her for undue emotional stress due to her losscoochieitis! She stays doing something strange for some change! I get the blame but not a dollar! Oh, hell to the no!

I hear it's lonely at the top but I'd rather be there then on the bottom trying to find out. Nowadays it's every bitch for herself and God for us all! I've got a good thing; she's not going to mess it up for me. No way! No how! Not to mention, Greg has become a very close friend to me. He's a good man. There are not too many brothers like him out here. When a woman wishes for a good man; he's what they mean. However, a man should have enough common sense to know when he's being played; Ray Charles and Stevie both can see this bullshit! How can he not know what she's doing? She must be extremely good!

Greg and now Simones' house is twenty minutes away. I left Rodney a note, grabbed Monica's old CD, jumped in my new cherry red Honda Accord; you know the one that Rodney co-signed for. I'm on my way singing, *"Love All Over Me"* at the top of my lungs. I need something to relax me before I have to deal with this chick, for real. Hold up, before I go to Simone's, let me stop past my old apartment and see how my cousin Trina's doing since she's moved in. I didn't tell you that? Oh yeah, I let her and her man sublet from me. My aunt, Heather, put Trina out for getting pregnant; so I let her move into my old apartment. You know people are so full of shit, fake self-righteous hypocrites. My aunt got pregnant at 15 and dropped out of school. At least Trina is still in school and her boyfriend is sticking with her. I still pay half of the rent to help out; until she finishes her paralegal classes. Don't get me wrong, by no means am I rich but family is family. I took my furniture out of storage and let them use it. Now that I don't have to pay for storage anymore; I'm using that money to help them with the rent. It balances itself out in the end. Also, the money I save by living with Rodney is making me break even so its okay. Two good things about it, she'll be finished school before the baby comes, and I'll always have a place to go. Gotta' keep a spot in case this doesn't work out; you feel me? Technically, I'm living in his house. He can put me out anytime he gets ready. My name ain't on jack; not even a light bill. Shit, my momma ain't raise no fool.

"Wassup cuz...how's it flowing?"

"Girl, I'm makin' it. These classes are a mother! I've been studying this case, Brown vs. Board of Education for the last five hours and I'm still not finished. How have you been?" Trina asked.

"You know me...I've just been. You wouldn't believe what's been goin' on. Where's Keith?"

Keith is Trina's fiancé' and soon to be husband. He's twenty, six foot five, and funny looking. He looks like a lanky Elmer Fudd with Will Smith ears. To me, there ain't nothing cute about him. Sometimes, I wonder how she could have a baby by him, then again I know; he worships the ground she walks on. He loves her and he's loyal. That boy would jump in front of a moving car for her without thinking twice; and she'd do the same for him. They really love each other. Trina's only eighteen and has been with Keith for four years. It's a first love kinda thing. He's a very gifted artist who plans on eventually becoming an architect. For now, he works at Popeye's while he takes classes at U.D.C. I know that in the end Trina and Keith will be alright; watch what I tell you. They're survivors! I still think it's pitiful, how my fake ass aunt turned her back on her daughter. She put a man before her daughter! I would never do no shit like that to my child. Thank God she's not my mom! Things ain't been right with Heather and Trina, since Trina told my aunt that she woke up in the middle of the night to find my aunt's boyfriend, Sticks, in her room beating his dick while watching her sleep. To this day, my aunt still doesn't believe her. She took his side and at this very moment, she's still with that pervert to this day. Yeah, you heard me, it's fucked up ain' t it?

"Keith's at work. Hanging out with the chickens! If I see or have to eat another piece of chicken, I swear I'll cut somebody then call the police on my damn self. That's my baby, though. What's the dirt? Spill it."

"Simone and Greg are getting married."

"Get the fuck outta here; you're lying, for real? Is that why she moved out?" Trina asked.

"You know it! If I'm lying I'm flying and I ain't even moving. She's gon' marry him."

"Girl, he must don't know that Simone's legs be open like an IHOP, all night. We heard her having sex with the moving man the night she moved out."

"You're lying! That bitch is so scandalous. I know Simone and that furniture move was free!"Ha Man! Dumb is you!" I replied.

"No...dumb is he! You're right, I don't believe this. What did water head Rodney say?" Trina asked.

"Rodney was so mad you could see the smoke coming from his ears. He never did like Simone from day one. Now he really can't stand her. I'm the one stuck in the middle. He wants to ask me so badly if Simone is using Greg; he's choking on his tongue."

"Cuz....you should have Weezy'd her ass! She's definitely *"On One"*! She's dripping Drake from her pores!"

"Did what? Dripping what? What are you talking about?"

"Weezy said... *left her ass on the bench until thebus come!*"

"Trina...your ass is crazy."

"What you gon' do?" She asked.

"Pray and play it by ear."

"You know damn well that she don't love him?"

" I hope and pray she does." I replied.

"Well your knees are going to get mighty ashy and sore. Simone loves Simone! I just told you she fucked the man to move the furniture for free. If Greg didn't have all of that money we wouldn't even be having this conversation… and you know it."

"Yeah…but what can I do? Simone is my best friend! She was there for me when I was down and out. Greg is my friend and my man's best friend! If Rodney ever finds out that I knew what Simone is doing it's going to put some serious strain on our relationship. I ain't trying to lose my man over her bullshit!"

"Cuz, cut her off."

"Yeah, I wish it was that easy."

"You know what, just stay out of it. Talk to Simone and see if she's really dogging him. If she is, then play the back. Wash your hands of it. C.Y.A….cover your ass!"

"You know you're right. Girl, how'd you get to be so smart? I was just thinking the same thing!"

"I had a fly teacher…you!"

We embraced as I left. Trina's making a lot of sense. I tried to prepare myself for the upcoming confrontation with Simone. *"Big Girls"*, by Stiletto is on repeat as I ride to battle. Every note locked inside my Honda by the closed windows. Shaynna is singing the hell out of that third verse! I just pray that I can control my temper. I feel like punching Simone in her mouth. What! Man, I'm telling you, if Simone's shit makes me stink; I swear that I'm going to give her a World Star worthy ass whipping! I can't believe she's got me in the middle of this shit. I'm not losing Rodney over her. I love him! Did you hear what I said? I love him! Love is a very powerful thing. It makes you do some off the wall shit. Huh, some people lose all grips on reality; will I be one? You can bet your last dollar that I'm going to be newsworthy if she fucks up my happy home! Believe that!

Simone and Minyon have just taken over poor Greg's' house. Minyon has toys everywhere. Things are still packed in boxes. Simone never has been one for cleaning. She's always been a little on the trifling side. Wherever she takes something off at; that's where she leaves it at. I thought that she'd at least try to keep a clean house to impress Greg. Wrong! That was my brain thinking! Cleaning is the furthest thing from her mind. I haven't even got into the house good and she's bragging that she's convinced Greg to hire a cleaning service called Andy's to come three days a week; did she say a maid? This bitch here is a pimp! She should teach a class! This bitch done talked up on a cleaning service! One part of me envies her ruthless nature; while the other part of me despises everything she stands for. I can't fake; she's working her shit. When is enough going to be enough? I only hope for Greg's sake, he remains the number one salesman at SJM Realty. If homie ever hits a slump; Simone will make him a human speed bump. Talk about rolling out, she'll leave skid marks on his ass. No joke! Peace!

Her drag for today consists of a silk Versace blouse, leather pants, and these bad ass chocolate brown, crocodile, knee-high boots. She looks like she's jumped straight out of a Rodeo Drive catalog. This week she's doing the blonde weave thing with her hair. She thinks she's giving up the Beyonce/ Barbarella look. Sike! It's a shitty mess. She looks like who did it and what for! Whoever sewed in her tracks must really hate her they set her ass up! It sitting too far back off of her already too big forehead and it's too thick. Eww! What do you think? It looks like a dry hunk of honey blonde hay. If I was her, I'd try to get back to CHOW with the quickness. She's in definite need of some water, conditioner, oil sheen or something. She better not stand too close to a match, or poof; she'll be up in smoke. I wonder if I light this lighter in my bag if she would just breakout running. Then she has the nerve to ask me about it. Hold my tongue! Before answering, I took time to think, I decided to be on the safe side. I'd better be nice before she messes up my hair, accidentally on purpose.

"So what do you think? You like?" She asked pointing to her new do."

My mind is screaming *HELL NO* but I didn't say it.

"It's a bit much for me but you're working it."

"You don't like it do you?" Simone asked.

"You know that I'm not a big fan of a lot of hair, that's all. Where's Greg?"

"Are you trying to change the subject?"

"Yep... where's Minyon?" I asked.

"Forget you...she's at her grandmother's house. Greg and his father went to the National Harbor. He better bring me something back."

"What you mean he *better*?"

"Rhonda honey... understand this... Greg knows if he ever goes anywhere that has a mall, he better bring me something back. Jewelry! Shoes! An umbrella or cotton candy; I don't care what it is! He has to bring me something; let me know that you're thinking about me!"

"You must really love him? I mean, you accepted his proposal and everything."

"What? Girl, you got me fucked up! This is me! Simone! Love?! I don't love anybody but my daughter and her father. I just accepted his proposal 'cause his mother and father were there. I didn't want to make him look bad. And, let's not forget this big ass rock! Plus, I want him to get me a new truck. Bitch, this ain't love, it's a business transaction!"

"But you're going to marry him, right?"

"I might... I might not! It depends on how I feel that day."

"Simone, if you don't want to be with him you shouldn't string him along."

"Mother had him, mother fuck him. And, why are you so concerned anyway? This is my world and you must pay for the nuts you bust. This is business! I didn't tell know that he was going to propose; but thanks for the ring. Diamonds really are my best friend; especially big ones."

"You really are serious? You're not the least bit fazed by the fact the Greg is madly in love with you?" I asked.

"Nope! Not one damn bit!"

"Simone, girl you're cold blooded!"

"Cold as a Section 8 apartment in the projects of Alaska; when the heat's turned off in January! He's the one that got all serious. I mean let's be realistic, how in the hell are you gonna be madly in love after fifteen days; give me a break. Greg is stuck on stupid! Wit' his pussy-whipped ass!"

"You can't put a time limit on love. Some people just know what they want."

"Yeah well, I know I want…I want to hurry up and finish your hair. A sista's trying to roll out before Greg gets back. I'm supposed to meet Chuckie at 9:30."

"You're still seeing him?" I asked, being nosey.

"Yep… him and his best friend! What? It's not a game!"

"Are you serious?"

"Serious as a pipe head with a pocketful of money; I ain't faking."

I'm convinced! This bitch has no heart. She just don't give a fuck! I hope for her sake Marvin Sr. never finds out. She'll be on the six o'clock news. He'll kill her. Marvin never expected Simone to be a nun while he was locked up; he didn't expect her to be a whore either. Trust, Simone has slept with about 32% of DC. The rest, she probably just milked for their loot. Everybody done ran up in her; her box is hot as fire! Her pussy has got to be stretched out of shape. Uugh! She's nasty as shit. The bad part is that you can't help but laugh at the way she colorfully expresses herself. Use what you got to get what you need. It's more like use what's left until you catch a disease.

She really just don't give a fuck. She uses every whore phrase in existence to justify how she's living. I hate to admit it but I can't help but laugh when she gets to talking that shit. How she treats some of them dudes is hilarious. I understand when she says they do it to us; shit it's been done to me! Trust me a part of me feels her; but she's just so ruthless. She be working these dudes to the concrete. They're gonna pay to play whether they want to or not. She's comical but dead serious.

My pity for Greg has reached new heights. He's riding the poorhouse express and don't even know it. Slowly, I'm realizing that my actions give Simone the impression that I agree with her lifestyle. By hanging with her, laughing, and joking about her rendezvous, in a way, I'm condoning it. I've played codefendant and covered up a lot of her shit. By doing that I've been giving her my approval. I don't feel the way she does so, why do I hang with her? This makes me just as guilty as she is because I know about it. I've got to throw shade Simone's way. I want no parts of this shit! I'm not gonna play sidekick to her demented emotional crimes. Oh hell no! I'm not going to mess up my happy home. I've paid her back every dime of the money she loaned me; so I'm out of it. I knew what she was going to do to him from the beginning; I should've never introduced them. I shouldn't say any more than I already have? Why me?

9

Ho! Ho! Ho! Happy holidays! Jingle Bells! Merry Christmas! Happy Kwanza! Feliz Navidad! All that shit! My president is black and so am I. This year I've really got the holiday spirit. Mostly due to the fact that; this is the first Christmas in a long time that I won't spend divided between four and five women. Each one thinking that I'm their man; with all of their mothers' praying that I would soon become their son-in-law. Mother's are a trip. If you take a chick out more than two times, she's changing her FaceBook status, posting pictures with hearts and shit! Her mother is already picking out a wedding dress, and naming imaginary grandbabies. Are they really that damn pressed to get their daughters married off? I've had bad luck with females and their mothers. Out of all of the serious relationships I've had; two of the girls had drug addicted mothers. Those two relationships changed my life! Yvette's mother turned tricks; she had a pimp and everything. The other was Kenya. Her and her, based-out mother used to get high together. Now she's one piece of pussy, I definitely should have passed up. Every day that goes by I wish I would've kept my anaconda in my pants.

Not this time! Our flow is real smooth; it feels like this is what I'm supposed to be doing. Our shit is on point; no fighting, no arguing, just loving and chilling! Finally some peace! Tomorrow will be the best Christmas she's ever had; I'm gonna make sure of that. Everything is on point. Tonight, I'm cooking dinner for her. We'll drink some DP, eat something fly, and do something that's very unpredictable in front of the fireplace; yeah, that's the plan. I've gotta remember to take the Charde's Destiny soundtrack in the house. Sounds like a winner to me. I can think of nothing better than relaxing at home on a cold night with my baby keeping me warm; ain't no heat like body heat. I'm trying to get my grown man on; you hear me!

Driving down Benning Road, I decided to pick up some food from Levi's. Anyway, who am I fooling? I ain't no G. Garvin! My specialty is Steak-umm's! I should've went to the food truck "D.C. Dives" but I don't feel like driving all the way over to Rhode Island avenue. Rhonda loves that joint. I'm there so often Khalani knows the order and me. I left Levi's and drove back to Hechinger Mall's Redbox, for a flick. I'm considering getting a freak joint but with the intense passion between Rhonda and I already, it would be a waste of money. We stay stimulated. What should I get? Maybe I should rent Saw IV. I know that I've seen it fourteen times already but that shit is hilarious; Jigsaw keeps their ass in a fucked up predicament. I always wonder what I'd do in that situation.

Yo! I know that you're cracking up. I ain't never seen no Redbox like this! Man, they have everything: Black Caesar, The Mack, Cleopatra Jones, Dolemite, Willie Dynamite, and J.D.'s Revenge. I'm as happy as a recipient on the first of the month. I finally decided on *Django* and *Let Me Explain*. I know that ain't who I think it is? Guess who I see as I make my way to me? Someone I haven't seen in about six months; my cousin.

"What's up playa?"

"Your world! I'm just a squirrel trying to get a nut." He replied.

"You the man!"

"No, you the man…If I had you hand I'd cut mines off. I'm just out her trying to keep from getting my wig split or filled up with hot shit, you know. Playa hater's stay busy."

"I'm hip. That's why I'm mostly at the crib, you know, lounging with my lady! It's real hectic nowadays."

"It's crazy. Looka here champ, I'm 'bout to make this freak move. Hit me on the cell later and we'll hook up, go to the strip joint or something?"

"Bet! I've gotta get your new number. Let me put it in my phone. I know that you still change it every year!" I suggested.

"Walk with me to the car so I can get yours too." "Anyway, I want you to check out this lil' freak I got. She's an anything bitch! Down for whatever! We're 'bout to go to the hotel. I can't even front, she be having me climbing the walls. No bullshit! The head is official! You want to go? I'm telling you, she's a straight roller! She's wit' whatever, anything goes. It'll be like the old days."

"Naw man, I'm cool…I think I'll pass on that." I replied.

The closer we're getting to my cousin's Maserati, I can't believe my eyes. You ain't going to believe this shit! The live freak that he's talking about is Simone. Yes, you heard me, Simone! Greg's' Simone! My best friends' new fiancée is fucking my cousin. What! When Simone spotted me, she immediately turned sideways like she was going to magically disappear and began trying to cover her face. She turned sideways like I can't see her ass; is she serious? That ass is busted! I couldn't wait to get to her, so I started walking faster over to the car. She's hella nervous! I know she's shitting and pissing on herself at the same time.

"What's up Simone baby?" I asked.

"Juice you know her, Cuz?" asked Chuckie.

"Know her? Damn right I know her…come to think about it you're the dude that she's been telling me about."

"Oh yeah! Wassup?" Chuckie inquired.

"Naw see, when she bought me these Lebron 11's I'm rocking right now, she was talking big shit about how she got the money from this trick that drives a Maserati. That bitch was talking plenty of shit. Champ, she called you all kinds of little dick tricks, and spent your money on me."

"What! Yo bitch! Get your cum drinking ass out of my mother fucking car before I stomp a mud hole in your tricking ass."

"Chuckie baby he's lying! I don't even know him!"

"I ain't trying to hear that shit bitch! That's my damn cousin and he ain't got no reason to lie on your thirsty ass. Get the fuck out of my car! Now! You ain't moving fast enough!"

Chuckie snapped snatching Simone out of his car by the back of her weave, and slammed her to the ground face first; damn! He face smashed against the tar roadway like the sole of a shoe. He gave me five, told me good lookin' out, and skidded out the parking lot before the cops came. Lucky for her, he's calmed down a lot. The old Chuckie would've stomped her into the concrete. To Chuckie, Simone is what you call a lifestyle perk. With or without her, he's not gon' lose any sleep. As long as he has cars and money, girls like Simone come a dozen a dozen. I was so mad that I hawk spit on Simone and we both left her lying in the middle of Hechinger Mall's parking lot; face busted and all. Freak bitch! That's what she gets! Let me get the fuck out of her before the police come.

I drove around the city in silence for about an hour trying to figure out how to tell Greg that his woman ain't shit. Why me? My chain of thought was broken by my *"Call Me Right Back"* ringtone. Who is this? 555-2668? I've never seen this number before so I ain't answering that shit. It's probably Kenya playing again. I pulled into the 7'11 parking lot to get me some Black and Mild's. My mind is swimming with thoughts of Simone, Greg, and Chuckie. Curiosity got the best of me so I called the number back.

"Yeah, did somebody call me from this number?"

All I hear is someone screaming and crying on the other end. It's Simone! She's not calling me from Greg's house. She's at a hotel on New York Avenue, threatening to commit suicide if I don't meet her there. Like I give a fuck! Go head bitch, kill yourself! Twice! She says she wants to talk about Greg. I really don't want to hear nothing she has to say. She's been living with my partner for less than twenty days, she's accepted his proposal, and I catch her going to the hotel with my cousin. On the real man, why did I have to be the one to catch her? I wonder does Rhonda know about the shit she's been doing. This is a fucked up situation that I want no part of but I'm driving to meet her anyway. Why? I don't know. For real, I don't care what she says, I'm telling my boy! She ain't gon' use him like that!

Knocking on the motel room door, I'm pissed off to put it nicely. I feel like punching her in the face as soon as she opens the door; I just might. This chick has some balls! I mean, what can she possibly have to say to me? When Simone opened the door she looked like warmed up shit; she's all messed up. She has a big ass knot sitting up on her forehead from being slammed into the concrete. Her lip is busted and I swear it looks like she's rocking a chipped tooth. Remember when the boxer Rahman' head swole up like a damn watermelon in that fight with that dude? That's exactly what her head looks like. It looks like she has a two heads, her eyes are red and puffy, her fake lashes are barely hanging on, her skin is visibly stained with tear streaks, and her clothes are hanging off. She has a bottle of Conjure and a shiny .38 revolver on the table beside the bed. I know Luda don't want this chick drinking his cognac! This bitch looks crazy like the chick from, "The Ring".

She immediately began begging for forgiveness and apologizing; saying how much she loves Greg. She's claiming that Chuckie's been stalking her and won't leave her alone; we both know that's a lie. He's got 100 more freaks like her on speed-dial. I sat on the edge of the bed; she sat beside me and leaned on my shoulder. I snatched away and scooted further down the bed; she followed and again placed her head on my shoulder. This time she turned on the waterworks and began to cry on my shoulder. Even though I really want to snap her neck, for some reason I began to comfort her. Don't ask me why; it just seemed like the right thing to do. I calmed her down enough to pour myself a drink. She told me her life story and why she never thought she'd have a man like Greg. Either this bitch is crazy, or she thinks I'm crazy! We began to work on that Conjure. I'm starting to feel kinda nice. I think it's time for me to go; besides the bottle is empty anyway.

"Rodney, I'm sorry…I really love Greg. Please don't tell him. It would only hurt him. I swear, on my daughter, I won't do this again. I love him! After this, I know Chuckie will leave me alone. I don't want to lose him! Please don't tell him! Please!"

"Simone, even though I can't stand you, I'm gonna take you at your word. I don't want to tell my partner that the woman he loves ain't shit! But if you do that shit again then you're going to answer to me." I warned.

"I swear…I promise…never again…..
Then she looked at me very strangely; like she had something on her mind.

….well, maybe one more time."

Next thing I know, Simone's mouth hugging my meat; busted lip and all. I know this is wrong, dead wrong! It just feels so good; I can't stop her or me. Four positions later, now I'm paranoid. What have I done? I've just betrayed my best friend and my woman in one stroke; okay it was a couple of strokes. Oh yeah, and the rubber broke. Does she have something? Did she give me something? Man, what the hell am I doing? I'm supposed to be helping my partner. Instead, I'm helping myself to his woman. However, I must say, I see what the fuss is about. Simone can sure put a hurting' on a mattress. That sex was cold bomb! Baby girl can be a porn star easily! Every part of me is drained. I hope Rhonda ain't trying to do a lil' something, something tonight. If she is, she's short. I'm through booking for the night! Did I mention that Simone warned me that if I ever told Greg, she'd tell Rhonda; that's straight up blackmail! Man, she's playing real dirty! Ain't this some shit! How did I get into this?

By time I got home, the food from the Levi's was ice cold. Lucky for me Rhonda isn't here. She left a note saying that she'd gone to the mall with my mother; last minute Christmas shopping. Good! I ran and jumped into the shower and began to scrub so hard, I thought my skin would come off. I have to wash the smell of Simone off of me before Rhonda gets back. I'm never going to let Greg or Rhonda finds out; I'm taking this one to the grave! Placing my head under the shower nozzle; I drifted away into thought.

The beads of water hitting against my body rejuvenated me. I have to tell you something. I know you're going to be mad but a part of me really enjoyed being with someone different; new pussy is always good pussy. I just can't help myself. Do you think that I need to see a sex therapist or something? Maybe I'm a nympho? Stop laughing; I'm serious. What's that? Did you hear something? Somebody is here.

It's a good thing I've had some time to rejuvenate and begin to regain some energy. Rhonda has eased into the bathroom and as we speak, she's joining me in the shower. I went through the motions of making love to her. I don't know how I keep getting myself into more shit! I wonder can she tell what I've done? I know that she senses that something's strange. Every time I look at her, I see Kenya or Simone! Guilt! My mind's playing tricks on me. I went straight to bed using the excuse that I was worn out. What have I done? I wonder could Rhonda tell when I kissed her. Can she taste Simone? Women always know when something ain't right. Why is it that everything in my life that's good, I destroy?

Rhonda's grabbing on my arm and placing kisses all over my face. Its Christmas morning! My baby is so happy. For me, Christmas cheer left when guilt moved in. I can't forget what happened last night. I can't get it out of my mind. I don't even want to look at Rhonda. I put my game face on and faked it.

"C'mon baby…let's go downstairs and unwrap your presents."

"First, I have something else that I'd like to unwrap."

"C'mon baby… we have plenty of time for that."

"What? Rodney? Are you turning me down?" asked Rhonda.

"Naw baby! It's just I want to see your expression when you open your gifts…C'mon."

"Okay….okay."

Yeah! I was thinking fast as hell! I had to freestyle on that one! I just don't feel right making love to her after what I've done. I can still feel Simone on my skin! I need another shower. If it was anyone except Rhonda then I wouldn't have a problem with it. With her it's different; I guess I really do love her.

10

"Sometimes you gotta lose…to win again". I know
that's a strange song to be playing the first thing on
Christmas morning. I just turned on the radio and here she
is, Fantasia; singing her heart out. Rodney gave me so
many beautiful Christmas gifts. I really wasn't expecting
that much from him since; he'd just helped me buy my
Honda Accord. I got a black leather coat with fur
trimming, 2 suede suits, Chanel No. 5, Hypnotic Poison, a
certificate for Sak's, a Badgley Mischka handbag, and
some money. Either Rodney Claus is definitely in a good
mood, or Rodney Hughes has been very bad. I gave him
some Legna Ec'urb gear, to add to his already extensive
collection, 2 Gucci shirts, jeans, Gucci tennis shoes, and
$500.00. I did it real big! Shit, I started buying Christmas
presents in September. He still has one more box to open.

"Baby girl, you didn't have to spend all of this
money on me. I told you that this was your Christmas."

"It's your Christmas too and I love to see you
happy. Can't I do something nice for the man I love?"

"I love you too."

"Hurry up….open your box."

"Alright…alright. Wassup wit' this? Baby booties?
Oh damn! Rhonda are you?"

"Yes! We're having a baby! Are you happy? Merry
Christmas."

"What? When?"

"Sometime around August 10th, Rhonda and
Rodney make three."

"Yes! I'm going to be a father!"

"You okay?" I asked puzzled by the look on his
face.

"Yeah baby….I'm fine! I just can't believe that I'm
finally going to be a father! C'mon we've got to call my
mother; better yet let's go tell her."

Rodney's overjoyed; he's grinning' from ear to ear. I must say, I'm super relieved about his reaction. I really didn't know what to expect. In the back of my mind, I was prepared for him to mention an abortion, or comment on not being ready to be a father. News of a pregnancy can bring the worst out in people. For a while there, things with us have been a little shaky. Our relationship has really been tested. Once I moved back in after the cabaret incident, everything's been lovely. I've received breakfast in bed, hot oil massages, and "just because" gifts; all the pampering a girl could want. It's been almost too good to be true! I can't shake the feeling that at any moment something or someone is going to burst my bubble. When it feels too good to be true; it usually is. But for right now; I'm just going to enjoy the moment. I'm not going to look for trouble. I deserve to be happy and nothing is going to steal my joy. I put on "*I Like It*" followed by my man Two Chainz and danced around as I dressed.

It's only been twenty-five minutes since I've told Rodney; he's acting like a fool already. He doesn't want me to lift anything, he's in the mirror practicing how he's going to break the news about his upcoming son, already complaining that my jeans are too tight and might squeeze the baby. Lord, please don't tell me that I have to spend the rest of my pregnancy like this. We cruised the city listening to the SJM Records Christmas album. Rodney can't keep his hands off of me. I don't ever want to forget this feeling. He kept his hand on my stomach as we drove to his mom's house. Greg lives only a few blocks away from his mom; so I suggested that we stop there first to drop off gifts. Rodney's' whole demeanor changed but he agreed anyway. I wonder why, all of a sudden, he doesn't want to see Greg? I know he doesn't like Simone but does he hate her that much? Does he know that Simone's playing Greg like the Wizards? I wonder what he knows.

You got to be fucking kidding me! Are you serious?

Do you should see this? Yes, Greg did buy her a black '14 Range Rover. My mind's spinning 100 mph as I look in amazement at this truck in the driveway with a big red bow on it. Talk about tricking! This doesn't make any damn sense; homie is beyond whipped! Rodney looks like he's seen a ghost. I guess he can't believe it either. His bottom lip is hanging. He is in total disbelief! We're both in shock. No joke! Total disbelief! Simone has taken this gold-digging situation to a whole new level. This girl is working her shit; you hear me! I ain't mad at her; I respect her level of skill. But, I feel so sorry for Greg.

Rodney and I, both agree that we no longer want to go inside. We're just gonna throw it in reverse, roll out quietly, and go to his mother's. Rodney allows the car to drift backwards. Damn! Minyon busted us trying to leave. She came flying out of the garage in her new motorized Lexus mini car. She's screaming my name at the top of her lungs. Damn! How can I continue to face Greg; knowing what Simone's doing? I'm so glad it's not my life, it's hers. But give credit where credit is due, she is working his ass! I got out of the car and walked over to meet Minyon. I kneeled down beside her and she squeezed my neck for dear life. She's so excited about Christmas.

"Hey doll baby…where's Mommy and Greg?"

"Mommy and Daddy in the house…see my new car."

"Ump humph….it's real nice."

"Did she call Greg daddy?" Rodney whispered.

"Ump humph." I replied.

"Man, this is some foul shit!"

"What's wrong sexy?"

"Nothin'…just go in there and drop the presents off. Tell them we'll see them at Coco's."

"Alright…I'll be back as quickly as I can."

I grabbed the presents from the back of the car. For some reason, Rodney appears to be a little more than pissed off. Is it because Minyon called Greg daddy? Well, honey if that upset him, he'd hit the roof if he saw the full-length chinchilla and Celine bag that she just modeled for me. One of those animal rights organizations is going to get her ass! We ain't even gonna talk about the 5 carat pear shaped rock that she's calling her engagement ring. Which, did I mention, also happens to be surrounded by a cluster of one hundred smaller diamonds? Though I know what she's doing is wrong, I have to give her props; she's making cash registers ring. I just wish that Greg had been anyone else; except Rodney's' best friend.

Nothing else was said, between Rodney and me, about Greg or Simone. I know that we are both still in shock; I know I am. I mean what kind of person am I, to knowingly let her dog him? He has become my friend also. I'm just as guilty as she is. What should I do? The fan is getting closer and closer and the shit is about to hit it! He's a good dude! They're not too many good brothers out here as it is. I think that Simone is so wrong for treating him like this; but who am I? She's just mad at the world because Marvin got locked up and left her to raise Minyon alone. She vowed that she'd never love another man; it appears she's sticking to her word. She says that love leaves you broken hearted. She is one heartless, cold blooded, gold-digging broad. Maybe she'll change her mind? Maybe she already has? It's obvious that he loves her but it's not looking too good for him right now. He's the biggest fool in D.C.

I love spending time with Mrs. Hughes. She's a cool old lady. As soon as we arrived at the door, we hear The Temptations singing, "*Silent Night*" sounding like true heavenly voices. The stereo is blasting. She answered the door wearing a colorful sweater, black corduroys, a pair of beautiful knee- length black boots, and a Santa hat with a ball on it. Oh, can't forget the extra-large glass of Mr. Boston's eggnog in her hand.

"Merry Christmas baby…'bout time you've made it over here to see momma."

"Merry Christmas… Mrs. Hughes!" I said extending my arms for a hug."

"Now Rhonda, didn't I ask you to call me Ma…you're a part of this family!"

"Ma, is Coco here? We have something to tell you."

"No …he better be at home waiting on us! Why is something wrong with my son? Is something wrong? Is everything okay?" She asked worried.

"No ma…it's nothing like that. It's good news…right baby?"

"Yes."

"Boy… y'all are about to make my pressure go up! Well…don't string me along…spit it out."

"Mrs. Hughes…. I mean…Ma… how would you feel about being a grandmother?" I nervously questioned.

"A what?" She asked before covering her mouth with her trembling hands.

"Rhonda's pregnant! We're having a baby!" Rodney shouted.

"Congratulations! Aw, God bless you child. God is good! I'm so happy for you. I've been waiting for a grandbaby! Oh, Rhonda you've made me so happy."

"What about me? She didn't get pregnant by herself!"

"Oh Juice. I'm so happy for the both of you."

I really love Rodney's' mother; she reminds me of my mother. She's always cheerful, very wise, and she always has something positive to say. She can be your best friend as long as you don't get on her bad side. Well so far, I'm four for four. Everyone seems excited about the baby. The fifth and final test is Jean; my mother. Please God, let her be happy about this. She's really been pressing me to go back to school. I'm gonna go. It's just, in the back of my mind, I'm still holding on to my dream of opening a restaurant. One day, mark my words; I'm going to be a restaurant owner. After exchanging gifts, once again we all piled into the car. The destination this time is Coco and Kiki's new condo.

Damn! This joint is laid out. They have some seriously top flight shit up in here. This place needs to be in a magazine. You can tell he's Rodney's brother; these men sure have good taste. Their new home is a split-level sixth floor duplex, floor to ceiling glass windows, the finest hardwood floors, Versace furniture, marble, crystal chandeliers, a hand painted oil picture of them and Jason, and a 70' plasma mounted over the fireplace. You name it, they got it! African art, 7 foot elephant leaf plants, Persian rugs, a fish tank that mimics the Baltimore Aquarium and a sixty five hundred dollar stereo center built into the wall. This is a long way from Shifton Terrace. I want one! I want a house like this! I've got to get cracking on opening my own restaurant; that's the only way I can afford something like this.

They deserve it and much more; I'm so happy for them. Coco must be holding onto some major paper! This shit in here costs so much I'm scared to touching anything. This is black love at its finest. This is how it should be done!

"Lil' bro got it going on something lovely up in here. Oh yeah...I likes! I likes!" Rodney proclaimed.

"Something small...something' small! Wassup Sis? Merry Christmas." Coco stated as he gave me a family member type embrace.

"Merry Christmas!" I said returning the hug.

"Or should we say, Uncle Coco." Rodney added

"Oh shit! Juice, you gon' be a daddy?" Coco asked.

"And you know it."

"Kiki...guess what?"

"What?" she hollered from another room.

"Juice and Rhonda are having a baby." Coco yelled

Kiki came flying around the corner like she was on the run from the police or on the *"First 48"* or something.

"Stop playing...for real? Go 'head girlfriend...congratulations!"

"Juice man, I know you want a son. Me and my nephew gon' be hanging tough."

"And you know this!" Rodney shouted.

"Well... I'm sorry... but we're having a girl. So you and your niece will be hanging tough...right Kiki?"

"The world always needs another African queen."

"I don't care if it's a boy or girl, long as it's a healthy baby. Now momma has spoken. Let's eat. Where's my grandson... Jason...Jason... I swear that boy moves quicker than roaches." Everyone laughed.

"He's in the room playing with his toys." said Kiki.

"Jason." Mama Sandra yelled.

"Yes...Grandma?" Jason yelled still fixed in his position in from of the TV.

"Come on in here... baby we're about to eat."

Jason bolted into the living room carrying a DVD in one of his hands. The DVD is titled, "We Are The Children of Kings and Queens". It's a cartoon for ages five and up with black characters telling black history stories. His face is filled with frustration as he came out to join us; the poor baby is almost in tears. He couldn't get the DVD to play. It would be an understatement to say that he's anxious to watch it. Kiki had given it to him so that he could learn his history and obtain a sense of self-worth at a young age. These are the types of things that I'm gonna do for my child. I know that as long as Jason has Kiki and Coco, he'll be alright. He's going to grow up to be somebody great.

Sandra agreed to start the DVD for Jason since the food wasn't quite ready yet. But now he won't watch it unless everyone joins him. This child is our future and Kiki is the only family he knows. It's important that we embrace him and he gets an early understanding of unity and real family so, we agreed to join him. Child, I had more fun watching the movie than Jason. I was a firm believer that a child couldn't teach me anything. Wrong! Jason told me about the pyramids and sphinx. Who was who and where they lived. Damn! I feel so stupid. I feel like I'm on "*Are you smarter than a 6 year old*". A sister really needs to break open a book more a little more often. I'd better get on the ball before my child gets here. There's so much I need to know.

I know that this is off of the subject but seeing how Kiki pulled herself out of a terrible situation, I've decided that if I have a girl I'll name her Kinesha; after Kiki. She's a beautiful, strong, educated black woman and that's what I want for my daughter. Now what was I saying? Oh yeah!

I know Sandra wants me to call her Ma but I just can't. I don't want Rodney to think I'm rushing him. You know, trying to get in good with his mom's to keep him. I don't want to come across as pushy. So, for now, I just call her Sandra. It's hard though because she feels like a mother to me. She's so sweet it's unbelievable. Sandra and my mother have become very close; they clicked immediately. They're just like old friends; add Ma Wheeler and you have three birds of a feather. That surprised the hell out of me because my mother doesn't really like many people. She says that Sandra and Betty are good people; real folks, not all uppity and phony. What made me think about this was the fact that when I went to call my mother, Sandra was already on the phone with her. Though, my mother was the first person I'd told of my condition, she's still the last one that I'll get a response from. Sandra gives me the message that my mother says she doesn't need me to come pick her up. That Ma Wheeler and Otis are already on the way to get her. Well, excuse the hell outta me!

Praying that my mother will share in my joy, I impatiently awaited her arrival. Everyone else is so happy.

It would be awful if she doesn't approve. Imagine going through nine months of pregnancy knowing your mother didn't approve. That would kill me; worrying if she'd ever really accept your child. Now I know how Trina feels. Talk about stress. I'm beginning to O.D. on stress, just thinking about it. She likes Rodney so she'll approve, right? Forget you! Well, my wondering is now over. Here she is, in the place to be. Otis, Ma Wheeler, and my mom have just arrived.

　　As soon as she came through the door, she didn't say one word to me. Not hi, fuck you, you stink, nothing! She dropped some presents on the couch, snatched up Sandra and they rushed into the back with a present. Damn! She hasn't even taken her coat off. I know she doesn't approve, I can tell. Everyone else just mingled while we waited for Greg and the gold digger crew to stroll in, late as usual. Oh! I'm gonna cry! Don't cry Rhonda, don't cry! Suddenly, tears begin to form in the wells of my eyes. I'm getting the feeling that my mother isn't as happy as everyone else about my pregnancy. I'm fighting these tears with all of my might. I don't want to mess up this joyous occasion but I can't help it. She hasn't even looked my way since she's arrived. She's been locked up in that room with Sandra for almost 10 minutes.

　　I sat on the couch and laid my head upon the armrest. Fighting back tears with all my might; determined not to mess up Christmas. I closed my eyes drifting off into thought. I don't know how long I was inside my mind but now someone is standing over me, clearing their throat. I looked up to find Sandra and my mother both wearing #1 Grandma on their new sweatshirts. My mothers' pretty brown skin was wet with tears. I think that she'd started Sandra crying or vice versa. Jean had brought the sweatshirts two weeks ago. She said she knew that I was pregnant before I even told her. She had a feeling; a mother's intuition. As she kissed Rodney on his cheek, she thanked him for making me happy. Now her life is complete, she says. Rodney is even getting all teary-eyed. Kiki and Ma Wheeler are already crying. Coco and Otis are toasting. Oh, we are so emotional. Doesn't it just make you sick? A bunch of cry-babies! At least I know my baby will be loved. I can't fake, I was worried up. Mom's had me going for a minute.

"Hey...hey...hey! Wassup family! Greg's in da' house."

"Merry Christmas!" Simone added.

"Yeah Simone, sure looks like you're having a merry little time. Nice coat and is that a Celine bag?" Asked Coco.

"Yes and yes! Thank you. The love of my life, my fiancée gave it for me. Isn't it beautiful? It's two of my favorite presents." Simone replied.

"Well if a fur coat and a Celine bag is second and third, I'm scared to ask what your favorite is." Kiki added.

"Daddy bought Mommy a truck." Minyon chirped in.

All at once everyone, except Rodney and I, went "Daddy"? I don't even think they heard the part about the truck.

"Yeah... I bought my baby a truck." Greg boasted with his chest stuck out full of pride.

"Son, all that's well and good but what's with this daddy business?" asked Otis.

"Since we're getting married, Minyon asked if she could call me Daddy."

"The child has a father. All of this is just moving too fast for me. Now don't get me wrong, Simone, you seem to be a very nice young lady. I like you and you seem like a very nice young lady. However, this is a bit much jewelry, cars and now your child is calling my child daddy. I raised my son to be a good man. I also respect his decisions. But so that there aren't any future surprises, I just want to advise you that I can be the best friend you ever had or, the worst enemy you'll ever want to make. Hurt my son and even though I'm a church-going woman, I'll personally take you for a slow walk through hell. Put that on my life! A very long one! I ain't always been in the church! If you hurt my son I'm going to beat you until you light skin and whoever you bring with you! Believe that!" Ma Wheeler warned.

"Yeah…and I'm gon' be your tour guide." Added Otis.

"Ma and Pop's, it's not like that at all. Simone loves me. I love her and we both love Minyon. Why is everyone so upset?"

"I sincerely hope that's all there is to it. This is too much, too fast. You're buying her all of these expensive things. What did she have when you met her? What has she given you? And, who the hell is Celine?" Otis warned.

"As the Deacon in the church says…Well!"

"Well." Everyone chirped in sarcastically.

"Since everyone's here, let's eat." Sandra interjected trying to change the subject.

Making our way into the dining room, Simone appears to be very uncomfortable; nervous as a hooker in church. That's what she gets! What did she expect? I mean, strutting in here like she's Joseline Hernandez. Sorry, had to say that, that's my chick! Yes, her and that damn accent are everything! Anyway, back to what I was saying. Oh yeah, then she has her daughter calling a man that she's known for less than five months Daddy. Driving a brand new I don't know how many thousand-dollar truck. Did she really expect his mother to do back flips? I wasn't expecting Ms. Betty to go that hard but she went in and let have! Simone should know that she's been dogging him from the word go. I don't even know why she bothers to come to family events when she knows she's going to drop him anyway. Girlfriend, please get a life! What the fuck is she thinking? Any fool knows that you don't parade stuff that a man's worked hard for in front of his mother, especially, not with the attitude that he owed you that. To Betty, Simone could've fallen out of the sky for all she knew. We ain't even gonna kick the fact, that Greg has never met any of Simones' family. Not even her mother Boodie and they are thick as thieves. You know she is helping Simone spend that money. They are a true example of the apple not falling far from the tree. Shit, Boodie taught Simone everything she knows. Come to think of it, he probably doesn't even know her real name! Cause it ain't Simone, that's her middle name. Her real name is Tierra.

11

I can't believe everyone's tripping. Why is everyone monitoring how I spend my money? Even my mom's flipped out on Simone. That shit was crazy. Why are they so worried about Minyon calling me Daddy anyway? What's wrong with that? I don't have a problem with it so why does anyone else? I want to be her father. I want her to call me Daddy. So what, I bought my fiancée a truck, a handbag, and a fur coat. It's a small thing. I got it like that! I can do that! It's my money! They just hating! It didn't cost them a dime. I worked for that money. I can wipe my ass with it if I feel like it. My mother sure knows how to get to me. Boy, she's working overtime this round. She basically threatened, no promised, to whip up on her for nothing. Wondering if she likes Simone is pushing me over the edge. She knows how much her opinion means to me. I respect her judgment. I want her to accept Simone. I want my woman to feel welcome around my family and friends. They're treating her like she's Bin Ladins' sister or something. Opinions are like assholes, everybody has one. And, everyone has an opinion on Simone.

All of my life I've had a very special relationship with my parents. By me being the only child, I was always very spoiled. My parents have been together for 30 years. My father owns a trash company and my mom is a retired teacher. We've always had money. Being one of the very few children on the block to have my real father in the home allowed me a lot of advantages and experiences. I was lucky to have a very stable environment and a positive view of what a male/female relationship should be. No matter what happened one was there to see the other one through. I know what two people in love can accomplish together.

Dad raised a man! My father taught me respect for women and myself. My mother showed me how great a real woman's love could be. So they, of all people, should understand why I treat Simone like a queen. They raised me to be like this. It hurts me to think one day I may have to choose between Simone and my family. I hope it never comes down to that. The way I feel right now, I would choose Simone. My parents have made their decisions. They've lived their lives and have each other. I, on the other hand have only just begun. I want what they have. I'm only twenty-five and Simone is whom I choose to spend the rest of my life with. The bible says, a man who finds a wife finds a good thing, right! There's no other woman out there for me. She's the one! So they better accept it! I'm a grown ass man! Nobody's going to tell me what to do or who to be with. I love her and she loves me! Case closed.

Take Rodney, now we've been boys since we were in pampers. Even he has turned on Simone, when he was the one that introduced us. Man, ain't that some shit! We used to hang out every day. Now he tells me that he no longer feels welcome at my house. He's like my brother but all of a sudden he doesn't feel welcome at my house? What kind of shit is that? Even Rhonda's acting funny. She and Simone barely speak anymore. They used to stay on the phone for hours now they don't hang out together at all. It's almost like they never were best friends. When Rhonda came over on Christmas and told Simone that she was pregnant, Simone blew her off. They're totally different from the way they were. It's like they hate each other. What the fuck is going on?

When I first met them, they used to be as close as titties in a push up bra. Talking! Sharing secret! Hanging out and shopping together. Now it seems like they're in competition; like they're trying to outdo each other. Rhonda moves with Rodney. Simone moves with me. Simone and I get engaged. Rhonda and Rodney are having a baby. Rodney helps Rhonda get a car; I buy Simone a truck. Rhonda wants a leather jacket; Simone wants a mink. When will it end? I think all of this confusion between Simone and Rhonda is driving a wedge between me and my partner. So, today is men's day. Coco, Rodney, and I are just going to hang out. Chilling! Letting our nuts hang; shooting some hoops and shit. No females!

We met up at the gym. It wasn't long before we got next on a lil' three on three against some scrubs who'd won the game before. We schooled them. Beat'em like they stole something. We got this gym rocking like an And 1 tour. The score was thirty-two to twelve. Once again I taste sweet victory. Who's your daddy! I know you can't believe your eyes. Did you see when Rodney hit one bamma with a head fake, then came back wit' a sweet as finger roll? You know that was a helluva move; especially since Juice got that big ass head. Then I hit CoCo off with this pretty half court pass that set up the slam. Booyah! The last play of the game, Coco took it straight up the middle and hit 'em wit a baby Jordan reverse dunk. We started looking like the old Bulls team. Ump, ump, ump! School is in session! The bamma's got so mad they started hollering foul. Foul deez nuts! They tried to say we cheated. Nigga please, stop crying like an old biiiiaatch! You lost. Release the grip on my nut sack. Get your sorry ass off the court. Next!

The next two games were basically the same. Eventually we got tired of whipping ass, not to mention tired from being out of shape, so we decided to roll out. Winners of course! Kiki's out attending some black awareness conference and since Coco lives the closest; we went to his crib, showered, changed clothes and tried to figure out what we'd do next. The only thing we agree on is tonight we're gonna end up in somebody's club.

"Wassup G! What you trying to do?"

"I don't know."

"What about you Juice? Strip Club?" Coco asked

"Let's go to the Convention Center and check out

the car show." I added not in the mood for strippers.

"You know that joint gon' be off the hook."

"Fly ass cars, oh yeah ...I'm game!"

"Don't forget the bitches." Coco added

"I thought you supposed to be on Kiki so hard? Juice man, you hear your brother?" I joked.

"Don't get it twisted I love my lady. She just ain't walking around with my nuts in her pocketbook like your people. You whipped!"

"Nothing wrong with looking long as you don't touch." Rodney added.

"Ain't nothing wrong with touching as long as you don't get caught! Besides getting your dick sucked ain't considered cheating! No fingerprints, no crime."

"Man, y'all some trifling ass dogs... I'm gon' call you Rover and you Fido."

"Woof!" Rodney replied

Coco came out the bathroom with a tampon and threw it at me. They burst out laughing. I can't find the humor.

"Oh, you think that shit is funny huh?"

"Yeah."

"Coco man, why you trying to carry me?"

"Cause you acting like she the man and you the female. She got you whipped! Pussy whipped! Your nose so open you don't know shit from shoe wax."

"She's running your life. You can't see that she's using you? Stevie Wonder can see that shit C'mon! You acting like you ain't never had any trim before! What does she have on you? I bet you had to get permission to hangout today, didn't you?" Rodney asked.

"Simone don't tell me what to do ...I'm the boss!"

"Sure you right"

"Aw Juice man, I don't know why you talking. I know for a fact that Rhonda clocks your every move. I can smell a lil' scent of pussy on you too playa, playa!"

"See lil' bro that's where you wrong cause Rhonda

ain't petty. She don't even trip off of shit like that. She does her thing. I do my thing and we do our thing. When you grow up, if you're lucky, you'll be like me."

"Bullshit! Rodney, you're shoveling so much shit you can wax these hardwood floors." I clowned.

"Naw, but on the strength though, I think Simone is on money. Watch her! I know some dude's that know her and her rep ain't good! Word is she's a gold digging freak. No disrespect just watch yourself." Coco added.

"I'm wit Coco! G, we want to see you happy. Just don't buy it. Whatever you do I got your back".

"Double that!" Coco added

"I hear you."

"Don't just hear us. Man, check yourself and watch Simone." Juice warned.

"With both eyes! Coco added.

All the way to the car show, I couldn't stop thinking about what they've been saying. Half of Drake's new CD had played; yet I haven't really heard one song. Is this the way everyone feels about Simone? Is this how my parents feel? Why do they feel that way? What's up? Do they see something I don't? The more I think, the more confused I'm becoming. It got to a point where I just stopped thinking and turned my brain off. This shit is giving me a headache. I keep reaching the same conclusion, I love Simone. I like how she makes me feel. She loves me. We're going to get married and that's the bottom line. I don't want to hear no more mother fucking hating on my lady! I'm serious about that shit! Next one that says something wrong I'm going to put this size 11 in their ass. Enough is enough!

The car show is tight! Coco was right. There are plenty of women here. A lot of them in groups of 4 and 5! Why is it that women always travel in packs? Herded up like cattle. I guess it's to run interference. Cock block 101. We haven't been in here ten minutes and Coco has already trapped a hood booger.

"How you doin'. I'm Sherry."

"Well, I'm doing better now that I've met you. This is my brother Rodney and my cousin Greg."

"Hi." She waved poking her butt out so far I was waiting for her spine to snap.

"Wassup." Said Rodney

"Hey."

"So uh, do you think it's possible I can get to know you a little better? Maybe take you out or something?" Coco inquired.

"Ump humph."

"Let me get your number"

"Okay…just give me your cell number. Then I'll call you from mines."
I'm thinking to myself I know damn well he ain't giving her his number. He better shoot her a blank. He shouted out his cell number as she programmed it into her phone to dial.

"As fine as you are I know that you got a bitch somewhere?" She inquired

"Hell no! I got a queen…baby I'm married!"

"Then what do you want with me? You plan on leaving your wife or something?"

"You just seem like somebody I need to know! See, this ain't about me leaving my woman. This is about me getting to know you. You don't have a problem with that do you?"

"Nope. What she doesn't know won't hurt her. Besides, when I'm done with you I guarantee you'll want to leave."

"I doubt that. Play your position and everything will be mutually beneficial!"

"I most certainly will…point guard! I don't ride the bench so we will see!"

"Well…let me see you get drafted… make me a

believer then wit' your fine ass."

Now see this is why a lot of brothers don't respect women. She doesn't respect herself. She's gonna call him too, you can bet on that. He went through the motions of acting as if he was programming her number in his contacts. Bitches, will accept any kind of treatment from a nigga with a few dollars. The whole time she was talking she kept sticking her butt out and rubbing her titties on him; sucking on a cherry lollipop. I thought she was going to do him right there in the damn auto show. I guess she thought that shit was sexy or something. I can't lie, she is fine as hell! She got that video vixen look working.

Now she's a gold digger! Her eyes didn't leave the knot in his pocket the whole time they were talking. If they did manage to move they only fixed on his jewelry. She's willing to be number 2 or 52 on his list if it will get her a Gucci bag or some red bottom shoes. Coco looks like a big ass dollar sign to her. He has become very flashy like Rodney. He's wearing a Benz medallion with diamonds. A yellow diamond pinky ring and a diamond face Jacob watch. Funny thing is, when Coco was hustling he always looked broke. Now that he's not hustling he looks like he is.

Coco says he realized that fast money is not worth dying for. He's tired of looking over his shoulder. He got tired of seeing his boys killed over cars, bitches, and a couple grand. Petty shit like that. Besides judges are giving out years like candy nowadays. He was stacking for years so he got a nice bankroll. He was smart when it came to that. He had me get him a couple houses, etc. Wait, you didn't hear that. Forget what I just said. Anyway, now he just plays ball and chills, awaiting his return to school. The girl Sherry is going to blow his phone up. It's too bad that she doesn't know that she will never hear his voice again. That's one of them burner phones, it's his play phone. He deleted her number as soon as she walked away. He turned to us explaining that he was just making sure that his game was still strong. I guess it is. I know Kiki has his nose wide open. He talked all that shit and he's whipped just like me.

The club is jumping but for some reason I'm not enjoying myself. I wish Blak Erth would hurry up and start their set so that I can bounce. D.J. Gemini is rocking this joint though. That *"Dark Nights"* joint by Rhapsody is banging from the speakers. You know the song where the girl is rocking the joker face in the video and beating up the beat like a MMA fighter? I want to party but I'm just not feeling it! Coco and Rodney aren't having the same problem. They have more half naked chicks then a rap video. These are my boys and their opinion means a lot to me. Now that I have an idea of how they feel about Simone; I know how to carry it. I don't like what they said but at least now I know how they feel. However, I still can't find any reason to justify me wasting any more of my time or energy in this club. I'm going home and waste my energy the right way; making love to my woman. That's what I'm gon' do. Call me whipped, call me what you want. Just call me later cause I'm outta here.

When I got home, Fatz was on. *"Sex On The Late"* was playing. Minyon is over her grandmothers' and Simone is butterball naked in the bed asleep. I got into the shower knowing that when I get out; she's going to have to wake up. I placed some ice on my tongue and let it explore her legs. I worked my magic until my lips began a seductive French kiss with special place. She awoke groaning with pleasure. We spent the night making some good love. You know like you're never going to see that person again kind of sex. She was wild! It's like she's trying to eat me alive. Her groans are driving me to dig deeper and deeper into her wetness. She wrapped her legs around me; I lift her onto me and began to walk around the room with her. Her juices dripped down my thighs as her body released over and over again. Tears filled her eyes as she dug her nails into my back begging for mercy. Hello no! By the time we'd finished I'd fallen for her all over again. I ain't gon' fake, she got me open! Coco and Rodney are crazy. They don't know nothing 'bout a love like this. Whoever ain't feeling our love can kiss my ass. I'm feeling like J. Cole and Trey right about now, *"Can't Get Enough"*. This is for keeps she hits the spot! Fuck anybody that ain't feeling our love! This is my woman and my life. I'm not listening to them fools, especially Rodney's ass. Talking 'bout the blind leading the blind!

12

Is this fool blind? Stupid? Or, is he just slow as hell? For the last week, I've slowly been moving out of here. I told him that I was redecorating. He went for that shit hook, line, and sinker. He hasn't said a word. Oh well, I got what I wanted. My Dior bag runneth over. Greg paid me like a Casino Live slot machine. I really do hate to break his heart but life is about pain. I got to do, what I got to do. I like him, I really do, but I'm not in love with him. I love Marvin and even though you may not understand or approve of this everything I've done; I've done for Marvin. I had to make sure we got off to a good start. Anyone will tell you that money or lack thereof causes undue stress in a relationship. I don't want Marvin worrying about playing catch up. I want his full attention on me! Marvin gets released from prison today and that's where I'm heading. I'll be posted up at that gate like a security guard. I gave Greg some goodbye pussy, right? He'll be alright? He'll bounce back. His family will help him get over me. Shit, those mother fuckers didn't like me anyway. His mother lucky that she didn't get chin checked for that little warning speech she called herself giving me.

Rodney will be there for him. Come to think of it, I wish Rodney was here for me. I sure wouldn't mind having another round or two with him. I see why Rhonda is tripping. I can think of 10 1/2 real good reasons. Brother' is slanging some grade A meat. I do feel bad about that, sike? That bastard was going to cheat anyway. He's a dog! His dick controls him that's why I knew he'd come to the hotel when I called. Shit, better me than the next bitch. That's what friends are for. If you look at it, I was helping her out! I was just setting him up anyway. I wouldn't do it again. Okay I'm lying, I'd surfboard his ass again in a heartbeat! Believe it!

Now let's see if I'm all set. Notified my clients

about moving to the new shop? Done! Settled into my new Bowie condo? Done! Pawned Greg's ring? Doing. Changed tag number? Done! Yes, the title is in my name in case you're wondering! Moved all clothes and toys? Done! New bank account? Done! Letter to Greg? Done! Douche? Need to do. Twice! Yes indeed I've got to shrink it up before Marvin dives in. Greg has me so open; Marvin might drown if I don't. I need to soak in a vinegar tub; real talk. Greg was eating and beating it up! My baby Marvin ain't had none in so long you know he's going to be so pressed to tear it up. Ain't nothing like that fresh out of jail sex! Shit, its ten o'clock already. I need to get a move on. I know I'm going to be late to my own funeral and you'll better be there when I get there. What? I'm supposed to pick up the truck at noon. I have to be at the pawnshop and finished by one so that I can pick up Marvin at three o'clock. I need to get a move on.

Let me go over this letter again and make sure I didn't forget anything. I hope this doesn't hurt him too bad. He really is a good man but he's just not the one for me. What? For real, I do! I know he's going to be devastated. His family is going to flip! Then again, who am I trying to fool; I don't give a flying fuck if he's hurt or what they have to say about me. *"What the business is? Stay up outta mines!"* I'm carrying it Trap-house style like French and them. Men have been using women for years. Fucking up their credit! Leaving them to raise babies alone and heartbroken! I'm just returning the favor. Payback is a bitch and her name is Simone. Don't get mad because I beat him to the punch. Eventually, he was going to turn on me anyway. He couldn't keep up that nice guy act too much longer. There's no *"Couple Of Forever's"* here! This ain't a damn Chrisette Michelle song, this is life! There is no such thing as forever when it comes to love. It's good while it last and then you move on! Period! I've got to get the hell out of here before he comes. Let me go over this

letter again. I don't want to leave anything out.
Dear Greg,

I'm leaving you. Don't try to find me. Shit
happens, you know. It just didn't work out.

C-Ya,

Simone

Works for me! I can't lie. I am going to miss two
things about Greg; his money and how freely he spent it on
me! Well, let's make that three things. Brother does have
a mean stroke. Oops, can't forget the tongue. No man,
Marvin included, can use a tongue like him; he should
register that joint. After only five minutes of his tongue in
my spot child, I needed a diaper to hold back the juice flow.
Maybe I shouldn't leave? Sike! I like Greg but I love
Marvin. There's a difference.

Marvin and I were high school sweethearts. We
met at Southeastern High School. He was a 12th and I was
in the 10th. Marvin was so damn fine. He was tall, dark
skin, with curly hair, and hazel eyes. Ump, he's gorgeous!
He was the most popular dude in the whole school. All of
the girls wanted him but I got him! I gave Marvin
everything I had; even my virginity. Yes, I was beyond
determined! I also was young, sprung, and dumb. I didn't
care if he cheated on me as long as he came back. And,
trust me; there were a lot of other women. It was my first
love. I swore that my coochie had magic beans and I would
change him. We broke up so many times during our five
years we've been together; I've lost track. I am sure we're
in the record books somewhere. I would get tired of the
cheating and physical abuse, pack my shit and leave. He'd
cry, tell me he loved me, and fuck me so good I couldn't
spell goodbye. I'd forgive him and the cycle would begin
again. He's my personal kryptonite. I'm addicted to the
drama he brings. I can't leave him alone. I'm convinced
that no man can fill that space in my heart; so I stay with
him.

When I got pregnant with Minyon, we decided to work harder on saving our family. That's when I got turned out on money. See, Marvin got deep into the hustling game. You know, selling drugs. In no time flat he was kinging it. He had an Uncle that was big in the game and he fronted him some kilos. Marvin hit the ground running. The money was rolling in like waves on water. Non-stop! We went from living in the projects to a lavish hi-rise in Silver Spring. Nothing was too expensive for Marvin; everything had to be the best. From Don P, couture clothes, and diamonds; it was all at my fingertips. No longer was I riding the bus. I cruised through the city in a silver Mercedes CLK 350 at 17 years old. Bitches hated me and I loved every minute of it. I stayed shopping on Wisconsin Avenue at the finest stores; buying $600.00 pairs of shoes. We vacationed in all the hot spots. It was nothing to be ringside at the fights in Vegas. You name it; we did it. I got strung out on money. I was hooked. I jumped head first into the lifestyle. Child, I'm the reason they came up with the title, "Ghetto Fabulous"!

When Marvin got locked up he left me in a fucked up position. I had nothing. Zero! Not a pot to piss in or a window to throw it out of. The police took everything. My life of luxury was a memory. The money was gone. House in Potomac gone! All I had were my clothes on my back, an infant in diapers, and my car. The very same car I had when Greg bought me this truck. I'd dropped out of school to run the streets balling and keeping a close eye on Marvin. What family I had washed their hands of me over different money disputes long ago. Mostly, because they knew I had it and wouldn't give there greedy asses any.

The only person I broke bread with was my Mom. That's my road dawg! That's where I get my game from. I grew up watching her work men out of money. When the shit hit the fan and I lost everything I went to stay with her. She helped me get up the money for an apartment. I went to hair school in the morning and took classes to get my GED at night. I was barely making ends meet but I couldn't get the thirst for material things out of my system; so I was always behind on my bills. Luckily, for me, my Mom's is and was just a fly as me and my size, so I rocked her gear until I got myself together. That's when the dudes came into play. The first two years he was gone I was celibate. After that the need for money took over. I had to have it. A baller and money! What did you think I meant? I know watching all those rap videos didn't help. The world had changed. They only made me thirstier and money hungry. Random chicks were getting butt shots and plastic surgery and coming up left and right. The same chicks that couldn't carry my shoes back in the day were now flyer than me. Groupie was the new job and my city was knee deep in ballers. Even my mom had a retired NFL player at that time. Shit, I even thought about being a stripper for a minute. Between you and I, the only reason I didn't do it was I needed a gig with daytime hours.

Don't get me wrong; being a hairdresser was making me some nice money; I just needed more. I was not always in the mood to pull those long hours. I craved the lifestyle that I'd become accustomed to. I had to catch up with my mother. She was doing it! Her label collection was outrageous. I've always wanted to be like her. She could turn any mans' pockets inside-out with a kiss. I've always been a fly bitch and I had to keep my rep up. Marvin's leaving had left a hole in my heart and pocket. So I used my other holes to fill it. I started juggling men to keep clothes on my back and food for my child; until I got things the way I wanted them. I have a different man for different needs. I never intended to get so deeply involved with so many dudes; I really didn't. I just wanted one or two sugar daddies and to live well. Except for the apartment part; I moved into a small four-apartment building that I could afford with or without a man. I have a fear of becoming homeless. I knew Marvin was coming home to me so I had to have my own spot. Ain't no dude moving in with me, nor will he ever know that he had control of my living situation. Believe that! Never ever will I depend on a man to pay my rent, even though they did and still do! They just didn't know or get credit for it. That's where I met Rhonda. She lived directly across the hall from me.

Let me tell you that story. Rhonda and I hit it off instantly. We became closer friends when she started dating my cousin Patrick. I tried to tell her that he was not the one but she has always been so thirsty for love. I don't know who was happier when their relationship ended, me or her! I got tired of watching him take her for bad and beat her ass relentlessly. Their relationship lasted only five months but our friendship continued. I've always had a lot of respect for Rhonda because no matter what happened in one relationship, she never carried it over into the next. If she had, Rodney would have nothing coming because Patrick dogged the shit out of her. She's just so stupid when it comes to money. She doesn't want a man to take care of her. I don't know where she got that shit from. Rhonda's always had a hard time taking a man's money. She watches too much Oprah. She's been listening to that independent woman shit. That's why she's inde-broke and inde-struggling! Not me! Humph, give it up! How much ya' got? How much you giving me? Let me get that up off you playa! Pussy ain't free. You gotta keep it clean, manicured, fruity fragranced, take it to the doctor, and wrap it up in silk and satin Gucci and Victoria's Secrets. That shit cost money! Despite our different approaches and ideas on love/finances we still became best friends. She was my confidant and babysitter. For a long while she like vicariously through my sex-capades. Man, Patrick left that girl fucked up in the head. I felt so bad for her and a little guilty.

Many of nights we'd cry on each other's shoulder

over Marvin and Patrick. She'd always have something positive to say. Every storm had a silver lining in her eyes. She truly knew how to be a friend. I've always wanted her to be happy especially after Patrick. That's why I kind of feel bad about what happened with Rodney; I really did. But you have to understand that I was only protecting my investment, right? He was going to tell Greg. I have to complete my mission before Marvin came home and he was going to ruin everything. I couldn't have that; now could I? Rhonda wouldn't understand that it wasn't personal it was purely business. She's naïve when it comes to the hustle. Usually, I don't give a fuck but she's the one person that I would never intentionally hurt. Oh well, I had good intentions. Shut up! I know what the road to hell was paved with!

I'm so glad to put all this chaos and drama behind me. Driving down the highway to pick Marvin up, I feel free. Like I'm the one getting out of jail. Like I'm finally free from myself made prison! I can't fake my lifestyle was getting a little out of control. I was running out of nigga's to work. Shit, between you and me, I did a whole lot of tricking. See I'm over here running my mouth. Let me get out of here. I jumped in the truck, slid in the *"Getting To The Money"* joint by Two Chainz and was on my way. That's my new theme song! *"I been getting to that money where the fuck you been. Bought a new crib just to fuck you in!"* Hell yeah! My new Range Rover became one with the road. After Chainz I listened to a little Red Café then went straight to my favorite, *"Belly of the Beast"*, CD which rode with me the rest of my travel. I parked and leaned against the truck, hoping to catch a glimpse of Marvin as he exited. Here comes my baby! You see him, yeah the one that Gucci down. Don't get any ideas, he's mines. Open that mother fucking gate! Damn he looks so good! Whew! He's cut up like a bag of dope. Muscle rippling! Skin glowing! All tatted up! I can feel my panties getting wet as I blew the horn.

"Marvin...Marvin, over here baby!" I screamed
"Damn, it's so good to see you...

He immediately opened my blouse and slid a breast
into his mouth. My knees weakened and body jerked from
the pleasure of his touch as I melted into the truck frame.
Inmates were banging on the windows; watching us.

...girl get me the fuck away from this joint. I've
got five years backed up in me. I can't wait to get up in
between. Damn, baby you looking real good! Where's my
daughter?"

"With my momma. You drive and let me give you
some highway!"

"That sure sound good to me but I ain't had that in
so long I might fuck around and crash into somebody. Not
to mention, I ain't got a bicycle license. You trying to get
me violated my first few minutes home. You so crazy!
Damn, I missed you!"

"I know baby! I just want you inside of me so
badly, I'm not thinking straight."

"C'mon let's go, get me away from here."

Child, you know, I broke every traffic law in
existence! My mailbox is going to be full of speeding
tickets. I want him as much as he wants me. Just the
baritone in his voice saying my name made my body throb
with anticipation. Now that's some powerful shit, am I
right? Thought so! I don't know how we made it to our
new condo in one piece. By time we reached the parking
lot, I couldn't take it anymore. A bitch is about to burst! I
refuse to wait until we get inside. I want him inside me
right here, right now. You know I'm prepared so I'm not
wearing any draws. I swung into a parking space, threw the
truck in park, hiked my skirt up and climbed atop my
personal piece of heaven. He pleased me right in the
parking lot. I almost blacked out from his touch. I screamed
so loudly when my body released, we better hurry up inside

before the neighbors call the police.

Barely making it inside, Marvin looked around our new condo. You know, the one that Greg paid for and furnished. SSSSSShhhhhhhh! Don't say anything! He's so impressed with my hard work.

"Baby, you did all of this?"

"Worked my fingers to the bone. It was hard but where there's a will; there's a way."

"Well, baby you're struggling days are over, your man's home to take care of things now! We're 'bout to get this money, you feel me? I'm 'bout to get shit jumping!"

"I know baby."

"You wasn't out here faking! You must've been handling your business to get all of this. A new truck! Fully furnished joint! None of that cheap shit either. Everything top flight! Taking care of the baby, you, and keeping money on my books. Shit, baby you was getting busy!"

"Busy as a motha! It wasn't all good. Some days were better than others but we made it."

"I know, I remember I used to call sometimes and the phone was cut off and shit. I'm sorry I left you to deal with all this alone. Raising our daughter by yourself! I'm going to make up for everything. I promise you baby. I love you girl." He said pulling me into his strong arms.

"I love you too Marvin! I know what kind of man you are and now that you're home, I know everything is going to be fine."

It was all worth it. Marvin's home now and has no idea how I got the money and I damn sure ain't going to tell him. I'm taking that info with me to the grave. He thinks I was working hard at the salon. Well I was a working hard, just not at the salon. Now he's back to take care of us. Everything will be back to normal. What he doesn't know won't hurt him. Matter of fact, it won't hurt me either. So you better keep your mouth shut. If Marvin ever finds out about the things I've done, that would be all she wrote. Child, I would surely come up missing. He ain't into sharing. It would be some drama for real. Just thinking about it makes me nervous. I need to pee.

These first two weeks have been like living a dream. Screwing constantly, confessing our love, and even eating dinner together as a family. I know that sounds corny but it's been wonderful. Especially showing him off to all the haters! I'm on a high and no one can bring me down. We laid in each other's arms and talked of marriage and buying a house. Making plans to rule the world. We laughed at all the fake friends who'd turned their backs on him when he was locked up because now he's living and looking better than them. You know I had a fly ass wardrobe waiting for him. I gave him a $1,000.00 diamond pinky ring as a welcome home present. Yeah, my baby is still the flyest mother fucker around the way. It was like; I was living every love lyric in *The Three Year Engagement.*

It wasn't long before the bottom began to drop out from underneath me. Now things are changing. The newness has worn off. Using the excuse that he's getting shit set up to start getting money he's been gone more often. He's always in the streets with his friends; drinking. I think I fucked up by letting him drive the truck with no license. I just didn't want him to have to ask anybody for anything. I wanted them to know that he doesn't need shit from their fake asses. Now he's just gon' wild with it. In the morning he drops us off and picks us up in the afternoon, at first it was cute. He has the truck all day to supposedly handle his business. When he picks us up in the afternoon, we go home, he fumbles around for about an hour on the phone and then he's gone until 3 or 4 am. Coming home drunk, talking loud, wanting to fuck and I've got to go to work in the morning. At first I let it slide, I knew he'd be in the street trying to play catch up but now I'm getting sick of this shit! All this time in the street and I ain't seen 1 dime. I know him and he ain't out there for nothing. He's getting money! He ain't paid one bill in this house. No cable! No phone! No nothing! But he's got money to buy bottles and new clothes every day. He comes home every night with new shit! It's always a hook-up from one of his men. What? They didn't have any clothes in my size? What kind of shit is this? Is this what I waited 5 years for? You've got to be fucking with me! This has to be a joke!

What happened to happily ever after? My dream ending is quickly becoming a nightmare. Marvin has become obsessed with drinking, the streets, and that damn truck. I've got to do something. I haven't driven my own truck in I don't know when. Last night, or should I say this morning he came in at 4 am. He was drunk as hell! He woke me up to confess his love. I'm getting tired of hearing that old shit. I've decided that it's now time to change the game. He thinks he's going to drop me off this morning but I got a trick for his ass. He's already gotten up and is preparing himself to take us.

"Oh baby, that's okay. Get some rest! You don't have to drop us off this morning. I have a lot of running around to do, so I'm going to drive myself."

"Alright!" He growled

He crawled back into bed and put the pillow over his head and growled something. If looks could kill; I'd be dead twice. He's fired up. That mother fucker must've forgotten whose shit this is! How's he gonna catch feelings over me driving MY TRUCK? I know Marvin like the back of my hand so I already know what he's going to do. Our rule is, "never let the sun catch you on the wrong side of the door". He knows I don't play that shit! Because I took the truck, he's going to stay out all night. He'll use the excuse that his best friend was too drunk to drive and he doesn't want everyone knowing where we live. I'm already waiting on that move. That shit is old and played out. I'm hip to his shit! He can run the streets all he wants but it won't be in my shit. I've burned so many bridges trying to make his return home comfortable. I never thought he'd show his ass like this. This behavior was not part of my fairy tale. He's not paying me any attention. The loving has decreased to next to nothing. I'm using toys to please myself when I have a man lying beside me. This is some bullshit! Just like I warned you, true to his character, Marvin isn't home yet. It's already 3 a.m. and I haven't heard from him since I left this morning. I wonder who picked him up. Hold on a minute, the phone's ringing. Let the games begin.

"Hello". I whispered trying to sound asleep.

"Simone, this Peanut. Marvin is drunk and passed out. I'm too drunk to bring him home."

"Okay that's fine. It's better that y'all are safe! You don't need to be driving anyway." I replied in a sugary tone.

"Are you sure"? Peanut questioned in disbelief. He can't believe he just told me that my man ain't coming home and I'm so calm. He knows I don't play that shit.

"Of course! It's not a problem. Y'all both get some rest. I will talk to you tomorrow. Thank you for taking care of my baby." I sweetly added before hanging up.
They got me fucked up! Who does he think I am? You can't out slick a can of oil. Hold on the phone is ringing again.

"Hello!"

"Are you sure? This shit ain't right. Let me see if I can I get him up....Marv...Marv....
You can hear the fake ass snoring in the background.

...he's out...I tried." Peanut explained.

"I told you it's okay. I'll see him tomorrow. It's fine!"

"You sure?"

"Of course I am! It's cool! I don't want y'all out in

the streets driving around like that!"

"Alright then". Peanut replied angrily because their little plan isn't working out the way they planned.

Fooled his ass! I changed the game! He expected me to go off! Cursing, offering to get out of bed to pick him up, and having a fit! Meet the new Simone! I knew what he was going to do before he did. I told you that I know him like the back of my hand. I didn't just meet him. See, the purpose for staying out all night was to teach me a lesson. Lesson being, if I he had the truck; he would've been able to bring himself home and not have to depend on anybody else. You got the wrong bitch! I ain't having it! I'm so tired of your shit; I don't care if you never come back. Wit' your drunk ass!

13

Times like this I wish I still smoked. Cause, right now I'd be as high as Coody Brown! Naw, fuck that, no I don't! I'm glad I'm off that shit. The crack head look was drastically decreasing my pussy portions. It's just that I feel bad for my boy. Did you hear what happened? Man, Simone carried him. She just up and left! Leaving him a note that basically said fuck you. That bitch is cold blooded! She carried the hell out of him like a flunkie. Since she left Greg hasn't spoken a word. He won't eat, hasn't been to work, won't answer the phone, and won't accept any visit from us. We eventually had no choice but to go over his house. We had to practically break the door down to get in. When we finally get inside, he's walking around in his boxers holding a picture of her, him, and Minyon; crying like a bitch. The shit is pathetic! I never thought it would go down like this. I damn sure didn't help the situation. I knew that she was using him and what did I do? I slept with her too. I don't need you to remind me; I know what I did. Man I'm telling you if my boy doesn't bounce back from this I'll kill Simone my damn self! I tried to tell him, you can't turn a whore into a housewife. That's gospel! He should've known better. Every woman ain't no got damn queen! Females just as doggish as dudes! They just cover their shit up better. Simone was so see through she was like gas. They say birds of a feather flock together. Rhonda can try me if she wants to.

Who's this? 555-1200? I don't know this number but I answered anyway. When I finally answered the lady on the phone said she's calling from Doctor's Hospital so I told her she had the wrong number and hung up. They're probably trying to page a doctor or something. She's calling back again. Let me tell this woman she got the wrong number.

"Hello." I answered.

"Hello, may I speak with Rodney Hughes?"

"Yes...this is Rodney Hughes?"

"Mr. Hughes this is Nurse Hill from Doctor's Hospital. We have your fiancée here. She's in labor and asked that we call you to come to the hospital. Can you come right away?"

"I'm on my way."

The woman is still running off at the mouth about something when I dropped the phone on the passenger side floor. I bucked a U turn with the quickness and floored it. Oh shit! Something's wrong with Rhonda and the baby. Do you think she lost the baby? She's only three months. All of this is my fault. I've been doing a lot of dumb shit, you know stressing her out. Please let her be okay. I swear that I will never cheat or leave her side again. This car in front of me is making me mad as shit. I banged on my horn. I was on some Ludacris get out of the way madness. Move bitch! I've got to get to the hospital! Don't let her suffer because of me. Please God! I've never really prayed before but now is as good a time as any to start.

"Dear Lord, It's me Rodney. Look, I know that you're very busy but I got this situation and I need help with the quickness. And, God since you **are** the man I'm asking you to please hook me up. I know I've done a lot of things wrong but please don't let Rhonda and the baby suffer for my mistakes."

I continued this prayer over and over all the way to the hospital. Please let my woman and my baby are alright. I never knew how much I really loved Rhonda and wanted our baby until right now. The thought of losing them is weighing heavy on my mind. At this moment I get it! Now I know what I want. A family! With Rhonda! This can't be happening. I've heard stories about women dying after miscarriages are they true? C'mon man, we can't go out like this! They can't leave me. Not today, not on Valentine's. I have a special evening planned and everything. This is some bullshit!

I came speeding into the circular entrance way, threw the car in park, and jumped out of the car. I got to the spin-around door when I realized that I'd left the car running with the driver's side door wide open. I somehow gathered my composure, went back to my car and parked. I rushed straight to the information desk and asked how to get to 2NE. The lady told me to take the elevators behind me to the second floor and make a right. I heard the directions but this is definitely a Charlie Brown moment. I found the elevator, it came, and I boarded and pressed 2. I'm caught up in a whirlwind of emotions and when the doors opened I didn't even realize it. They were beginning to close as I dove out. I almost missed my floor. Then my brain shut down. Everything is a blur. I don't know which is the correct nursing station so I stopped at the first nurses' station I saw. I ran to the desk. *"Yes, I'm Rodney Hughes."* The nurses hurried me into this scrub room. I put on one of the hospital getups and flew into delivery room 8. Hold on Rhonda baby I'm on the way. I ain't no sucker or nothing but the tears won't stop flowing. I wish they'd hurt me; not my baby. Now I know understand what people mean when they say that, it really is how you feel. The room is cold and sterile. I feel like I'm in an episode of *"Hawthorne"*. I forced my way through the doctors and nurses. I am so focused I can't hear a word they say.

Through misty eyes I bent over to kiss my baby on the forehead to let her know that I was here. Hell no! What the fuck? Man, this ain't my woman! I don't believe this shit! Guess who it is? It's Kenya! Yeah, Kenya! You mean to tell me I practically killed myself getting here for this bitch? I'm out of here! What is she up here telling these people that would make them think I want to be here for this? I snatched the mask off of my face and stomped off heading for the door. At the same time my hand touched the door, I heard a smack, and then the baby began to cry.

Should I turn around? Man, fuck that! That ain't my baby anyway. I kept walking without looking back.

"Mr. Hughes, where are you going? Would you like to cut the umbilical cord?" The doctor asked.

"Hell no!"

"Don't you want to hold your son?" A nurse asked.

"He's not my son!" I shouted back.

I stormed out of the delivery room pissed. This bitch is a new kind of crazy. She's gone too far this time. I'm going to get my little cousins to whip her and Simone asses. Why me? Why do I always get the nut case? Well now that the baby is here, I can prove once and for all he's not mine. We are going on Maury or something. I'm not wasting any time getting the DNA test done. It's time to get her off of my back! I should turn around and see if the doctor can do that shit right now but I'm so mad that I'd choke her out again and end up in jail on Valentine 's Day. I feel sorry for that baby because he has a nitwit for a mother. How is she going to just make me be a father? I doubled up! That baby ain't mines! That's one night I wish I would've slept. I wish she would just leave me alone. She's on some fatal attraction type shit. Dizzy bitch! She can't take care of herself, let alone a baby. That's what I hate about women; they always trying to trap a somebody. I don't care what she does; she can't make me deal with that baby or her. If the baby is proven to be mines, I'll cut a check. That's it! That's all!

Once again, I almost ran every light rushing straight home to Rhonda. I raced upstairs where I found her sleeping. I crawled in bed and laid down beside her. I began to rub her stomach. My baby's okay! Thank you God! Good looking out! My mind's going 100 mph trying to figure out what to do next. What do you think I should do? Should I tell her or not? Yeah, I hear you! But, that is a definite no go! I drifted off to sleep with my hand on Rhonda's stomach. Rhonda woke me up in what felt like a couple of hours later. In reality it probably was 45 minutes.

"Happy Valentines sleepy head."

"Happy Valentine's." I replied

"I love you sexy."

"Oh yeah, how much?"

"Enough to mess up my beautiful body carrying your baby. Know what?"

"What?"

"I'd do it again in a heartbeat."

I grabbed Rhonda and pulled her close to me. So close, I could feel her heart beating against my bare chest. I'm holding her so tightly; I know that she can tell something's up. But she didn't say anything she just returned the embrace. We started kissing. I need to get my shit together now; right now! I'm starting to get on my own damn nerves. Then the O'Jays, *"Cry Together"* came on the radio. It's as if the DJ Frank Ski knows exactly what I'm experiencing at this moment. Tears streamed down Rhonda's face. I wiped them away. Every time I see her cry, I think of all the things I've done wrong. Guilt is fucking with me.

"Rodney, I thought I'd never know a love like this."

"Ssssh! Come here boo!"

We began to make love. This time it was intense. I took my time wit' it! I was begging for forgiveness through my lovemaking. Every touch was planned to drive her crazy. I coated her body with kisses and licked every inch of skin on her. As my face nestled between her thighs I was a man on a mission. I licked and sucked her until her wetness called for me. All movements were slow and defined. With every thrust I tried to say that I was sorry. Pleasing her should have been my only priority; not pleasing myself. I've done wrong and I'm sorry. Ain't no way I'm going to lose this woman. I don't know how I managed to get the words out but just as my thrust drove her into a frenzy. I slid the ring on her finger and asked her to marry me. She said yes. Afterwards I asked her again because it was kind of hard to tell what she was saying yes to. Ecstasy has taken her somewhere else. She hasn't even realized that I slipped the ring on her finger. She finally snapped back into focus and caught a glimpse of her hand.

"Yes!" She screamed and burst into tears after finally noticing the ring on her finger.

Rhonda's overjoyed to say the least. She screamed so loud that you'd think I was killing her in here. Did I really just do that? No turning back now. Time to turn in my playa card! I'm done! I'm serious! No more fucking up! I don't remember asking for your opinion! You heard me! I'm going to do the right thing! And no, I'm not just doing this because Greg asked Simone or because I cheated; I really want to spend the rest of my life with her. Looking at that two-carat, oval shaped diamond lets me know to the penny, how much I love her. I have to! It's going to take me a couple of years to pay for it. I don't care though. She's worth every dime and then some. As I kissed the ring on her finger, I slid my manhood back into his favorite place. We kissed passionately as our bodies wrestled for dominance. Today would've been perfect if Kenya hadn't pulled that stupid shit earlier. Why can't she just find her real baby daddy and stop fucking with me? She knows that baby ain't mines. Even if it is, like I said, I'm taking the cut the check route. No interaction at all!

We showered together making plans for the future as Raheem set the mood. Our wedding! What we would name the baby if it's a girl. What the name would be if it were a boy; Rodney Jr. of course! Now this is how it's supposed to go down, two consenting adults who both want the baby. Remember, that shit she said about putting a hole in the rubber? What kind of shit is that? I tell you this, that's the last time I'll ever let a female put a rubber on for me. I'm telling all my boys to put it on and take it off yourself. Shit, take it with you if you have to. I don't care if she is using her mouth to do it. Nobody should a trick you. I should charge her ass with rape. Sperm-hijacking! Something! A child should come from love not deceit; right? Nothing or no one is going to come between Rhonda and me. Does she think that baby will make me want to be with her? I've never really been in love before and I refuse to let her destroy this for me. When we finally got out of bed, we called around telling everyone the news of our engagement.

We got dressed and I took her to her favorite spot, The Cheesecake Factory to celebrate our engagement. Later, as we lay in bed, I stared at the ceiling above with her in my arms knowing that nothing will ever match this feeling. I can't lose her! I won't lose her! Kenya is not going to cost me everything! I need some time to think! I've got to figure out my next move. I can't play checkers when this nit wit is playing chess. So I'm taking the rest of the week off. Thursday and Friday belong to me! I feel a 2 day sickness coming on. That's what leave is for right? Time to take a couple of slick, my bad, I mean sick day. I might as well have went to work because all I did was drink and trying to find ways to kill Kenya without getting caught!

Monday morning came entirely too quick for me. I'm still not really prepared to deal with the unnecessary stress and problems of work. I feel like a walking time bomb! That feeling faded fast when the realization hit me that I need money to survive and pay for that ring. Let me get my ass up! Time to get up, get out, and get something! Rhonda has already left. She's working from seven to three today. I fumbled around the house preparing for work. Still trying to figure out how I got into this predicament. Better yet, how am I going to get out of it? Man shit! That baby ain't mines! Can't be! I strapped up! I only have one child and he isn't even born yet. He's still in Rhonda's stomach. Kenya is trying to destroy me. I'm not going to let her.

She must've forgotten who she's dealing with! I'm not a toy. I'm not some little boy. I'm a grown ass man! How's she just going to make me the father of her child? Where do they do that at? What kind of shit is this? I always knew she was a few cards short of a deck, but damn! She's tripping. See I told you; there are hazards to being a hell of a man like me. I got 99 problems but laying pipe ain't one! I used to put it on Kenya so proper that I've driven this chick off the deep end. If you don't know; now you know. Big daddy lay pipe like an Exxon oil worker. I tried to warn her that this pole was addictive but she didn't listen. She thought she could handle it. See what happens when you don't listen. You end up like her. Hard head = crazy stalker. I never thought she'd flip out like this though. I guess I can't blame her; I'd miss me too. Who wouldn't?

All the way up to and through my lunch hour my mind is consumed with thoughts of Kenya and that baby. It is driving me crazy. Man, I wonder how she's going to carry things. While entering my office I got a bad vibe. You see that? Yeah, right there? What the fuck is that on my desk? It's something small and white sitting atop a stack of papers on my desk. What's that? It wasn't here when I left out! The closer I get, I realize it's a photograph in a white border. The top border frame reads, "World Please Meet". The bottom reads, "Mr. Rodney Hughes Jr. What the fuck? Man, I don't believe this! Do you know that crazy bitch still named that baby after me? She's pressed! She named him after me; last name and all. I didn't sign the birth certificate is that legal? A million things are running through my mind right now as I hold this picture. She's going to make me catch a murder beef! This ain't my damn baby! But Shorty is cute though. Between you and me, he has this crooked little smile and one dimple in his right cheek; just like me. Maybe, he is my son? I mean, I was tapping that ass on the regular. Did I just say that? What do you think? Naw, fuck that! Ain't no way. I ain't claiming nobody! My man stayed strapped. How did this picture get here anyway? Man, I'm telling you, she's trying to ruin me.

Instantly, I became paranoid. Do you think anyone else has seen this picture? The baby? Her? Does somebody in the hospital know? Does Kenya know someone that works here? Who put this picture here? Is Kenya still in the hospital? Did she go see Rhonda? Oh shit! I flew out of my office like I had diarrhea in the club. Diving head first into the elevator I reached for the B button. My tie got caught in the closing doors; almost chocked the shit out of myself. I have to get to the emergency room. I have to get to Rhonda. I should've taken the stairs.

When I got the emergency room Rhonda had already left for the day. Patrice, the triage nurse, said she'd left about a half an hour ago. She also told me that five minutes after Rhonda left some light skinned girl with a baby came by asking for her. She wants me to give Rhonda the message. My mouth replied sure but my mind said I ain't telling her shit. Yeah right! Either Patrice is crazy or she thinks I am. That's it! I called Kenya from my cell and left her a message to meet me at Dr. Berton's office right now. We're going to squash this baby mess once and for all. Shit, I don't care what it cost! We're taking some test, today! Not tomorrow; today! I consider this an investment in my future. I am not trying to deal with her dingy ass for the next 18 years and lose my woman. She called back laughing and agreed to meet me. I immediately and made an appointment for 4:30. I left work early and headed for his office.

Driving to Dr. Berton's office I couldn't keep my focus. DJ Flexx was banging that Clapper joint "*Shorty Got A Big Ole Butt*" with Wale, Nikki and Juicy J. Then DJ Reddz hit a mix that included everything from Da Water to Da Butt! Vintage go-go! I was in my car partying like a lunatic. I tried my best to forget my problems and get lost in the music. All of my thoughts are being interrupted by plans of different ways to kill Kenya. Have you ever wanted to kill someone before? Man, I'm telling you, I can see myself digging a hole and putting her in it. Nobody would miss her. I'm telling you I can get away with it. I know I'll never do it but I'm sure enjoying thinking about it. This chick got me in serial killer mode. Sitting across from Kenya in the doctor's office; I'm really feeling froggy than a mother fucker. Like at any second, I'm going to leap over there and choke her ass out. I can barely manage to restrain myself. She's sitting over there smiling and shit! What the fuck is she so happy about? Does she think I'm happy about this? Man, she's on joke time. I don't want to make a scene. I'm trying my best not to make a scene. It took me about twenty minutes to even look at her. Between you and me, Kenya is looking kind of healthy. She must've stopped smoking because she's picked up a few pregnancy pounds. I haven't really seen her since that day at my mother's house. Every pound is in the right place. Damn she's looking good for someone who just pushed a baby out. My dick is so hard that I can use it to cut diamonds. That ass is looking nice and juicy. Real good! She's staring at my print so she knows she's turning me on. I tried to cover my print with my suit jacket. She giggled with joy at my arousal. I might have to hit that again? What am I saying? That's how I go into this.

Since Kenya started all of this drama I've been a walking time bomb. I'm anxious, irritable, and nervous as Tiger Woods when his wife found out. Dr. Berton said he could have the results in 48 hours. I told him that I'd be back in 47 hours. What time is it now? It seems like this day is never going to be over. What time is it now? Good, let's go find out. I hauled ass over to Dr. Berton's.

"Hey Doc, are the results in?"

"Sure son, they came back from the lab this

morning. Since you didn't want any calls, I didn't try to contact you."

"Alright. What the deal? Is this my baby or what?"

"Yes, son it is."

"Oh hell no! What? Are you sure? C'mon Doc...you can't be serious"

"The results are 99.9% positive that the baby is yours." He responded

"This is all messed up! I don't want a dog with her never less a baby"

"I take it that congratulations are not in order. Remember, all children are a blessing. A child is a gift from God."

"Doc, please tell me that you're wrong!" Can we take it again? Maybe the samples got mixed up or something?"

"I'm sorry son but the tests don't lie."

Dr. Theodore Berton has been my fathers' best friend since they became Q dogs while attending H.U. My pops was there on a basketball scholarship; that's where my little brother gets his game. I can talk to Doc about anything and he always had the answer. This time Doc left me hanging; even he can't get me out of this one! Aw damn! What am I going to do now? I damn sure can't tell Rhonda about this baby cause then she'll know that I've been lying the whole time. She can't say I've cheated on her because of the time frame but lying is just as bad. I've got to do something because Kenya is not going to back off. She's going to press the issue. Now that those results came back positive she's going to show her ass. She's going to tell the world! Eventually Rhonda is going to find out. I can't afford to let Rhonda find out from somebody else. She'll never forgive me if I'm not the one to tell her. So much drama; so little time! You know what? I'm just going to keep my mouth shut for now and pray she gets hit by a bus. Yeah, then I'll just act as if I just found out about the baby, tell Rhonda the situation, and adopt him. Who am I fooling that shit will never happen but it is a great dream anyway.

14

I knew from the embarrassment alone, Simone's leaving would hit Greg hard but not like this; he's damn near suicidal. Any minute he's going to snap, I just know it. He's on the fast track to the mental ward. Rodney's been spending a lot of time with him. Personally, I can't even look at him. I feel like shit! I did him wrong as well. I mean, I did introduce him to the gold digging bitch. I should've never introduced her to him. When I called to check up on him earlier he wouldn't even talk to me. He just mumbled something and dropped the receiver. My conscious is fucking with me so badly; I left work an hour early. When I got home there was a message on the answering machine from someone named Kenya. I don't know anyone named Kenya. Kenya? She says that she's an old classmate. I don't remember her. She said Patrice had told her about my party when she'd stopped past the hospital today and if she was still in town she'd come. That's mighty bold of her. How's she just going to invite herself to my shit? Who is Kenya? And how did she get my number?

Whoever she is she better have a good present. Oh, it must be Kenya Turner with her crazy butt. That was my girl in school; me, Pam, and Kenya used to cut up. She wanted to be the next Nikki Minaj. She was always rapping and singing. Child she would wear some outfits that would flip you out. She definitely had her own style. With dreams of fame or a rich husband she packed up and moved to Atlanta right after graduation. And when I say right after graduation I really mean it. Girlfriend had her car loaded up on graduation day and left on her journey from the Verizon Center. Okay! She sure could blow; voice like Monica. I wonder what she's doing now. I hope she found her dream. She was really sweet and deserves to be happy. She's one sista who had a rough life. Boy does she have a story to tell. Why didn't she leave a number? The caller ID just says cell phone. I called back but nobody answered. Oh well, I can't focus on that right now. I have to help Greg, plan my party, and not get stressed out. I do miss her though. I can't wait to see her. My birthday is a month and a half away. I can't wait to see her. That girl is crazy. She used to keep me in trouble at school. I can't wait until you meet her. You're going to love her. That reminds me, I need to call my girl Kim Evans also. She moved to Georgia to start her own PR firm. She's down there killing it too. I wonder will she be at home during that time. Yeah, just remind me to call her later. I erased the message from Kenya. Ate! Then I went to lie down.

Why is it that when you're trying to sleep everybody starts calling on the phone. It's like they can see you. Don't you hate that! It hasn't been fifteen minutes since I've laid down and the phone is ringing off of the hook. See what I'm saying! It's ringing again. They hung up. The phone rang again. I looked at the caller ID. This time it's my mother. She's asking if I've heard about Greg. Heard what? What's wrong? Oh no! Apparently, sometime after I had talked to him his mind snapped. He's jumped out of his second floor bedroom window; holding on to Simone's picture. No bullshit! He jumped out the damn second floor window! He survived the fall with only a few bruises and a broken ankle. But he's had a nervous breakdown and is considered a danger to himself. He's in the mental ward at Hobson under suicide watch.

I must be dreaming. Breathe, Rhonda, breathe! I'll just close my eyes and open them back up and everything will be okay. No! This is not a dream because I'm still holding the phone and Jean's still yapping away in my ear. My brain is so fried right now I can't understand her at all. She sounds like Charlie Brown's school teacher. Womp! Womp! Womp! She wants Rodney and me to meet her at the hospital. All of this drama has caused Ma Wheeler to pass out and she's also at Hobson in the E.R. This is all my fault! I can't go! I can't face Greg's parents. Suppose Greg never snaps out of it and never comes back to normal? I don't know what I'll do. What should I do? This is not happening.

While I was getting the scoop from Jean, the other line clicked. I managed to tell my mom to hold on and clicked over. It's Rodney! I told him to meet me at the hospital but I didn't tell him why. The last thing I need is for him to have an accident trying to get there. He didn't really ask any questions he just agreed and said he was en route. I clicked back over and told my mother that we were on our way. Then I called to tell Coco and Kiki as I was heading for my car but they knew and were also already en route. Lexie's boyfriend Chris answered the phone when I called. He'd come over to pick up Jason. He and Coco are good friends. They've been close buddies for years, just like Rodney and Greg. So naturally, he was concerned about Rodney. I explained that Rodney didn't know what happened but he was on his way to the hospital. He agreed that not telling him was probably was the best way to handle the situation.

Shaking and crying uncontrollably, I made it to the hospital by God's will alone; accident-free. I don't even remember driving. I can't see a thing. My eyes are red and puffy like I've just smoked a pound of loud. Good thing I know my way around the hospital; my vision has taken a temporary vacation. I feel light headed. Straight to the ER, I went to check on Ma Wheeler. She'd just been released. Everyone here is staring at me like I have a booger hanging from my nose or something. I caught a glimpse of myself in the mirror. Oh my God! Now I see why they're staring at me. I'd run out of the house in Rodney's Nike boots, a doll baby nightie, and a trench coat. Thugarella! Gaining my sense for a moment I borrowed a scrub outfit. Talk about embarrassing. Child please! This is too much for me! They're going to be talking about this for weeks. I looked like I should be checking into the mental ward.

On the elevator ride to the eighth floor mental ward, I feel like I'm about to lose it. It feels like the walls are closing in. By the time I rounded the corner to the waiting room entrance I was through booking! Shaking! Crying! My palms are sweaty and I'm having a hard time breathing. My legs feel like spaghetti. I feel like I'm having an asthma attack and I don't even have asthma. I gotta piss! You should see Rodney! He's bawled up in the corner rocking and crying. This is not happening! I've seen Rodney let a tear or two sneak down his face but I've never seen him breakdown. He's bawling like Greg's dead. Oh no is he? I rushed straight over to comfort Rodney. As soon as I hugged him, he cried even harder!

This waiting room feels like a morgue. It's so cold and dreary in here. Everyone is in a daze; like chocolate zombies! We look like we should be the patients! Jean and Sandra are trying their best to comfort Ma Wheeler. Otis, poor Otis, his head is hung so low he looks beheaded! It's understandable though, I don't know how I would feel if that was my child in there. I'd probably be the same way if not worse. Simone really did a number on Greg. She reached into his chest and literally pulled his heart out. Karma is a bitch! She will get hers! Damn, I wish I never introduced her to him. In my wildest nightmare, I never expected it to end like this. I knew Simone would hurt him in some way but not like this. I think that he's more embarrassed than hurt. Either way, he's not doing well.

Rodney's going off! If he doesn't calm down he may end up becoming Greg's roommate. What the hell am I supposed to do? I don't know what to do and I really don't feel comfortable being here. Since Simone was my friend, I know they blame me. Whether they say it or not, they're probably thinking that I'm just like her trifling ass. You know guilt by association; birds of a feather flock together. I know they do! I know I would if I was them.

Maybe, if I had done something different I could've stopped this. I should've said something! I knew she was up to no good. This is one time I should've butted in. I just thought it was best to mind my own business. Now it's too late. He doesn't deserve this he's a good dude! All he did was try to love her undeserving ass. They say bad things happen to good people, now I'm witnessing it up close and personal. I also know that I don't like this one bit. How can I continue to face these people? Her shit is making me stink. They're bout to question me to death, I just know it. What am I supposed to say? Yes, I knew she was using your son? I'm all in the middle of this and she rolled out; leaving me to clean up her mess. Best friend my ass!

This will definitely go down as the longest night of my life. The tension and emotion in this room is so thick you can cut it with a knife. Pacing and crying! Crying and pacing! I'm a nervous wreck. By time the doctor returns to talk to Ma Wheeler, I'll have walked a bald spot or at least a pathway into this tacky corporate carpet. Guilt has wrapped itself around my throat and is choking the shit out of me. Everyone wants me to go home because of the pregnancy. I can't! I won't! My black ass ain't budging! They're going to have to literally carry me out of here. It's my fault! I've got to know how Greg is. I have to hear it for myself. He's got to be okay! Wait a minute; here comes the doctor.

"Mr. and Mrs. Wheeler?"

"Yes...we are the Wheelers."

"Would you come with me please?"

"We're all his family. You can talk to us here doctor."

"Are you sure?"

"Yes." Otis replied in his *did you not hear me* tone.

"Well, the only way to tell you this is to be direct."

"Okay."

"You're son is in a very agitated state. He's suicidal

and is considered a danger to himself at this time. As we speak he's restrained and has been sedated to calm him down."

"Wait one damn minute. Are you telling me that you got my boy chained down like some got damn animal?"

"*OH JESUS!*" Ma Wheeler screamed.

"Mr. Wheeler your son is paranoid, delusional, and suicidal. He had to be restrained to protect him from harming himself. He's had a severe breakdown. Once the medication kicks in, well be in a better position diagnosing him further. Tell me, was there a recent tragedy the may have triggered this?"

"The girl he was in love with just up and left him. He's been devastated and heartbroken ever since." Ma Wheeler managed to mutter through the tears.

"Doctor, may we see our son?" asked Otis.

"I'm sorry but for the first couple of days there can be no visitors. His condition must be closely monitored. Anybody can upset him and increase the severity of his condition. So we allow no visitors at all. I'm sorry but its hospital policy. We just want him to rest right now."

Ma Wheeler fell to her knees and called out for the Lord to let her take her sons place. Coco snapped punching a hole in the hospital wall before storming out on a hit mission to find Simone. I know he's going to get Chris! This shit just officially went left! The entire waiting room turned into an angry lynch mob. Simone is the target of their venomous rage. She's public enemy number #1. They want to kill her and hang her head on a lamp post on Benning Road. Right about now, I am more than willing to help them. How could she do that to him? She had no right. Talk about fucking somebody over! Now, Greg's strapped down in a mental ward while Simone's sipping Don P somewhere strapped down with Marvin. There is no way possible that this is fair. You deserve better than this for loving someone. He gave her the world and all she gave him was her ass to kiss.

It's been at least an hour since the doctor told us to we couldn't see Greg but, with the exception of Coco, we're all still sitting here. Stuck! The reality that the hospital staff wasn't going to let us behind those locked doors finally set in.; we started to leave. Rodney and I both have to work tomorrow. We assured Ma Wheeler and Otis that we'd find a way to sneak in and check on Greg; that gave them some relief. It wasn't much though. These hospital walls feel like they're closing in around me. What once was a spacious room now feels like a jail cell. As if someone fired a starter gun we all began to stream out. We headed for our separate destinations; all in a state of disbelief. Everyone clearly had their own intentions on how to deal with the situation. The only common thread involved harm to Simone. I got in my car and cried as I drove home. This is so fucked up. Tell me this is not happening! This is not happening? Future's and Rick Ross's jam, *"No Games"* has a whole new meaning right now. I threw on Casanova to calm me down. I need to hear some love songs. I'm already turned up! I have got to calm down for my baby.

The closer I get to my front door my feet are sticking to the pavement more and more with each step. I feel like I'm wearing cinderblocks. I'm terrified. Rodney has beaten me home and I know that he's going to give me the third degree about Simone; I don't want to go in here. Do you think he's going to question me? Me too! I turned the key bracing myself for whatever may happen next. Lord, please be with me! Rodney's in the living room sitting in his favorite white leather chair. He's looking at an album of old pictures of him, Coco, and Greg; tears are gushing down his face. I've never seen him so hurt. He looks zapped out; like he smoked a dipper or something. Is he about to have a breakdown too? What am

I supposed to do? I've never been in a situation like this. I'm not prepared to handle all of this! Fuck it, if he asks me I'm just going to tell him the truth. The version of the truth where I don't know anything and never did. I'm not going to let her mess my shit up! The only problem is that the truth is I knew what she was doing the entire time. From the word go, I knew she was working him. Damn, this is fucked up!

"Rhonda, what happened to Greg? Do you know?"

"Huh? What do you mean, sexy?" I asked acting like I didn't understand the question.

"What made him snap like that? Can loving someone make you lose your mind?"

"People love in different ways, some harder than others. Most people can't handle betrayal, especially from someone they love." I replied trying to avoid any further questioning.

"What about you? How would you react?"

"Well, I don't really know. Why? Why do you ask?"

"Just curious…what would you do?"

"I guess I'd survive. I pray that I'll never have to find out but if I loved someone as intensely as Greg did I suppose there would always be a possibility. Love can be a deadly weapon if you're not in the right frame of mind when it's used against you."

"Baby, I'm sorry." Rodney proclaimed.

"Sorry for what, baby? You haven't hurt me."

"Rhonda, no matter what happens always know that I love you." He replied.

"I love you too…what do you think is going to happen?"

"Nothing! Just letting you know, I really do love you. I always have and always will! You're my world!"

What is that supposed to mean? This whole night has completely drained me. I tried to eat for the baby's sake, showered, climbed into bed, and finally fell asleep. Truthfully, I don't how to get out of this situation. I'm totally clueless! Simone snatched away the frying pan and dropped my ass right into the fire. It would be a lot easier to deal with the pressure if I'd reaped the benefits. I didn't get a dime, pocketbook, shoe, or nothing out of the deal. But I have to pay the price for her actions. I don't believe this is happening to me!

15

"Kitty what time is it?"

"1:30"

"Tony?"

"What?"

"Can you cover my 2:00 for me?"

"Oh no... Ms. Thang! I have things to do...trade to work!" He responded with a finger snap.

"Telephone!" Kitty yelled.

"Who is it?"

"It's Kecia."

"Tony, you ain't right ho! That trick ain't going nowhere! You know you could help me out! You make me sick!"

"Ump humph! Whatever! This queen wants her meat! Momma needs to be fed!"

"Hello...oh, for real...okay...sure we can reschedule...okay...bye."

"Who was that?"

"Kecia...she wants to reschedule...so there Ms. Thing. I didn't need your help anyway!"

"Uh uh! Ms One, slow your roll! Let's not get beside ourselves. First I will read your tired ass for life then I will beat that ass!"

"Whatever! Jump!" I dared.

I grabbed my purse, car keys, and exited stage left. I have to get out of this shop. I should've gotten Greg to help me get my own shop before I left. I'm just not feeling this shit today! I can't concentrate. My mind is on Marvin. I'm really getting sick of his shit. Child, I get a migraine every time I think of how he's been acting since he's been home. He's really been overplaying his hand. Every since he's been home it's been a mixture of heaven and hell. He's matured so much since he's been locked up; yet a lot of shit stayed the same. He sold me that jailhouse con and I fell for it. He came with some new ideas on how our relationship was going to go; he should've asked me! It's like we're starting all over again; but I don't know this man. The new Marvin is every woman's dream and my reality/curse. He's drinking too much and I don't like it. I'm trying to be cool about it but I ain't really feeling this shit. When he drinks he's too aggressive and rough with me. He claims he's going to do right by me this time; whatever that means. We've been talking about getting married. Minyon is so happy about her daddy being home; she follows him around like a puppy. She's been glued to Marvin's hip every day. I'm happy that she's happy; they look so cute together. He loves playing daddy and she loves being daddy's little girl. Although, Minyon still asks about Greg often; too often for Marvin!

My contact with Rhonda and them has completely stopped; since I left Greg. I wonder what they've been up to? I'm going to call Rhonda eventually. I miss my girl. We've been through hell together. I know that she's mad at me for leaving her holding the bag. But she's still my girl and she knows the game. I know that she's holding me down. I'm sure Greg is on the bounce back tip by now. I guess he probably took it kind of hard at first. He's strong. He'll brush it off and roll on with his life. Between you and me, I kind of miss him. He was fun to be with and he treated me like a lady. He was always making me laugh. We had some good times but he just doesn't do it for me like Marvin. Greg's a good man and he'll find someone to return the love he has. It just wasn't me. There is only enough room in my heart for one man. Marvin has that spot locked down. I guess if the situation had been different I may have allowed myself to care for Greg but it wasn't. It was just bad timing. I know Greg doesn't want to see or hear from me but let's just drive past his house and case the joint. You know, check on the situation. Do a little tree boxing. You and I, both know there's a possibility I may see Rhonda, Rodney or maybe even Greg. If I do see one of them; I'll just act like I don't and keep driving. Yeah that'll work. They won't know it's me especially since I've painted the truck red now and all the windows are tinted.

I really don't know what I'm expecting to see other than a house. I mean, if he is missing me he wouldn't advertise it on the lawn. Suppose he had a big ass sign reading: "Come Home Simone- I Love You". That would be too damn funny. I turned on my radio and Angie Ange provided me with some much needed musical courage. "*Give It All To Me*" by Movado featuring Nikki was pumping. That reggae vibe gave me some Bob Marley type strength. In the back of my mind I just know that there's going to be another car in the driveway besides his Vette. Some bitch is probably up in there as we speak, living in my house; trying to fill my shoes. Payless feet don't belong in Jimmy Choo's! The thought of that alone is making me mad as hell. Wait a minute! What am I getting jealous for? I left him! I came out on top. He's the one missing me; right? A part of me really doesn't want Greg to be over me that fast. I want him to miss me longer. Shit, with the way Marvin's acting I don't know if leaving Greg was such a good idea. Real talk!

As soon as I turn the corner, I spot Greg's Porsche in the driveway. I guess he's home! I wonder if he's alone. If someone is here, he had to have picked the whore up. The cheap bitch can't even afford a ride. Now that's what you call low income; he got one of them bus pass bitches. What's that? You see that? I wonder if he got robbed or something? Something must've happened! Why is his second floor window broken? What happened to the front door? I wonder what went down? Some kid probably threw a football or something like that. Yeah, that's probably what happened. Right? Nah, it has to be more to it. That couldn't be the reason because Greg would've had that window fixed immediately. Something ain't right! It also looks like the front door frame is broken. Something definitely jumped off over here!

I better get up out of here; before someone comes outside. I talk a lot of shit but I'm not really up for a showdown; not today! Let me get my ass home. I wonder did Marvin find out where Greg lives? Oh, I pray that Marvin hasn't done something stupid. Greg ain't no match for Marvin and Marvin is so jealous he would really hurt Greg. Especially for the way Minyon has been going on and on about him. I know for a fact; Marvin can't stand to hear his daughter praising another man.

Driving home the sounds of Wiz and Juicy J, "*Smoke Ass Nigga*" bounced around my Range Rover. jumping from my speakers. I thought about Marvin as I drove. I have so many things to make up to him, as he does with me; we owe each other. For the five years he was away, I took tricking to a new level. I am firm believer in cash for ass! I was officially whoring. It wasn't my initial intention it just spiraled out of control. The only thing I was missing was a pimp. See, what you don't know is that Marvin and I had a discussion when he first got locked up. He never asked anything unreasonable of me. He was realistic. All he asked of me was that I never went out with any of his friends. You know how it is, as soon as a man takes a fall their main girl usually ends up with his best friend that's still on the streets. The closest get the mostest! You know the game. I swore to him that I wasn't going out like that. Secondly, he asked that I didn't have a rack of dudes around his daughter. He didn't want Minyon to see a lot of different men with her mother. He said it would make her lose respect for herself as a woman and think that was what a woman was supposed to do. Now that one I did do! As far as the first one; I tried. It's just a matter of supply and demand. Between jail and the drought, finding a baller was like finding Nemo; it took some work. Now don't get me wrong, there is definitely some long money in the city. It's just; the lifestyle I demanded required a large supply of men with money. I wanted all the money I could get. Everyone with money was fair game; including his friends. Shit! Coochie is a commodity.

"Can't Raise A Man" that's the jam. K. Michelle is singing her face off! Music is a funny thing. Ain't it weird how a song can tap into your emotions and say what you're feeling? Marvin has got me sprung! Gone! He keeps me moist all day and night! I really want everything to work out for us. I didn't do all of this for nothing; I want my happy ending! But if he keeps drinking and running the streets I don't know what's going to happen. I can't stand a drunk. As good as he looks I know bitches are throwing themselves at him. And, I know, his little fucked up friends are encouraging him to get as much new pussy as possible.

This drive home is working on my last nerve! No matter how fast I go it doesn't seem fast enough. I just should've taken my ass straight home instead of stopping past Greg's. I can't wait to feel Marvin inside of me. He better be here too because mommy needs to be fed. All that he had to do today is take a urine and get a haircut. He left early this morning. Men are not like women; it only takes his barber fifteen to twenty minutes tops! I know that he's home by now. Finally here! Home sweet home! I can't wait to feel his touch. I just want to be happy with him and keep our family together. Is that too much to ask for? I may have went the wrong way to get it I know that.

The living room lights are on; so he's here. Oh yeah, did I mention that the pawnshop gave me a pretty penny for Greg's ring. What did I do with the money? Now there's a little trivia for you.

"Hey boo…how was your day? Did you miss me? I asked as I hugged him and placed tiny kisses all over his face and neck.

"Humph...wassup!" He growled.

"Wassup...what's wrong with you? Why you sound like that?" I purred while straddled atop his lap.

"Like what?" Marvin snapped pushing me off of his lap onto the floor.

"Why you barking at me? What's wrong?" I asked from the floor confused.

"Let me ask you something...while I was away how many bitch ass nigga's did you say you dealt with?"

"Two! Greg and Troy...why?"

"I'm going to give you one more chance to tell the truth. You know I can't stand a liar." Marvin warned.

"What the fuck is that supposed to mean? I'm telling the truth!" I answered defensively.

"Simone... you didn't fuck Pierre?" Marvin snapped as he walked off into the kitchen.

Pierre was Marvin's right hand man and hustling partner before Marvin got locked up. Hell yeah! I slept with Pierre but how did he know?

"Who told you that?" I questioned in full denial mode.

"I went around the way today. A hot day brings everybody outside. You'd be surprised at who I ran into!"

"They lied...mother fuckers always lying! The need to mind their business! They're just jealous of what we got!"

"Oh really? Well, Pierre's baby mother, Tiffany told me how Pierre left her for you. Yeah but she's doing all right now. She's got a new friend; his name is Chuckie. Don't you know him? What about Dave; Chuckie's walk boy? Or, maybe Russell; some girl named Kitty's uncle. My little cousins; Tweet and Dee! From what I hear you've fucked half of the city? Shall I continue? The list goes on."

"I know that you don't really believe that shit? Marvin, somebody's just hating on me! Probably trying to

171

get even with me because I wouldn't give them none.
Mother fuckers can see how I held you down. So many of
your so called friends were coming at me while you were
gone! They're jealous that's all. Don't feed into that
bullshit! You know me! You know I wouldn't do no shit
like that!"

"Well how come every last one of them knows you
have a birthmark on the inside of your left thigh; right by
your twat? Huh? How do they all know that you have my
name tattooed on your ass, huh? What about big head
Roy? I guess you didn't give him head in the car? My
motherfucking car! The car I paid for! I hear they call you
the *Deep Throat Slot Machine!* You was out here doing
something strange for some change! Huh! Did you think
that you could do all of this shit and get away with it? D.C.
is too small to be trying to get over; especially on a player
in these streets. Everybody knows everybody! You just a
whore! You just a dope man's trick! I'm outta here and
I'm taking my daughter with me! You cum drinking
bitch!"

Marvin grabbed his coat, the keys to *my* truck, and
started for the door. I know he don't think he's going to
leave me in my shit! I grabbed his arm trying to stop him.
He snatched away; then pushed me by my forehead onto
the floor. I jumped up screaming it was all his fault. He's
the one that left! I screamed that he wasn't man enough to
face his responsibility the right way and get a job. He
chose to take the easy way out; hustling! He was the one
who left me alone to raise our child. Marvin snatched free
from my desperate clutch. Before I knew what I was
doing; I swung on him. My left arm apparently has a mind
of its own. It turned into a wild haymaker and I punched
him right in the jaw. Oh shit! He wobbled a little then he
grabbed me by my throat. He's squeezing so hard I can feel
my esophagus crushing. His eyes are filled with hurt and
hatred. He's breathing like a mad bull. I can't breathe! I fill

light headed! He's going to kill me in here! Attempting to free myself; I crashed my knee into his nuts with all my might. That's where I fucked up! Marvin doubled over in pain and let go of my throat. But when he rose back up he brought an uppercut with him. He hit me so hard I slid across the floor and hit the wall; knocking my newly replaced front teeth out. Yeah, the one that was chipped! I sat on the floor crying, screaming, holding my busted lip and watching him walk out my life. Toothless! What have I done?

"Leave my truck!" I screamed.

"Go fuck for another one!" He yelled back.

He came back and stomped on my tooth crushing it and me in one move. The door slammed. Now I'm a bloody crying mess crawling across the floor. The side of my face is throbbing. It feels like I have a rock band inside my head; Tylenol 3 can't help this. A cold reality filled the room as I realized I have no one to call. My mother is in Vegas and I have no other family that deals with me; no support system. No family! No friends! I've burned all of my bridges. I'm all alone! It wasn't supposed to be like this. I know I didn't do all of this to end up like this. I didn't kill myself out here hustling these trick ass fools so that he can live well; for him to pass judgment on how I got money. I need someone to talk to. I'll call Rhonda! That's my girl. Even if she is mad at me; she'll at least listen to my side. She's always been there for me. I know she could care less about how I carried Greg. She would never put him before me! All the shit I've done for her. We go history and she's still my best friend! She hasn't forgotten. She'll be there for me; I just know she will. Yeah, I'm calling Rhonda. I somehow managed to dial her number.

"Hello." Rhonda answered sounding angry.

"Rhonda?" I muttered through the tears.

"What!" She snapped.

"Rhonda, it's me Simone. Can you talk for a

minute? I need someone to talk to. Marvin and I had a fight. He found out about the things I did while he was locked up. He just left and I don't think he's coming back."

"Good bitch! He should've left your trifling ass! That's what the fuck you get! After what you did to Greg, Marvin should've beaten your ass unconscious!"

"Rhonda, I'm serious. Stop playing!" I replied.

"Does this sound like a joke? Greg jumped out of a fucking window! He tried to kill himself over you! And, you left me behind to clean up your shit! So excuse me if I don't have any pity for you. I'm all out!" The phone went dead.

"Hello…hello?"

Uh! No she didn't! I know this Rihanna wannabe ass bitch didn't just hang up on me! Did she just turn her back on me when I need her? After all the shit I've done for her? Rhonda's supposed to be my best friend; not Greg's! She got me fucked up! Who is she to tell me how to live? She's overstepping her bounds! Miss High and mighty! So what I used him; I'd do it again! Who is she to pass judgment on me? Greg's dumb ass should've died! Just for being so damn stupid. Am I right? I mean c'mon now, ain't no way I'm going to hurt myself over somebody. Fuck that! Child please! I might kill somebody else but not myself! How is that my fault? I ain't know that he was weak like that! I mean if I had known he'd react like that; I would've taken out an insurance policy on the fool. That would've been the ultimate payday if I was as conniving as they say. I'd have gotten paid off him in the present and afterlife! Humph! Dumb is you! I feel two ways about it:

1) I'm sorry that he's having a rough time but things change.
2) If you're stupid enough to try and kill yourself, then you deserve to die.

No pussy or dick in the world is worth all of that. Well, except this one! Ha ha! I didn't push Greg out of that window; he jumped; of his own free will. He believed he could fly! How is that my fault? Everybody keeps kicking this love bullshit to me. They weren't in our house; in our bed. I don't remember seeing them at our dinner table! Never once, did I tell Greg that I loved him. Those words never came out of my mouth! I ain't going to lie to you. Never! When he would say he loved me I would just kiss him; I never responded. He assumed I loved him and that's where he fucked up. HE wanted Minyon to call him daddy! HE wanted to get married! HE wanted to live together; I didn't.

All I wanted was his money and think what you want but Greg knew what was up! He wanted a fairy tale. I told him that my mother had already raised me and this is who I am; but he really thought he could change me. Now I've got all of these self-righteous motherfuckers passing judgment on me! Trying to make themselves look big by standing on top of me; well it ain't going to work. I told Greg from day one; I didn't want a relationship. I told him that I was in love with my daughters' father; he ignored me. He took it upon himself to create the rest! Now, I'm supposed to be the bad guy? Oh no, fuck that! He created this happy relationship in his mind; I never lied to him. I never told him the truth; but I never lied either.

You see how people are? Rhonda had no problem with my getting over on tricks when it helped her pay her rent. Her shit was a breath away from the sidewalk; okay! Her ass was nervous as hell; crying and shit! I should've let her stupid ass get evicted. Oh but see, I would've been wrong then. Fuck her! And, the high horse she rode in on! I don't need her. She ain't never did shit for me or mines! To think, when I slept with Rodney all the way up to our second encounter; I actually felt guilty. I don't owe her shit and anything over 30 seconds is too much time spent worrying about another mother-fucker's feelings! I just thought she was my girl; then she's going to turn around and choose them over me? Greg ain't nobody! Rodney definitely ain't nobody! With their trick asses! She's got the nerve to be strung out on that no good bastard; the same Rodney that's been screaming my name and begging for sex since Christmas Eve. That's right; I still break him off at least once a week. He's been wearing my thighs like earmuffs on the regular. Every time she kisses him she tastes my juices. In the word of the Notorious B.I.G., *"if you don't know, now you know!"*

You know what; whoever wants to get with it can all pitch in on a case of Chapstick; pucker up and kiss my entire pitch black ass! They got the game fucked up! I came into the world by myself and I'm going out the same way. I can't wait until she finds out about the real Rodney; he's going to break her heart and I hope I get to see it. He's a cheating bastard! I'm going to laugh right in her face. Humph! Then I'm going to beat her ass for turning on me while bragging on how I've been fucking the shit out of Rodney; regularly. Watch me! I can't wait to tell my mother this bullshit! Rhonda knows the game! She better not even look like she's thinking about expecting some sympathy from me. I wouldn't give that bitch sympathy if it came with a free oil change. I can't wait til the day her cookie crumbles; I'm going to laugh my ass off. Ha. Dumb is ya?

Trust me; I'm telling you some good shit! She's in for a rude awakening; Rodney loves no-one but Rodney. It won't be long before her happily ever after turns into a nightmare. And, if there is a God he'll let me see it happen. Dusty bitch! I don't need her. I never needed her; she needed me. That bitch ain't do nothing for me! It was always me helping her; doing her hair! Paying bills for her broke ass! Matter fact, I want my mother fucking money back; all of it. She still owes me $120.00. She got the right one this time. She's going to feel my wrath. She is officially on my shit list! I'm not going to stop until I ruin her; I promise you this! She's going to pay for turning her back on me! My mother told me she was too soft and would crack under pressure. That bitch is dumb as a box of rocks! She ain't know shit about the game until I taught her. Mark my words; RODNEY IS GOING TO MAKE A FOOL OUT OF HER!

16

Happy Birthday to me! I'm the big 28. I'm glad to report that my birthday is starting out great. So far, so good! We found out yesterday that Greg will be coming home sometime next week. He'll miss my birthday party tonight but that's okay; we'll have another party just for him. Oh yeah, guess what, do you know Simone had the nerve to call me! Yeah a couple of days ago! She was crying and shit. Apparently, Marvin had tapped her on her jaw after finding out how hard she was tricking. Man, I tell you no lie, she's slept with half of D.C. while he was locked up. Ms. Loose Booty was always willing to do something strange for some change. Serves her ass right! That's what she gets. I'm not even going to waste anymore of my time discussing that bitch! Moving on!

Anyway, I'm about to go get my hair done, Lexie's treating me as a part of my birthday present. She's trying to convince me to get a weave. I don't know about all of that; maybe or maybe not. I not one for a lot of hair; but I promised her I'd think about it. I do need a makeover. A whole new persona! I'm five months pregnant and not feeling pretty at all. I've picked up what seems like 45 pounds already. Since my pregnancy; I've become overly insecure about my looks. Maybe a new look is just what I need; a weave may be just what the doctor ordered. It's my day am I want to feel flawless! Go Rhonda! It's my birthday! It's my birthday!

Hey, "*I Like It*", go Fatz. I'm with that! I don't care how pregnant I am; I'm going to climb my big ass on top of that dresser tonight. Bet on that! Sing your song. Do you like that song? That joint is cranking! Hooo! That "*Move That Dope*" joint is on; that's my theme song. Future, Pusha T, Pharell, and Casino was on one when they made that joint. The radio is cranking this morning. Hey, they

hitting some throwback jams. This used to be my theme song, *"Lollipop"* by Weezy F. Baby; please say the Baby. That's my man; I love me some Lil' Wayne. Umph, can I get a witness up in this mother or what? Let me get big my ass dressed before Lexie gets here. I'm so excited about my party tonight; I'm not playing with a full deck.
Say what you want; but I'm giving all haters the business tonight! Please excuse me! I'm so excited! I know that this party is going to be jumping; I can't wait until tonight. Everybody's coming! I'm going to stay on that floor tonight. I'm shutting the club down; watch me! I'm going to be looking fierce. Speaking of looking fierce; I saw these pictures on the internet last week of Beyonce. She is slaying broads! No I'm not a beehive stan but the truth is the damn truth! Success is always the best revenge especially when you look amazing doing it. Child, I stay on Bossip, Media Takeout, Necole Bitchie, and that damn crazy ass Funky Dineva; getting the latest scoop. Damn! That reminds me; I got to check out C'mon Son for this week's videos; Ed Lover be on one all day! He cracks me the hell up. Charlamagne be giving them hell as well. The truth shall set you free. That reminds me, I haven't been on Facebook in a minute. I need to go see which of my FB friends or former schoolmates is out there telling all of their business. People be over-sharing like shit on social media.

Oh yeah, I forgot to tell you this; talking about a nice way to wake up on your birthday check this fly shit out. Now of course you know; I had to handle the morning breath. Humph! I slept so good last night that my breath was kicking like Bruce Lee vs. Jackie Chan; wasn't nothing minty fresh about it. Girl, the taste woke me up out of my sleep. Shit! I was scared to talk to myself. Anyway, afterwards I climbed back into bed; then Rodney served me breakfast in bed. I had pancakes, cheese eggs, beef bacon, grits, and orange juice. The *"Three Year Anniversary"* was on repeat! While I ate he slipped into the living room returning with a three-foot tall birthday card, flowers, a Neiman's gift certificate, a special box from Kyndall Tyrelle Edible Décor and another real big box. Like about the size of a 27" TV box. Inside that box was another box. I went through five boxes; ending up with a wrapped up Tamar Braxton CD. A CD! I already have two downloads of this CD. Matter of fact, mother fucker's ain't even buying CD's no damn more! What kind of funky ass gift is this? I immediately became hot as fish grease. Now don't get me wrong I love me some Tamar; but not for my birthday. Where's the present? Okay!

"C'mon Rhonda baby! Are you going to play the CD for me? I know that you really like it."

"I don't like it that damn much!" I replied through gritted teeth.

"C'mon play the CD."

"Know what…you like it so much… you play it!"

I threw the CD at him as hard as I could. It flew into the air before finally becoming one with his forehead. It popped open and a 3 carat diamond tennis bracelet fell out onto the bed. Oooh! I feel like a fool! I should've known that he wouldn't just give me a tape for my birthday. That still not all he gave me! Next, Rodney gave me a bath and a full body massage, okay! Let's just say that when Tamar recorded that CD she was missing one backup singer; ME. He had me hitting all kinds of notes! This was some *Love and War* type of loving. My girl is singing my life in her songs. She knows exactly how I feel right now. Rodney makes me feel like a lady; a queen! I want to be so perfect for him. I love the way he pleases me. He opens doors and gives me flowers; candle lit bubble baths! Ump! He makes me feel so special! Just when I thought it couldn't get any better; he licked me like a Popsicle. Happy birthday to me!

Lexie's taking me to her hairdresser; her name is also Caprice but Lexie calls her Almighty Isis. Her salon is called "*CHOW*". Yeah, the same "*CHOW*" that fired Simone's dusty ass! She's the miracle worker that's supposed to transform me today. Besides, Lexie swears by her and her hair is always on point; like the hair Gods have personally blessed Caprice with skills like no other.

We're here! Okay here goes nothing; I settled in for my hair deliverance. She hooked a sister up; you hear me. I look good enough for TV! My wig is fried, dyed, and laying! Let me see how I can explain it; whose hair is like mine? Let me think! Child, I don't even know; but I do know I look fierce. Okay the weave is black with honey and light blonde streaks. And, its styled in a long feathered mushroom with bangs. All I know is that it's fly! Oh hell yeah! I been bald headed so long I'd forgotten how good I look with hair; wait until Rodney sees this. I know that he's going to love it. He won't be able to keep his hands off of me; I hope.

I must've thanked Caprice forty times before we left. She created a custom color for me and everything. I'm acting like I've never had my hair done before; I know she thinks that I'm crazy. It just looks so good! I needed a new hairdresser anyway; guess I've found her. You and I, both know I'm not about to let Simone get her hands on my head again in life. She'd scalp me on purpose; bald spots and all.

Cheesecake Factory is the destination to grub. On the way Lexie popped in a homemade CD that Scottie Beats had made especially for her. It's obvious the she's still heavily into old school hip hop. This CD had everything on it; "I'll Take Your Man", "Just a Friend", "Bonita Applebomb.", and of course we had some vintage 50 cent, and of course Dougie Fresh and Slick Rick! I'm dancing so hard in this seat; you can't tell me I'm not at the club. I know the people in the car beside us think I'm having some type of fit or something. It's the funniest thing you will ever see. It's my birthday; my day! I'm going to enjoy it. All of this dancing has made me hungry. I can't wait to get to the restaurant. I would say that I could eat a horse but everybody says that; so I won't but I could.

"What are you getting?"

"No you didn't ask me that! As long as you've know me what do you think?"

"Everything". Lexie sarcastically replied

"There it is! Girl, thank you so much for everything. This is really shaping up to be a beautiful birthday. It's off to a great start."

"No problem, you know how we go! You wanna stop at Mazza Gallerie after we eat?"

"Let me see… going to a mall… on my birthday with my multi-millionaire best friend…tough decision? Is water wet? Hell yeah! Matter of fact; I'm not even hungry anymore. We can go straight to the mall. I'll just grab something from the food court." I replied.

"You crazy." Lexie laughed

"Oh yeah… but I've got to stop and pick up my present from Uncle D.J. while we are out… do you mind stopping by Legna Ecurb?"

"No problem."

"Did I show you what Sexy got me?"

"Only fifty-five times." She joked.

"I can't wait until tonight. I'm going to be all over that floor."

"Just don't burst your pregnant ass because I will laugh; then roll you over". Lexie joked.

"You ain't right. Girl, you ain't right!"
Her cell rang.

"Chris is calling me. He must have the second part of your present."

"What you waiting for? Answer the damn phone. Move it!"

"Anxious are we?"

She reached into her crocodile Hermes bag and whipped out her cell. She's right; I'm beyond anxious. As you know Lexie is a "Benjamin" and you know how they roll; stacks on deck! The finest of everything! And, she owns an entertainment company, I can't say the name. I tease her all the time calling her the female Russell Corleone. She's more like a female mob boss mixed with music mogul; but you ain't heard that from me. She'd kill me if she knew I was telling you all of this; and I do mean that literally. She says when she accomplished what Russell has then we can call her that. Fuck that! I say my girl is all of that. Her motto is: Keep sleeping on me you're gonna wake up mad as shit"! Don't let the wheelchair fool you! By the time you finish reading this everyone is going to know her name.

Talk about shrewd; she's a vicious businesswoman. Matter of fact; she's just vicious. I often forget who she is until I go to her house, see that 380 in her bag or one of her brother's pull up with somebody gagged and bleeding in the trunk. You wouldn't believe the things I've seen hanging with her. All I can say is them Benjamin's are some bad mother fuckers; believe it! They'll kill you as quickly as they change clothes. It's so hard to believe that they do what they do. You know what; let me shut up. I'm talking too much! I don't know you that well to be telling you all of this. Forget everything I just said; I was welling. The Benjamin's are some nice hard working law abiding citizens. They're great community servants that wouldn't hurt a fly. That's my story and I'm sticking to it!

Yet, it's so easy to forget how rich she is because she's so laid back. We've been friends since I was seven years old. She was 12 and for some reason decided it was her job to look out for me. We grew up on the same block. My mom and their mom were best friends. My mom used to babysit all of them. Lexie was there for me then and she's still here for me now; protecting me. Nothing's changed! You know how some motherfuckers have a tendency to forget where they came from. Lexie, once told me that only a few people stuck by her after she got shot and those people will always be special to her; I'm one of those people. Shit! That's my girl! Money or no money! Wheelchair, walker, whatever! I remember I used to be up at the hospital so much they thought I worked there. She fought like hell for her life! She's strong! She's a soldier! No matter what she keeps pushing! That's what I respect about her; money hasn't changed her at all. I think she's been filthy rich since she was about 16; no lie. Her mother and father were killed by the police on her 15th birthday. Her father Brocco was as big time as they come! The police raided their house on Christmas morning killing her mother and father; I'll never forget that shit! She went straight to hustling to keep her four little brothers together until her Uncle Smiley or their Grandma Lil came home from jail to raise them. Lexie was determined they would never spend a night in foster care or be separated. Of course, they stayed with me and my mom first but Lexie was on a mission. I remember watching in amazement when she dropped 50k on my mothers' bed and asked her to go by them a townhouse and keep the rest. They had only been with us for one week. Moms took care of that, would sign the boys up for school and anything else that required an adult; the rest as they say is history. She's been running the game ever since. And when Bagz, I mean Uncle Smiley, came home it was a wrap. One thing for certain, my mother and I are two of the safest people in DC.

I don't care what she does she's still my girl; I will do anything she asks without a second thought. And the best thing about it is; I've always got a job. She cussed me out something terrible when she found out that I'd lost my job and was getting unemployment; back during the time I had to borrow money from Simone. You remember, don't you? Lexie never could stand Simone! Never! I know that she would've given me the money with no problem. I've just called on her so many times; I didn't want to bother her

with my problems again. Thinking back I wish I would've;
I shouldn't have taken a penny from Simone.

We cruised through Rock Creek Park. It's April;
the weather is nice and warm. The cherry blossoms have
bloomed and are filling the trees. Oh, did I tell you, today
is April 23rd. That's right; my birthday! Okay! Well,
anyway, it's about seventy-five degrees. Everybody is out
in the streets today; showing off their systems and rides.
Have you seen that new Chrysler? That joint looks like a
baby Rolls Royce. I've got to get me one of those.
Now that's another good thing about being with Lexie; the
ride gets much props! A snow white convertible Maybach;
this joint is wet! This joint got curtains and a driver! We
bubbling like a mug! What? Add two fine black women
and you got drama! We cruised up the Avenue to the
Legna Ec'urb Shop to see my Uncle D.J. I'm so glad he's
home. I missed him so much when he was locked up. I
can't wait to see what he's got for me; he gives great gifts.
We're here! I jumped out the car and ran straight into his
waiting arms for a hug. He's still fly as hell. He's decked
out in a red and black Legna Ecurb sweat suit and some
Gucci sneakers; looking like money!

He gave me a tiffany necklace, matching bracelet,
and a diamond clustered thumb ring. I knew that he'd give
me jewelry; 'cause that's all he knows. I squealed, "Thank
you", followed by a great big hug and kiss. I love my
Uncle! When he was locked up; I was miserable. I felt like
I'd lost my best friend. I know you've an uncle that's like a
brother? You know, one that you can tell anything and
always is there to get you out of trouble. If I can't count on
anyone; I can count on him, Lexie, and my mom. I love the
fact that he doesn't judge me. You know what; let me get
this show on the road. I better hurry up and get out of here;
before he and Lexie start talking about boxing or
basketball. We'll be here all day if they do.

"Wassup with your man Lamont Peterson?"

"He's passing out ass whippings…that's wassup with him. But Gary Russell Jr. is putting in that work! He's about to get a belt!"

If they get to talking about boxing I will never get out of here. I read about that Gary Russell dude in Upscale Live magazine. I like what he does for the kids. I've got to get her out of this store. Good! Chris is calling her on the phone; she's ready to go. Great! It's still early and I have plenty of time to prepare for the party; maybe Chris has my gift. I finally got her out of the store and we drove back to my townhouse. I wish her driver would step on it! Don't this joint do about 200 mph? Get this car moving! We're back at my house.

"Surprise". Lexie squealed

"Wassup C! Where's my gift? What you got for me?" I inquired leaping from the car.

"Damn! Wassup with you too? Nice to see you too!" Chris joked.

"I'm sorry…how are you?"

"Like you really care." He joked

"You're right…where's my present?" We all laughed.

"Baby, you didn't tell me Rhonda was a Chia pet. How did you grow all of that hair in two hours?"

"Forget you C!" Everyone really laughed.

Chris and Coco are waiting at my house when Lexie and I arrived. He opened up the back of his Hummer; all I can see is this big box with a huge white bow. I hope they don't try that same shit Rodney pulled this morning. I ripped the wrapping paper off the box; staring back at me is a picture of a 73' plasma TV. Oh yeah! A flat screen TV! They better not be fucking with me! I ripped open the top of that box with my bare hands; I got to make sure that there is really a TV inside.

I want to thank Lexie and Chris but my mouth won't move. I can't believe this; tears shot from my eyes.

I grabbed Lexie and squeezed her so tightly. No one has ever given me anything like this! Never! I'm so lucky to have a friend like her. Damn, she gives some great presents. First, I got a customized Louis Stewart set, a Celine bag of my very own; now this. Thank you Lexie! Thank you! Thank you! I got a TV! I got a TV! I unlocked my front door for Chris and Coco; so they could hook up the TV. Then I jumped back into the car with Lexie and off we went. That reminds me; I need some new DVD's and the True Blood box set. I love me some Bill and Sookie. Believe me; I plan on getting every drop of their money's worth out of that joint. I wish Rodney would touch it; I'll break his hands. Sike! He can watch it; sometimes. If he acts nicely!

We're rushing because Lexie has to pick AWOL up from National Airport Delta terminal at 6:30. You know AWOL right? Yeah, the 65 County Hound!". I thought so! It's already 5:45 and I've slowed her down with my movie detour; ain't no sense in taking me home first. I might as well ride. AWOL and Lexie have been working together on music for years. He's real cool peoples; real down to earth! They've been working together for about five years. *"Cold Blooded"* by Yo Gotti and J.Cole bumped as we made our way to the airport. Believe me when I tell you; they've made some major paper. They've been cranking out hit after hit; for a minute. AWOL jumped in and they went straight to work. She up some beats from another one of their partners, NevaSleep and it was on. It was almost like I wasn't even in the car. Anyway, back to what I was saying, when you see them together you'd swear they're family. They are so tight! Lexie has that kind of effect on people; especially dudes. That's all you really see her with is dudes. I know it has to drive Chris crazy. You can bet your last dollar though; that everybody knows Christopher Burnett is the MAN! It doesn't hurt that he's fine as hell either. Now you talk about love; she is one woman that is in love with her man. She loves the ground he walks on; don't get it twisted the feeling is mutual. As strong as their relationship is; I know it still has to bother Chris that Lexie keeps so many dudes around her.

She's one person who definitely doesn't care for female company. Average bitches can't understand where she's coming from. She says females' cause to much confusion. When you put too many females together you get jealousy, gossip, and someone willing to fuck your man just to bring you misery in a heartbeat.

I know what she means! It seems like Simone and I are always competing. Even though we tried to act like we weren't; we were. Nobody likes to be outdone and she's always trying to outdo me. Maybe, I should just hang out with Lexie from now on; might work out better. I'll tell you this; I'd hate to be the girl that tries to creep with Chris. That chick will be on her way to heaven before God got the news she was coming; you feel me? I've been with Lexie for six straight hours and not once have I heard; she said this or he said that. Stress free company is the best kind! I know I'm going on and on about her but she's a bad bitch. It's nice to have someone you can trust with your life to hold you down right or wrong; she would never let anyone hurt me. She's my big sister and I love her so much. Okay! Okay! Enough about that; moving on! They dropped me off at home to get ready for my gala! I'm so excited!

Party time! This party is off da hook! You hear me? If you're in D.C. or vicinity this is where you need to be. Everybody who's somebody is here! When I say everybody; I mean everybody! All of my friends, co-workers, and people that went to nursing school with me. This by far is my best birthday ever. I have everything a woman can wish for a party, a baby on the way, diamonds, Celine handbag, plasma TV, and a wonderful fiancé who loves me. Oh yeah, Happy Birthday to me! Everyone has been giving me so many props on my new hairdo; it's ridiculous. They love it! I look fabulous. I'm so lady up in here! What!

"Excuse me…everybody I'd like to make a toast. To my baby Rhonda, wishing you a happy birthday and many more. I promise to keep you smiling and as happy as you are tonight. I'm going to make sure of it!"

"Oh Rodney!" I purred

"To my niece…I wish you health, wealth, and good friends."

"Thank you Uncle DJ."

"To my partner in crime, one of the few females in existence that I can spend more than three hours with without killing! Thanks for my godchild. May all of your days be as happy as this one." Lexie added

"Alright girlfriend!"

"Excuse me……I'd like to make a toast?"

"Who are you?" I asked

"I'm Kenya." This strange girl replied with attitude.

Some bitch has bum rushed my party with her four hood rat friends and a baby on her hip. What the fuck? Is this a joke? How the hell did she get a baby in the club? I don't even know this chick. I've never seen this broad a day in my life. I waiting for Lil' Duval and a camera crew! Real talk!

"Kenya… go 'head with that shit! Don't come up in here with that shit!" Rodney threatened as he made his way through the crowd towards her obviously frustrated.

"Rodney, you know her?" Uncle DJ asked.

"No, I don't mind…go ahead." I said egging her on.

Anytime a chick brings a baby to the club she's on one and I couldn't wait to hear what she had to say. I know it better not be that baby belongs to Rodney or we are going to the next level with the quickness! Let's see what she has to say.

"To Rhonda and Rodney the happy couple…I wish you both wedded bliss and all that shit. I hope that there

will be room in your little family for my son; *RODNEY'S
SON*! Looks like your baby has a big brother or didn't you
know? Happy birthday!" She tipped her glass and sipped.

What! Wrong move! She spent around on her
bootleg red bottoms and tried to walk off. Oh hell no!
Where the fuck does she thinks she's going? Rodney's
mother snatched the baby out of her arms just as I grabbed
a hand full of her weave and yanked her back to me like a
yo-yo. Kiki stole one of her friends off the break causing
the girl to flip over a chair. Before she could hit the ground,
Kiki and Patrice dove on her ass. Lexie hit the big stud
looking broad with a Moet bottle; down she went. The
bottle broke so use your imagination to figure out what
happened next. I told you she was vicious and that's all I'm
saying. Karen and my other cousin Kita commenced to
whipping the asses of girls 3 and 4, while my mother and I
worked on the bitch with the fake shoes; Kenya or
whatever the fuck she said her name was. When I get
finished this bitch will never give another toast because her
mouth is going to be wired shut! Real talk! Security is
coming from everywhere. We turned Love into Hate. I
know I shouldn't be fighting while I'm pregnant but the
only thing I can think about is killing this bitch for
embarrassing me! 5th District is going see me tonight!
Hope you got some bail money!

"Rodney what the fuck is she talking about?" I
screamed over the shoulder of the sweaty 300 pound
security guard that was carrying me away; like a man
would carry his wife across the threshold.

"She's pregnant be careful with daughter! You hurt
a hair on her head and I'll kill the next three generations of
your entire fucking family!" Jean screamed continuously at
security meaning every word.

"Nigga what kind of games are you playing?" Uncle
DJ barked as he tried to get to Rodney. Rodney ignored
him.

"Rodney...Rodney! I know you hear me!"

"Rodney man you better say something." Coco advised

"You'll motherfuckers gonna make me catch a case over some dumb shit. I ain't got time for this! Come on baby let's go! This bitch is bleeding all over me!" Lexie snapped. Chris threw a jacket around Lexie, AWOL grabbed the broken bottle wrapping it in a t-shirt, and they disappeared into the night.

"Damn, you'll was rumbling like shit. Damn!"

"Y'all was whipping some ass!" Greg laughed.

"All the ghetto came out of y'all asses. Jean can sure throw them hands". Ma Betty laughed.

"Where my girl at...Kiki!" Coco yelled.

Security had already thrown us out of the club and the fight continued in the parking lot. Next thing I know; I see my mother and my co-worker Patrice ramming one of the girls head through somebody's car window. Kiki was stomping the other one on the ground like a roach. One girl ran away and Ms. Kenya, the one that started all of this shit; her punk ass was hiding in the club while her girls are out here getting fucked up. The po-po's are here. We are all going to jail tonight. Cell phones are recording like crazy. Oh, we making WorldStar! And, to tell the truth; I can't wait. I hope they put me in the cell with her ass. I'm gon' beat that bitch to death! Believe that! I put that on everything!

Everyone was trying to break up the fight due to my pregnant condition but I'm determined to get back inside and get my hands on that skank; baby or no baby! Here comes Rodney running towards me. I stood still, barefoot with my hands on my hips. As soon as he got within arm's reach; I popped his lying ass right in the mouth. You heard me right; I'm barefoot, pregnant, and whipping his ass. How dare he have some bitch crash my party-talking bout she got his baby? What kind of shit is that? Who else knew about this baby? I feel like a damn fool! Here I am, bragging on what a good man I got; and this motherfucker got babies stashed away. He knew about this baby! Why didn't he tell me? Why did I have to find out like this? That bitch brought a baby to the club just to fuck up my party! This is going to be the talk of the hospital. How am I supposed to face my co-worker's? I can't work there after this.

Here I am pregnant with what I thought was his first baby and this motherfucker already got a baby. Oh hell no! Did you know too? Well, why didn't you tell me? I thought we were supposed to be tight! I see that your just like the rest! I don't believe this shit! How could he do this to me? Why didn't he just tell me? As God is my witness; I'm going to kill him and her; but he's going first. I charged after him again like a raging bull. All I see is red! Every blow that connected only made me madder because I don't see any blood. Bleed you low down cheating mother fucker, bleed! I pounded on him with all of my might. Maybe if I hit him long enough, I can turn back time and erase this embarrassing moment from my memory. He keeps trying to grab me. I karate kicked him right in his mouth. The force was so hard I heard his teeth click together. The look in his eyes lets me know that he wants to kill me as much I as want to kill him. I punched him again crying uncontrollably. God, please make this pain go away!

"How could you keep this from me? I hate you! I wish I never met you!" I screamed as I pounded him; punch after punch.

I'm exhausted. I can feel my body shutting down. I swung a wild punch with what energy I had left. Lucky for me he was finally able to grab me because my body gave out and I was heading for the gravel paved parking lot. Oh my God! My stomach!

17

"Easy, it was easy for me to keep it from you Rhonda. I had to make sure the baby was mines first; before I told you. It was before I met you! Don't give up on us! That's what she wants to do; break us up. Please listen! I swear she tricked me; not only did I keep it from you I kept it from myself! I was just trying to protect you from the stress. I don't believe that baby is mines. On my mother, I swear she tricked me!" He pleaded

"Tricked you...how the fuck did she trick you? Did she do some Whodini magic and your dick magically appeared inside of her and released? I whispered from a hoarse voice still cradled in his arms trying my best to swing one more punch."

"She put a hole in the rubber."

"Please don't insult my intelligence! Please! Cut the bullshit!...You must think I'm stupid or something. You've hurt me enough don't insult my intelligence. Stop lying!" I punched him again

"I'm serious baby! No bullshit! I'm not lying. You've got to believe me! She's on me hard! She wanted to have my baby that bad! She knew that I was done fucking with her... I'd moved on. I'd found you! So she tried to find a way to keep me!" He pleaded.

"I guess it worked! Rodney why didn't you just tell me? Why did I have to find out like this? In front of all of these people! You said you loved me! You lied! Embarrassing me like this; you made a fool out of me!" I screamed.

"Fuck these people. Fuck'em! I'm fighting for my life. Baby, you've got to let me explain. Please, hear me out! Please baby! It's not like you think"

Rhonda smacked all the shit out of me. She better

not try that again though! That has to be the hundredth hit tonight and she box like a dude. I'm not trying to pop her. I know that she's mad and all that; but she's going overboard.

"You a sorry motherfucker!" She screamed.
Jean pulled up with the car and Rhonda got inside. They pulled off.

"Rhonda...Rhonda...Rhonda!" I yelled at the moving car.

I watched helplessly as my lady rolled out on me. I know I should go after her but I ain't about to play myself. Between, you and me, I've been fucking Simone on the regular. Who also happened to be my best friends' fiancée? I knew Kenya was having a baby that she screamed at the top of her lungs was mine; yet I didn't warn her. And, I was at the hospital when the baby was born. Rhonda is really going to kirk out if she finds that out. I guess I'm getting what I deserve. What goes around comes around. But damn it's a killer when it comes back around! I really fucked this one up. Talk about giving somebody enough rope to hang themselves; I thought I was a cowboy. My lies are causing me to lose the only woman I ever loved.

Here I am standing in the middle of the parking lot surrounded by all of Rhonda's family, friends, and a bunch of strangers with camera phones; looking like a damn fool. I'm trying to get the fuck out of here but my Gucci loafers feel like they've melted into the concrete. Dog is plastered across my forehead like a cheap tattoo. If looks could kill; my funeral would have been last Friday. We could have handled this like adults; but oh no, you can't reason with a crazy bitch! I wish I never fucked with her lunch box ass. I was just building up my courage to tell Rhonda. So much for not messing up her birthday! Man, shit! What am I going to do now? How am I going to get out of this? Can you believe she brought Lil' Rodney to the club with her? I ain't never seen no shit like that in my life. In my mind I tried to picture how it would go down if Kenya and Rhonda ever had a confrontation; I never pictured this. No one could have predicted this ending. Rhonda is never going to forgive me for this shit.

I couldn't get away from that club fast enough. The happy partygoers had turned into an angry lynch mob. I'm lucky I got out of there alive. I can't lie the shit was kind of funny. Especially when Rhonda, Jean, Lexie, Kiki and even Patrice put the ass whippings on them! Those girls can rumble. And, Jean was working out. Man, let me tell you something; don't let the gray hair fool you. Shit, Jean box like she 27; looking like Laila! I know I ain't got nothing coming. Let me stop talking to you and get down here so I can bail out Coco and Uncle D.J. They got locked up for rumbling the security guards that were grabbing Jean and Rhonda. Man, this has been one crazy night.

The police said they weren't releasing Coco and JD until tomorrow; they will have to go to court in the morning. That's not good because D.J. is still on parole. I hope they don't violate him. I sat outside 5th District police station in my car and prayed. I've found myself doing that a lot lately. What? Praying! What, I can't pray or something? I have to talk to my baby. Where is she? Who is she with? Thoughts of losing her are really began to sink in. I've really lost her, you think? She's gone? What about our baby? Do you think she's going to try to keep me away from the baby that I really want? I've got to find her! I've got to talk to her. It can't end like this.

William Casanova, "*Nasty You Out*" jumped from the speakers as soon as I turned on the radio. I hurried up and turned it off; screwing is the furthest thing from my mind. Besides, it got me into this position in the first place. I continued driving aimlessly around the city in silence. I have no idea where I'm going or what I'm going to do when I get there; I just know that I've got to do something.

I really wish Greg was here. He'd know what to do. He'd
help me get out of this shit. Who am I kidding? We both
know that I'm not ready to face Greg. I mean c'mon, how
can I? After what I did and am still doing to him? Did I say
that out loud? First Rhonda and now Greg! My shit is
getting out of hand. I'm going to lose everything. No
woman! No best friend! I'm going to end up alone; all
because I have no dick control. These types of thoughts
consumed me as I drove. It's like I'm on cruise control.
Dazed! I know I'm driving but it feels like the car is
driving me. Somehow; I ended up parked in front of the
Skylark. Even in the middle of all this chaos; females are
still on my mind. Oh well; might as well go inside. I know
what I said earlier but naked booty moving in slow motion
always makes me feel better! Watching it! Getting it! It all
works for me.

  The club is dark and smoky; filled with playas of
varied ages drinking and yelling remarks of undying one
night love for the strippers onstage. I found my way to the
bar and ordered a double shot of Remy; threw it down my
throat. I ordered another and walked over to a table at the
foot of the stage; I took a seat. Which one of you ladies
want to go with me tonight? What? What's wrong with
you? Shit, if life serves you lemons; you make lemonade.
All of this ass moving around; you must be crazy. Besides,
Rhonda is mad at me anyway. She ain't going to give me
none. I can't get into any more trouble than I am already in
so I might as well go out with a bang!

  This one chick in here has an unbelievable ass. I
wonder if it's real or she got some of that silicone shit. I
couldn't help but grab it. She ain't say nothing; so I
grabbed it again. She still ain't saying nothing! This time I
grabbed a handful and slid my finger into her personal
space. She jumped back and smacked the taste out of my
mouth. Before I realized what I was doing, I had my hand
around her throat crushing her windpipe. Next thing I

know; bouncers are coming from everywhere and some stud bitch is up in my face talking about, "I'm disrespecting her woman." What? I know she don't know me. If she did she'd know that if you act like a man; I treat you like a man. I broke free from the bouncer's chokehold and straight backhanded the taste of pussy out of her mouth before they grabbed me again and introduced me to the concrete outside. I know that I was wrong but I've been waiting to knock the shit out of someone all night. I guess she believed that looking like a man; made her a man. She ain't! She's a bitch! She bleeds once a month like the rest of them! Her stupid girlfriend rushed to her side to console her. Fuck both of them! They don't know me! This has definitely been the worst night of my life. I wobbled on drunken legs trying to stand up I think my back is broken.

I'm blown! After dropping $200.00 on the strippers and damn near $100.00 at the bar; I still ain't get no loving. I'm coming back to get each one of their ass. Especially, the miniature big, fake strong, ass dude complete with muscles and an extra medium shirt on. I know what he looks like. When I get myself together, I'm coming for him and that big cross-eyed ghetto Hulk looking mother fucker that threw me over his shoulder like Santa's bag and tossed me out onto the street; literally. That bouncer slammed the shit out of me. I keep trying to stand up but I can't. I'm drunk and I swear he broke my back; off the no bullshit!

Before you know it my ass is crawling across the parking lot to my car. There is nothing like being slammed into concrete to sober you up real fast. Bang! Bang! Bang! Oh shit! Somebody is busting off! I counted three shots so far. Who's shooting? Where's it coming from? I regrouped with the quickness and dove through the open driver side window into my car. Wait a damn minute; they're aiming over here by me. I see an image holding the shiny object; it must've jammed. Oh shit! It's that stud bitch and she's shooting at me. This bitch must think that she's Snoop from

HBO's *The Wire* or something. I don't want to die tonight; not like this! I managed to get my car started after fumbling for the keys. Bang! Bang! She just shot out my back window; glass flew everywhere. Lord, help me! I skidded out of the parking lot onto N.Y. Avenue.

The blazing sun hit me waking me up in my car covered with dried spit-up, no back window, a sore back, and a bad headache. I must've blacked out. What time is it? I got hurry up and get changed so that I can get down the court building. Last night was crazy as hell! That chick was trying to kill me! She better hope I never see her ass again! I promise you this, that's the last time; I will never underestimate another female. She went hard as shit! For real, I ain't mad at her! I was on some real disrespectful shit last night! I'm lucky that she missed.

This drive home is the most uncomfortable drive of my life. My head is spinning! My mouth has the taste of dirt filled sneakers! My clothes stink of vomit and alcohol; it's all over my neck. My back window is busted and there is glass everywhere. My nuts feel like they're stuck to my leg. I feel like shit! And, look like it too! The police must think the same thing. I guess that's why they're behind me with the siren on; gesturing for me to pull over. Damn! Oh we good! Everything is going to be cool; it's a chick cop. I'm about to Lil Wayne her; *Mrs. Officer.* I'm just messing with you. There is nothing sexy about me! I mentally began to prepare myself for a ticket or jail. I look, smell, and feel like shit.

I pulled over. She approached me with the usual bit, *"Let me see your license and registration"*. She asked me to step out so I got out and leaned against the car. I need to ask for an ambulance. My back is killing me. I can't help but check her out as she walked back to the police cruiser. She's a lil older than me but she still can get it! She ran my license for warrants before instructing me to walk a straight line and breathe into her machine. I began to try and explain my current appearance. She finally let me go with only a warning ticket after I'd passed the test. Even looking like this she couldn't resist the pimping. I can tell she want me to fuck the police! She wants this young meat in her life! I'm just joking! I am glad that she didn't give me a ticket. I just paid $500.00 in tickets last month to get my license back.

It's so good to be home. After a long hot shower; I changed clothes, taped a trash bag to my window, and headed for DC Superior Court to see about Coco and D.J. We're here! I guess we are too late because they've already left. The Judge had no papered the case and they'd left 20 minutes ago; good at least JD is cool. I would've felt some type of way if he'd gotten violated over that bullshit.

Rhonda hasn't been home in a week. This entire week the only thing I've had to offer the world is a heartbeat. I don't eat! I don't sleep! Thoughts of Rhonda and our baby consume every hour of my day. I don't know where they are! I don't know if they are okay or not! I hope she didn't get hurt. Man, I fucked up! I just should've told her! But not telling her wasn't lying; right? How did we end up like this? This is some soap opera type madness. I need my own reality show! I feel like my chances of tracking Rhonda down are slipping away. It's like trying to win a multi-million dollar lottery; virtually impossible. Where is she? No one will accept my calls not even my own mother.

I've looked everywhere. I've checked with all of her friends. I know they're lying for her. I even slept on Jean's porch for two nights; she left my ass out there too. They know where she is! I even went to her old apartment where I ran into her cousin Trina; who I didn't know was living there. I don't know what made me go over there; but I did. Rhonda must still have that apartment. The main person I need is the only person I haven't tried, Lexie. Rhonda had told me that she and Chris were going on

199

vacation after her birthday. I bet you that's where she is! Lexie would leave Rhonda alone in her house. I've got to find out where Lexie lives. I know that she just built a new house somewhere in Potomac. Who can I call? I know; I'll call Coco; he and Chris are tight. I don't know what I was thinking. I should've been done that! He should know the address.

"Yeah"

"Coco, man it's me." I said

"Wassup bro? Did you straighten that with Rhonda yet?"

"I would if I could find her."

"You mean to tell me that you haven't talked to her yet?"

"Naw…look here, I need Chris's phone number or address."

"I can't give you the number but I will take you the house."

"I'm on my way."

"Alright."

I have chills and pain running up and down my spine. Or, maybe it's the draft from the trash bag covered back window. This ride to Lexie's house feels like a walk to the electric chair. Then to top it off, my own brother blindfolded me. The only difference is that I have background music. I laid the passenger seat back as Raekwon and Lyfe, rocked that *"Catalina"* joint then Backyard filled my piece of reality with constantly grooving go-go beats. I feel like I'm at the go-go. I'm dreading the moment that I have to look into Rhonda's eyes. Man, she was so hurt. Maybe she's better off without me? You saw her that night! I'm constantly making her cry. I'm destroying this woman. All I bring is unnecessary trials and tribulations; maybe I should just turn around. Let's face it; my relationship with her has definitely bit the dust. There's no way in hell she's gon' take me back. How can I expect her to forgive me for this? I don't even think I'd forgive me. What would you do? Right! I hear that. But I'm still going to try. I've got to try! I really do love her. I can't just let her go without a fight.

I removed the blindfold as we're pulling into the driveway of Lexie's mansion; I see why Rhonda would runaway over here. I know I would! Lexie's got some major paper! This joint is off the hook. She's definitely a Benjamin. I heard they had money; but damn! This is some old Fabulous Life type shit! I'm speechless and I'm only in the driveway. I don't see Rhonda's car anywhere. Coco got out and knocked on the door; Chris answered. They both began walking over to the running car; where I'm waiting impatiently. Chris informed me that Rhonda had left earlier for a doctor's appointment. Bingo! She's here! Before Chris could finish, Rhonda came balling into the driveway; she never could drive.

Spotting my car she threw her Honda into reverse and skidded out. I jumped into the driver's side to chase behind her and the high-speed chase began. She's driving like a maniac. I'm doing about eighty trying to catch her. Slow down! Slow down! I hope she doesn't have an …NOOOO! Rhhhooonnnndddaa! I slammed on brakes and skid 40 feet before my car came to a stop. My heart is in my throat! I watched her car spin uncontrollably down the street. Then it jumped the curb and flipped completely over; landing in the upright position. I jumped from my car and ran to help Rhonda while dialing 911 on my cell phone.

"911… please hold…what's your emergency?"

"There's been a car accident on route 60. A pregnant woman is trapped in her car and she's bleeding from her head. I don't know what else is wrong, please hurry! Yes we're two miles past St. John's Pond. Use a satellite and find my cell signal; please just get here! Please hurry! Why are you asking me so many got damn questions? Send somebody out here. My woman and baby could be dying! Please help me! Hold on Rhonda baby; I'm here! Everything's going to be all right. Stay calm. It's all right! It's all right!"

The ambulance is taking forever! I snatched open the door to get closer to her. I want to move her but I can't tell where the blood is coming from. She looks like she's hurt real bad. What should I do? She's slipping in and out of consciousness. This airbag is in the way. The impact smashed her head into the drivers' side window. White chalky dust and blood is everywhere. I can't really see what's wrong. All of the extra hair she'd added is full of glass. She can't die! God, please help them! She and the baby have to be okay! They're going to be okay, right? Somebody help me!" I screamed

I watched helplessly as the paramedics and firemen cut off the cars' roof and used the *Jaws of Life* to pry Rhonda from the wrecked car. She's hurt really badly. It doesn't look like she's going to make it.

"God please don't let her die". I begged over and over again.

I feel so guilty. If I hadn't been chasing her; she wouldn't have been speeding. I should've never come here! I should've left her alone and waited until she was ready to talk to me. This is my fault! I climbed into the helicopter to ride with her. My hands are shaking! My body feels numb. I'm nervous as hell. God, please don't let her die! Man, what is happening? Does loving me mean that she might have to pay with her and our baby's' life? As the helicopter climbed high into the sky; I prayed for Rhonda, the baby, and begged for forgiveness as the paramedics worked frantically. I watched helplessly as tubes were inserted, a neck brace, and broke down when the oxygen mask was placed on her beautiful face. I held her hand while praying for a miracle. Drowning in tears of guilt and shame I began trying to man up and brace myself for the unexpected. I called my mom to pick up Jean and meet us at the hospital.

Once at the hospital, I called everyone that my fried mind could think of. They beat us here. Jean is beyond hysterical! She's crying and begging God to have mercy on her daughter and grandbaby. Everyone wants to know why Rhonda was driving so fast. They keep asking me questions. Lying got me into to this shit in the first place, so I decided to tell the truth.

"She crashed trying to get away from me. I just wanted to talk to her and tell her how sorry I was."

"What? You did what?" Jean screamed through tears.

"Juice... how could you do that to that child? Haven't you hurt her enough already? I never thought the day would come that I'd say this to a child of mine, you're sickening'! I'm really ashamed of how you've handled this situation." My mom added equally upset.

"Rodney, I loved you like my own son. How could you do these things to my daughter and grandbaby? If something happens to them, their blood is on your hands." Jean declared.

"Put it in God's hands. Rhonda's a fighter. She and the baby are going to be just fine. I'm sure Rodney is having a very hard time dealing with all of this as well. The Lord is going to protect her just trust in his power and mercy. He's going to take care of her and that baby!" Assured Ma Wheeler.

"I'm so sorry everybody! I'm sorry! All I wanted to do was to talk to her. I was just trying to get her to come home. She took off and I went after her. I never meant to hurt her. I just wanted her and the baby to come home."I pleaded.

"Are you the family of Rhonda Washington?" interrupted the doctor.

"Yes, I'm her mother. Is my daughter okay? Is the baby okay? May I please see her?" Jean cried.

"Well she's not out of the woods yet. We've just downgraded her condition from critical to stable. However, we are still going to keep her in the ICU unit. She has a concussion and has lost a severe amount of blood. We're running some additional test. The impact caused extreme bruising to the chest cavity. Fortunately the damages from the airbag were limited because she had the seat so far away. Right now she's resting comfortably."

"My baby...is the baby alright?" I asked.

"Everything is looking very positive right now; the baby has a very strong heartbeat and majority of the blood loss was from the face and head area. As I said, we're still running test on the both of them. We're doing everything we can for her and the baby. They are not out of the woods yet."

"What do you mean? Can she still lose the baby later on as a result of this?" I asked.

"A woman can miscarry at any point in a pregnancy. The risks are higher when the body suffers a trauma. So far, every test indicates that we have nothing to worry about. Fortunately, she is far enough along that if necessary we can perform an emergency C-section. However, we will be keeping her for a while to monitor her and the baby. Ms Washington is a very lucky young lady. It could have been a lot worse."

"Can I please see my daughter?" Jean begged.

"Yes...but I'm going to have to ask you to make it brief. Her head injury is serious and she needs her rest."

"Thank you Jesus! Thank you Doctor! Where is she?"

"Me and Betty are going to the chapel to pray. Please tell her we're here and we love her."

"I will...doctor can we go please?"

"Can I please go with you?" I asked Jean; wanting begging for her forgiveness and permission. She reluctantly agreed.

From that moment; I've been living at Rhonda's bedside. I literally moved into the hospital room with her; anything she wants I'm going to get. I'm going to be her nurse and anything else she needs. She's been sleeping most of the time. Around day 3; she's beginning to regain some strength. The doctors say the baby is doing fine. We talked about our problems; my problems! You know how much dirt I've done so you can imagine how intense the conversation was. I told her everything. Well, almost everything; I didn't tell her about Simone. She says the accident has given her a new outlook on life. It's reminded her that life is too short. It has also given her the ability to forgive me. I know I don't deserve it but miracles happen every day. She's letting me off too easy. I still can't shake the feeling of guilt. That accident was my fault! My conscious is still fucking with me. Rhonda keeps trying to convince me that it wasn't. She says that I had no way of knowing she'd crash. That's true but I still feel like shit. Her car is totaled. I think it symbolizes a new beginning. When she gets out of here, I'm buying her whatever kind of car she wants. This is our new beginning. We're using this time to clear the air. We talked, argued, laughed, and cried. Then we agreed to get a lawyer and deal with the Kenya situation, TOGETHER; as a team! I don't know what I've done to deserve a woman like this on my side. I'm telling you; this is going to be my wife. That's it! I'm keeping my dick in my pants; no more feeding the needy. I know when God is giving me a second chance to right my wrongs. I am not going to screw this up this time!

18

She didn't deserve that. What's up? I thought I was supposed to be the crazy one? Rodney has messed Rhonda's mind and heart up so badly that she's ended up wrapped around a tree. She and the baby could have died. What kind of shit is this? This is a helluva welcome home present. I know Rodney better than he knows himself! Yes he's a dog but he does in his own fucked up way love Rhonda. I could've sworn he told me that he'd told her about the baby. How could he carry her like that? I know exactly how she feels. I know that you've heard by now that she actually forgave him? She really loves him, she's really stupid or, she's really pressed for a man. Then again, who am I to pass judgment? My Captain Save A Hoe ass did jump out of a second story window over Simone. I guess I'm the wrong one to be giving somebody else relationship advice, huh? I'm the same one who didn't listen when everybody, and I do mean everybody, told me Simone was using me. Shit, she robbed me without a gun. She did more than break my heart; she slaughtered my pride, and tortured my trust.

As you probably already know, I've just been sprung from fruitcake central; rubber room city. Whatever you want to call it! Ain't no secrets around here so I know somebody already told you what happened. I took a temporary leave of absence from rational thinking. Temporary! I snapped back like Bootsys' Rubber Band. It's just that Simone threw me for a serious loop; not to mention serious loot. I figured before I hurt her; I'd hurt myself. I don't know how I came up with that one. It was like I was watching a movie or something. It was definitely an out of body experience. I felt myself walking towards the window but I couldn't stop. My mind was screaming **STOP**! I was on some other shit! Tripping!

I'm not making any excuses for what I did. I'm lucky to be alive, still walking, and have some sanity. I've now learned that there's nobody more important than me. I mean shit, just because I was in love with a nothing ass bitch, who am I to rob my mother and father of their child. I can't take my friendship away from people who care for me. Simone ain't worth it! Ain't no chick worth it! You know they say that pride can kill you. That's why it's one of the deadliest sins. My pride made me jump out of that window. I was too ashamed to face anyone. I didn't want to hear, "I *told you so*."

Now look, I'm going to run down the frame of mind I was in when I did the dumb shit. I will hit you with the highlights! Then we're going to squash it and move on, okay? Bet! As you already know, everyone had been on my back to leave her alone but I didn't listen. I convinced myself that they were wrong; they were just hating! They didn't know shit! I'm a grown ass man and nobody tells me what to do.

I had the whole night planned. I was going to cook her a romantic dinner. I was jamming to *"She Da Bomb"* as I played the night out in my mind. I stopped and bought white roses and Don P. I envisioned me wearing her out in front of the fireplace all night long. So, armed with my romantic premonition, I made my way to what I thought was a love filled home. Complete with a fiancée that I'd showered with my love and gifts and her daughter that I loved and treated like my own. I sat the bags down and opened the front door; the house was completely empty. I'm talking echo empty. Everything was gone. She'd taken her shit and my shit! Everything! All that was there awaiting my arrival was a tacky ass three line note that basically said; Fuck you Greg, I'm rolling out.

I loved this woman more than life itself. The only problem was that she didn't love me. I defended her tramp ass! I went against my family for her! All I wanted was to make her happy. Every word out of her mouth was a lie! I felt like the biggest fool in the world. She played me! You can't turn a whore into a housewife. Man, I'm telling you if I ever see Simone I don't know what I'd do to her! I've never hit a woman in my life but with her I'll make an exception. No, I wouldn't! But, it was sure nice thinking about it.

The embarrassment is, was, and always will be unexplainable. My world was crushed. Dreams crushed! Ego crushed! I know that I'm not one of them pretty niggas but I loved her. I guess it just wasn't enough. When it was all said and done I felt stupid as shit! She carried me and everybody knew it. All that "it ain't tricking if you got it" bullshit couldn't help me save face. I was official the biggest; dumbest trick in DC and everyone I love knows it. After that, instead of going to get the help I needed, I drifted away into a bottomless pit of self-pity. I wanted to pay her back. The only way I could think of was to make her feel guilty about my death forever. It didn't work out that way, lucky for me.

I know that trying to kill myself was a punk ass way to deal with things but you know how that goes? Knowing Simone's lil' dirty ass; she probably had an insurance policy on me. She was probably banking on some shit like that happening! I'm going to teach her a lesson. Since I failed horribly at suicide, I'm going to show her what she's missing. Success is always the best revenge! Everyone tried to tell me! Mom always says, "The same things that make you laugh, make you cry." Now I know what that means. A hard head makes a soft ass.

This whole suicide episode has put a speed bump in my plans to rule the world. I've gained fifty pounds. The medication they've got me on is making my face breakout. Then to top that off my friends, coworkers, and family think that I'm bat shit crazy! Every chance they get they let me know that they still can't believe I did what I did; well neither can I! But, I'm still breathing and I still have a job. Everything else will work itself out. Now it's just about picking up the pieces and moving on. Fuck that shit! It's over and I don't want to hear anymore about it. Got it? Good! Coco is here!

"Wassup champ...glad to see that you're still amongst the living."

"Yeah man, you ain't the only one."

"Man, what the fuck was you thinking?"

"I know! I know...my bad." I replied

"You're bad? Greg man...you scared the shit out of all of us and all you can say is you're bad?"

"You know what?"

"What?"

"I heard a song today that reminded me of you... He burst into his version of a K-Ci from Jodeci karaoke moment

...Take my money...my house and my car...for one hit of you...you can have it all baby."

"For real bro! "*Feenin*'"...Jodeci! That's some cold shit Coco!" I laughed.

"I'm just fucking wit' you man... but for real though... you had us scared. Your ass was almost outta here."

"Enough of that...c'mon were late for the movie." Kiki instructed.

"You're treating?" Coco asked me.

"I can."

"Look at you still giving up your money too easy! Haven't you learned anything? Sike! I'm just playing".

"We're treating! Tonight we're taking you out." Kiki replied.

"You mean to tell me that a brother has to almost die in order to get you to treat?" I inquired.

"Basically!" Coco teased.

It feels good to be out with my peoples again. Coco, Kiki, Rhonda, and Rodney practically lived at the hospital; every last one of them. Speaking of Rhonda, I know that she thinks I blame her for what Simone did but I don't. I can tell she feels bad about how Simone carried me. It wasn't her fault. Anyway, Juice is carrying her through enough; she shouldn't be worrying about me. I'm jumping out of windows, Rhonda's wrapping around trees; maybe we should've been together. Huh, what you think? Naw, I'm just joking. I shouldn't have said that now you're going to try and make more of it than it is. I just like her style. My next woman will be exactly like Rhonda. That sister is the bomb; mentally, physically, and emotionally. Damn! Any man would stick his chest out with pride to have her as his woman; except Juice.

DJ Flexx working out! WPGC is cranking as we drove to the movies. Kiki and Coco are my family. She's good for him, you know? By time we'd reached our destination we were hype and in a party mood. After hearing a throwback Rare Essence tape with Funk and Little Benny on it, we were ready for anything. Man, I miss me some Little Benny! We stopped at the sports bar first for some drinks since the movie didn't start for another hour. While at the bar Coco disappeared. He returned twenty minutes later; blunted. His clothes are reeking with the smell of loud. I thought he'd stopped smoking. He's super twisted. His eyes are bloodshot red and everything is funny. He's clowning big time! I can't help but laugh. He is fucked up!

Kiki obviously doesn't like it. If the grit on her face isn't an obvious clue I don't know what is. She won't walk with us. She's walking way in front of us as we cross the mall. I guess that she doesn't want anyone thinking that she's with us. Halfway to the movies a group of three fake thugs begin to approach Kiki. She still walking a little ahead of us and they're walking beside her. We speeded up our step to catch up to her. Yet, stay far enough behind to act is if she's alone to see what their intentions are.

"Wassup good looking?" Bamma 1 asked.

"Hi." Kiki replied curtly.

"Heading my way?"

"No, I'm sorry." Kiki replied irritated but still nicely.

"Aw c'mon now Shorty…sure you don't want to come with me?" Bamma 1 kept pressing the issue.

"No thank you."

"Man, fuck her! Bitch, thinks she's all that." Bamma 2 interjected.

Kiki stopped in her tracks and stepped straight to bamma two.

"Why I got to be your bitch?"

"Suck my dick bitch!" Bamma two replied squeezing his crotch.

The dudes began to walk away as KiKi stood there. One of the squeezed her right breast and another one hawk spit on her. Kiki punched him in the mouth with a nice right hook. Here and Bamma two began to tussle. She was whipping his ass.

"Mother fucker!" Coco yelled as he realized what was going on. He charged after the dude.

"Fuck you and that bitch! Motherfucker's always trying to be heroes! That's how nigga's end up on the news." Bamma 3 replied as if his face is in the dictionary right beside the word killer.

Coco punched Bamma 1 in the face so hard that you could hear the bones breaking and blood gushed from his nose. That was a one hitter quitter because dude is out cold. Kiki continued working on the one who spit on her. Then she kicked him in the balls; making him double over in pain. I know he's gotta feel like shit! He just got beat down by a female in public! Coco finished him off. I bum rushed the third one. He went from talking that killer shit to hollering that he had nothing to do with it. I didn't care. This was a chance for me to take all of my Simone frustration out. I finally eased up off of him to stop Kiki and Coco who are stomping the other two boys as they lay in the middle of the mall. No one is trying to break it up. I pulled them away because I could see the security running towards us, with their hands on their guns. Oh well, later for that movie. We've got to get the hell out of here! We started leaving. Someone is yelling at us. My first instinct was not to turn around and just keep walking; but I turned around anyway.

"Motherfucker! It ain't over!"
One of the bamma's that they'd been stomping has gotten up and is running towards us. Coco turned around and began walking back towards him.

"Oh you want some more? Work ain't hard"

"C'mon baby…let's go! He ain't worth it." Kiki pleaded pulling on Coco as she tried to hold him back.

Just as Coco broke loose from her clutches, the dude reached into his coat. Coco turned and began to run; I'm frozen. In one swoop he had Kiki shielded by his body as they ran. My feet are stuck to the floor paralyzed by fear. My eyes are glued as I'm watching him slide the top piece of the gun back to load the chamber. I still can't move! Shots rang out repeatedly. People are stampeding and screaming. The crowd of frantic people moved past me like ocean waves. It feels like everything is moving in slow motion. It's chaos at the fullest extent. I lifted my head and scanned the area. I finally see Coco. I crawled to Coco who was lying bawled up on the floor in a fetal position cradling Kiki. My heart stopped; as I get closer it seems as if he's not moving. Is he breathing? I start shaking him.

"Coco…Coco man you alright?" I screamed while shaking him.

"Yeah, I think so." He said patting his body for bullet holes.

"Did you get hit?"

"No…what about Kiki?"

Somebody from mall security had tackled the dude

from the blind side a second before he pulled the trigger. Three of the seven shots we heard went into the ceiling. One of the bullets ricocheted and hit Kiki directly in her chest. She's lying in a puddle of blood. I placed my hand over the hole; trying to stop the bleeding. I dialed 911. Fear is all over her face as she's gasping for breath. Her big brown eyes are wide open; staring at us. Coco is trying to keep her calm as he strokes her beautiful scared face. She coughed up blood as she tried to speak to speak to him. He put his ear to her lips and heard her take her final breath. Her body went limp dead in his arms!

"Nnnnnnooooooooo! Somebody help! Somebody help her! Kiki wake up! Kiki wake up!" Coco screamed.

His scream pierced my eardrums as I watched helplessly while Coco cradled her bloody lifeless body trying to wipe the blood off of her pretty face with his shirt. People are still screaming and running. Some are running away but some are running to offer help. Coco pulled out his knife and began swinging wildly; backing up anyone trying to get close to Kiki. I don't know what to do. Kiki please wake up! Somebody get an ambulance! Somebody help us!

Covered in Kinesha's blood, I pulled out my cell phone and called Coco's mom. She's screaming at the top of her lungs, "Why?" Then the phone went dead. After some questioning the police finally let us go. Coco keeps spitting up. He's going crazy. His woman was killed in front of his eyes, dies in his arms, and there is nothing that I can do or, say that's going to make him feel better. Finally all of our families arrived and Mama Sandra is here to comfort her son. I wish we never came to this damn place. Why did we have to go the movies? It's all my fault. If they weren't trying to cheer me up, Kinesha would still be alive. Why the fuck did we come here?

The next several days have been sad, depressing, and full of blame. Coco is in denial about Kinesha's death.

He keeps calling her cell phone just to hear her voice on the voicemail. He keeps waiting for her to walk through the door; saying she'll be home any minute. As you know Kinesha had no family; except Jason. Her mom is a junkie and we haven't been able to find her. He's in no shape to handle the funeral arrangements so Jean, Sandra, and my mother took care the everything. They picked out a mahogany coffin with white satin lining. The only thing that Coco has been able to say is that he wants her to be buried in her favorite dress; it's made of Kinte cloth and has a matching head thing. I used to love it when she'd wear that outfit. It made her look so regal; like an African princess. When Coco saw the program he lost it. I think that it's finally hitting him that it's real. She's gone forever! All because some hard head, disrespectful ass, wanna be thug couldn't keep his hands to himself. He couldn't deal with an old fashioned ass whipping. What kind of world are we living in? These kids have no respect for themselves let alone others.

　　While waiting for the funeral car, I logged into Facebook. Several posts from co-workers, classmates, friends and family filled her timeline. The day of the funeral came so quickly; it's here. A cold reality set in. I have no choice but to accept the fact that today I'm saying goodbye to an angel. Kiki is gone from this earth and taken her place in heaven! The news people have been covering the story everyday trying to find the other two dudes. They got the shooter but it still won't bring her back. I won't see that pretty smile again. I won't hear her speak so eloquently about our heritage. Man, she always made being black sound so beautiful. I won't get to hear that lil' crazy laugh! And most of all, I'll never see my man that happily in love again. Damn! She saved his life and now she's gone. The car arrived and we piled in like zombies. Coco is holding on to Jason for dear life. He's the closest thing that he has left to Kiki.

I'm sitting in this front pew frozen. Watching people as they march pass parade style to the casket saying their goodbyes to Kinesha. She's touched so many people. Everyone who knew her loved her. Flashes of her face on the news crowded my thoughts. Seeing her face on the news; it didn't look real. The sound of screams snapped me back from my daymare. Someone is screaming at the top of their lungs. The choir began to sing her favorite song, Donnie McClurkin's "Stand".

"Kiiiinnnnneeeeessshhhhaaa! Please God don't do this to me! Take me!" a voice shrieked from the entryway.

"Who is that?"

"Kiiinnnnnneeeeessshhhhaaa! Get up Kiki! Get up! I'm sorry baby! I'm so sorry!" the lady screamed.

It's so crowded in here that I still can't see who it is. What is going on? All of a sudden Coco jumped up from his seat and rushed to the back of the church to pick the woman up that had fallen out in grief onto the floor. I took off behind him as my mother grabbed Jason. Who is this woman? She's bawled up like a baby, crying, and screaming. She's wearing a dirty red dress and a dusty matted wig. She reeks of alcohol and I can smell piss on her from 10 feet away. She looks like she's homeless! Her legs are so weak they won't allow her to stand. She keeps screaming that she's sorry. Who is she? I still can't see her face. Coco scooped the woman into his arms and carried her out of the main parlor into the lobby area. I'm still trying to get through the crowd to follow him. Rodney is right behind me. I can still hear her screaming that she's sorry. I squeezed through finally making it out the door behind him.

Coco is sitting on a bench cradling the hysterical woman in his arms for dear life. As Rodney and I get closer we hear him reassuring her that Kiki loved her. The woman laid her head on his shoulder; he gently wiped the tears away. The way he's catering to her she must be somebody.

Finally, I get a glimpse of her face. Though it's obvious that she's had a hard life, too many fist fights, and more than her share of drugs; she still has a glow. Through all of that, you can still tell she used to be a very beautiful woman. The beauty is undeniable and very familiar. She looks exactly like Kinesha. It's her mother! Mama Sandra and my mother left Jason with Rhonda and came out to assist us with her. Not long after they came; since Rodney and I are two of the pallbearers we went back inside.

People are really moved by the services. The pastor preached! There was not a dry eye in the church. As we carried Kiki's casket; Kadejah began singing, Mariah Carey's *"One Sweet Day"* and the entire church broke down. As we loaded the casket into the Hertz, we released 25 doves in honor of every year God allowed one of his angels to walk amongst us. This is only the second time that I had to bury one of my friends and I pray to God that I never will have to again. Right now I can't help but remember Tonya Williams. That was my buddy! Everything I did, she supported. She's the reason I got into real estate in the first place. Why do bad things happen to good people? God, I know that I'm not supposed to question you and everything has a reason but how could you let this happen? Why would you take them away? My mind repeated this over and over as we rode to Harmony cemetery to say our final goodbyes.

The pastor read the 23rd Psalm and just like that a cold reality hit me; this could have been my funeral! I took a flower from her grave and promised to come back and see her. I tried to comfort myself with the thought that I loved her while she was here. It wasn't enough. I still find myself asking, why? As I read her obituary for the 50th time, I cried for her, Jason, and CoCo The love they shared that was taken away. I cried for her mom though I didn't know her. Tomorrow ain't promised. I love you Kinesha! Rest in peace!

19

Man, what's really going on? Can you believe this shit? First, Greg tries to commit suicide by jumping out of a damn window. Then, I almost lost Rhonda in an accident that I was responsible for. Now Kiki is gone. This shit is stressing me the fuck out. God must have both eyes on this family; he keeps saving us. I wish he would've spared Kiki because my brother needs her so badly. He's pitiful right now! All of these situations are a constant reminder of how quickly someone can be taken away. You know they say that you never miss something until it's gone; losing Kiki has changed me. I've decided to be more active in my son's life. You've got to let people know that you love them while they're here. Regardless of how he got here, he's here now, he's mines and he needs a father. I slept with her so I guess I'm the baby's daddy whether I want to be or not. Ain't that some shit! I'm going to man up and face my responsibilities. I don't mean just buying pampers and milk; I mean by really being in his life. I ain't fuckin' wit' his crazy ass mother though! For real, she can just give me my son and bounce.

Do you think I can get custody of him? That's what I should do; take her ratchet sperm hijacking ass to court. One problem, if they piss either of us the child will certainly end up in foster care. Between me and you, I've been getting blasted. The last couple of months I've been getting high as shit. I've got to get myself together before Rhonda finds out. I know Kenya is still fucking around. She'd love to hear that I'm smoking again. Don't say nothing! I'm serious! Keep your mouth shut! I don't even know why I said anything at all. You can't hold water let alone a secret.

Rhonda's being very understanding about Lil' Rodney; almost a little too damn understanding! The shit has got me kind of paranoid. First she beats the shit out of Kenya, now she's telling me that she will stick by me since I've decided to be a part of his life. Yeah right! I ain't falling for that shit! All that sounds great and I'll play the violin while she says it. I can smell a setup from a mile away. Ain't no way I'm going to trust her with my son; by another woman! Oh no! I know she would never do anything to hurt him but I ain't taking no chances. Fuck that! Don't get me wrong; I want to believe that she won't treat him any different than she would our child. I think she'll do the right thing but right now is not the time. I just want to let things cool off a little and then we'll start working on that part. I know she'll be a wonderful stepmother. She says she forgives me but forgiven doesn't mean forgotten. I guarantee you that every time we argue I will hear about that night at the club from this point on.

One thing I can say about my brother and me; we both know how to pick soldiers. When that shit went down at the mall, the night Kiki got killed, she rumbled side by side with my brother. She didn't run. Just like Rhonda, she's the type of woman that will stand beside me through this situation. But since the fight; I think it's better to keep them apart. Especially for Kenya! Rhonda beat the brakes off of her! I sincerely doubt that Kenya can take another one of those.

That's just why Rhonda doesn't know about me going to see Kenya and Lil' Rodney. I told her I was going to play ball with the fellas. I can't seem to shake the feeling that when I see her, I'm going to fuck her up. I still can't believe she tricked me like that. I hate her! I wasn't trying to be no father! From the day I met her ass; it's been nothing but trouble. You know how a person can just bring out the worse in you; that's Kenya. She's not the type of woman that's going to motivate you to do something positive. But she'll sure help you get habits that you'll spend the rest of your life trying to overcome. All she wants you to do is sell drugs, get high, fuck her, and beef with other dudes. That bitch is poison! I'm telling you she's Lucifer's daughter, niece or something. My life hasn't been the same since I met her. I guess that's what I get for trying to be a hero.

As I dressed, I glanced over at Rhonda who's lying across the bed watching Martin reruns; eating waffles and ice cream at ten o'clock in the morning. Who started that lie about all pregnant women being beautiful? She looks like a beached whale. She's fat, her titties look like droopy footballs, and she's gotten four shades blacker. I'm telling you the truth; ain't nothing pretty about it. Even her nose has spread almost across the entire length of her face. That joint looks like a two car garage. On the strength though, the day she drops that baby, her big ass is going on a diet. Jenny Craig. Slim-fast. Slim-slow. Slim-something! If she thinks that just because she's having this baby she is just going to lay around on me getting fat and not taking care of her; she's tripping. I want that body back in order, pronto! If I wanted a big girl, I would've gotten one off the break! Uugh man, look at her.

I know Kenya still wants me and I want her to know what she's missing. I put on a Solbiato sweat suit and my fresh new Foam's. Oh yeah, I know you heard about me! I know Kenya still wants me to smash her. Not going to happen! You know what? I'd rather lick a toilet seat. She can't even suck this pretty motherfucker here. Damn, I wish I didn't have a baby by her. I ain't never going to be able to get rid of this chick. I know that she's going to do some major stunting and drama bringing!

"Sexy, you're looking kind of good! You sure that you just going to play ball with your cousin? Since when did you start balling in Solbiato gear?"

"Rhonda, you know what's up. Don't start that shit!" I snapped because I knew I was lying.

"Why are you getting so defensive? I was just

playing! Should I be concerned?

"Naw man, it's just that so many things have been going wrong lately. I need to know that we are ok. I don't want any more surprises. I just want us to be chilling, I can't take no more drama!"

"Rodney, everything is going to be alright. Yes, things are rough right now but we'll make it.

"Ssssh! Come here baby?"

I kissed her and told her I'd see her later; before she could kick up a fact seeking conversation or try to get me to sleep with her. I know that sounds bad but I'm just telling you the truth. I rolled out. I had to get up out of there with the quickness. You ain't going to believe this; when I closed my eyes to kiss Rhonda in my mind guess who I was kissing? Naw, not Halle Berry? Kenya! All those drugs have fucked me up. I have lost my damn mind. I've got to stop smoking. I need to go to a meeting. I drove to Kenya's apartment mostly by reflex. In a daze, like I've just smoked some PCP or something. Jhene's, "The Worst", is playing on the radio. She's singing about something that has got a brother thinking? What? Naw, forget it. I'm not even going to tell you what I'm thinking! Well we're here!

There she is! I can see her looking out of her balcony window. I should throw a brick at her scandalous ass! From what I can see, she's half-dressed and she's looking kind of good. I knew she was going to try some shit like this; I should just turn around and leave. I've got a bad feeling about this; I shouldn't go in there? Then again, I think I should get a closer look. Climbing these stairs to her second floor apartment, I feel a mixture of anger and curiosity building inside of me. The curiosity about the baby and the anger is about the trick she pulled to conceive him. I still can't believe what she did! All I know is this; I'm through with Kenya. No matter how hard my dick gets; I'm not touching her! I knocked on the door; she yelled for me to come in. The door is unlocked. This is a cold blooded setup! Man, I'm telling you she's up to something. Knowing I should leave; I turned the doorknob.

Aw shit! I'm in trouble now! Kenya's standing no less than five feet away from me with her back against the wall, legs spread apart, and her hands on her hips. She's wearing only a fur coat and some high heels. Damn! She's butt ass naked. Before I could respond; my manhood already has. You know it has a mind of its own! I'm so hard a midget can do pull-ups on this joint! I feel myself moving towards her like I'm being pulled by a magnet. I've got to get the fuck out of here! I'm trying to leave but her body has got me mesmerized! She's phat as shit! Damn! This doorknob won't turn. I've got to get out of here! I can pick the baby up from somewhere else.

She grabbed me by my waist and pushed me back against the door. I know in the next few seconds my manhood will be playing ping pong with the inside of her cheeks so I just rolled wit' it. As she's drifting down to her knees she's unzipping my pants. She took me into the warmth of her mouth. I know I should stop her; but I can't. Ecstasy has me weak! I grabbed her head, the walls, and everything else I could. The pleasure she's giving me has my legs burning! My knees feel weak! The only words I manage to utter are groans of pleasure. Damn! She gives a mean mouth hug. As my body let go, I yanked on the doorknob so tight I almost snatched the front door off of the hinges. It's going to took me a couple of minutes to get myself together. Now here I stand with my joint hanging out and mouth hanging open; looking stupid! Man, what just happened?

While in the bathroom trying to wash away my guilt; I can't help replaying what just happened. Should I feel guilty? But for real though; I didn't do anything. I didn't touch her! It ain't my fault she did what she did! The way I see it, since I didn't sleep with her, I didn't cheat on Rhonda. Sucking ain't fucking; right? I appreciate how she was there for me! What? C'mon, let's go get my son and bounce. I'm taking him to my mother's and chill with him over there. Yeah, I'm going to roll out with lil' man; it's too dangerous up in here. If I stay up in here for five more minutes with her looking like that; I'll be taxing that ass. Hold up! You know what? I just realized something; I haven't seen nor heard the baby since I've been here. Have you?

The first thing I see when I walk in the bedroom is Kenya. She's butt naked in the middle of the bed, on all fours, and her ass pointing to the sky. She swung her weave like the shit was real and looked back over her shoulder at me; smiling! She's got a fat ass joint in her mouth. She turned over onto her back, spreading her legs apart, and began to play with herself. I can't stop watching! My eyes are glued. I need to get the fuck out of here!

"Kenya…where's the baby? Is he sleep or something?" I managed to utter.

"No! He's not here…come help me out." She purred.

"What you mean he ain't here? Where is he? You knew that I was coming over here today to get him!" I asked snapping out of my pussy induced trance.
She moaned from the pleasure she was giving herself. It's hot in here! My mouth is dry and watering at the same time!

"Yeah! And?" she replied crawling to the edge of the bed.

"Yeah my ass! Where is he? I snapped trying to sound unfazed by her performance.

"He's with my mother"

"You let that crack head keep my son? Call her now and tell her I'm coming to get him! She's probably somewhere trying to sell his pampers or some crazy shit like that."

"She's clean. She doesn't use anymore and I'll call

her when I get ready! We have some things that we need to discuss first." She whispered as we tussled for control of my belt.

"We ain't got shit to discuss. You better get my son right now!"

"C'mon baby... stop being so mean to me. You know you want to give me some of that juicy dick! Fuck me baby! My body's calling you. Look how wet I am."

She smacked herself on the ass; that joint looks as soft cotton as it jiggled. She grabbed my hand and placed it between her thighs. My finger accidentally slipped inside. She ain't lying! This thang is nice and wet. I snatched my hand back.

"You think I'm playing' with you? Get it through your head... ain't no me and you!" I argued through the kissing and rubbing.

"Ump humph! That's what your mouth says. You know you still love me. You know you want this!"

"Girl, stop trippin! You crazy! I ain't got time for this shit" I snatched free from her grip again.

"Oh I'm trippin huh...you know you miss this?" She reached up from the bed pulling my hand to caress her wetness again. I began to play with her as we kissed. My hands began to explore the softness of her body. The part of me that's controlling this situation is all in! I don't know why I did it but I did. The next hour or so was spent having hot erotic sex. Wasn't no love making; just straight up fucking. This was some porno movie type action. We went from the kitchen to the bathroom; stopping everywhere in between. I guess I must've fallen asleep because the ringing of the telephone woke me up. Damn! What have I done?

"Hey sleepyhead! You a little tired, huh?" Kenya laughed.

"Whatever man! You're playing too many games for me! You ain't going to trick me this time."

"I don't want to get you like that. No more games. I've got your son and I know you're going to be with me. But this time you're going to come to me on your own.

"Now I know it's time to go! Here's some money for the baby. I'll call you."

"I'm just sure you will."

Man, Kenya is on some ole brand new type shit! I guess she's trying to step her game up. She's scheming on a whole new level! She's one of them type chicks that'll call Rhonda and tell her what kind of draws I have on. How could I be so stupid? Thinking with the wrong head again! I jumped in the shower, put my clothes back on, and rolled out.

This drive home is reminding me of walking to the tree to pick out a branch for a whipping. I can't fake! I'm jive nervous! I'm tired! I don't feel like dealing with no bitching and whining. I just want to go home and go to sleep! I'm not the best liar. I know when Rhonda can tell I'm lying; by the way she looks at me. I have this feeling that when I open this door, Rhonda's going to be waiting. She'll probably ask me to drop my pants so she can smell me; or some crazy shit like that. I'm supposed to be coming from playing ball but I smell like Ivory soap. I should park and jog around the block a couple of times to get sweaty? That's exactly what I did until I broke a sweat. Man damn! I swear I don't feel like going in there!

I stared at the front door for about two minutes, took a deep breath, and went in. Well, here goes nothing! I cracked the door and scanned the living room. Good she's not downstairs! Sssssh! Be quiet! I tiptoed in the house like a burglar. Shit! Here she comes! I hurried and tried to sit down on the couch; why I don't know.

"Rodney don't sit down." Rhonda ordered.

"What?" I questioned.

"Don't sit down; I've got to check something out before we leave."

"Check what out?"

"Drop your pants and put your dick in my hand!"

"Say what?"

"Sexy… you so crazy. I'm just playing. I just wanted to check and make sure we still agree on the colors for the wedding. We have to be on the same page before we meet the lady. What do you think I wanted to check? You don't think I trust you or something?"

"You ready?"

"You didn't answer me!"

"As long as you're going to be Mrs. Rodney Hughes they can wear trash bags. I don't care. It's your day. Whatever you want is fine with me…as long as I have you!"

"Aw baby…come here boo."

Rhonda and I began to kiss. I wonder if she can taste the infidelity on my lips? What's really tripping me out; is that I know that I'll probably do it again. It's too easy; she doesn't suspect a thing. Big Daddy got it like that! She's on me hard. After everything we've been through; she still has blind trust in me. I know the right thing for me to say is that I'm grateful to have a woman like her in my life; I am. I'm also a man that likes variety. I can't stop thinking about Kenya. Damn that girl got some good head! Man oh man! The events from earlier today left an inerasable smirk on my face. Rhonda doesn't suspect a thing. If she only knew! I'm still shaking from that back shot I just got.

Work is just that; work. My personal life has become so complicated that everything else pales in comparison. Work to me has become an inconvenient necessity. I do the bare minimum and pick up a paycheck. I'm almost robotic. Today's no different. I've been here about twenty minutes and already I have a visitor. I don't see any interviews scheduled on my calendar. I bet it's Marilyn William! This woman has called me 100 times! I keep telling her I will call her when we start the interview process. Time to put my game face on! I instructed the receptionist to send the mystery visitor in. Guess who it is? Kenya! Yeah Kenya! I tried to tell you! She is really trying to put some shit in the game.

"Yes, I'd like to apply for a position." She flirted.

"Oh really…what position is that?"

"69." She replied licking her lips.

"Look Kenya…what happened yesterday was a mistake. It won't happen again. I love my lady and I'm going to marry her." I explained trying to convince myself.

"Who are you trying to convince me or you? You may think you love her but you're in love with me! You want me! You need me! Remember this Juice… she may fill the space but she can't take my place! Ain't no substitute for me! I know… you know that! I know the **real** you!"

"Yeah alright! You can bounce with that shit!"

"Baby…if you really wanted me gone… you and I both know I wouldn't be here now."
Rhonda walks in.

"Hey baby, wassup? I said quickly to Rhonda reaching out for her to come to me.

"I'm on my break… I came by so that we could pick out the wedding invitations. What is she doing here?" She asked while giving Kenya the look of death.

"I just came by to congratulate you'll on the wedding! I really hope that we can be friends since our children are related. I'm all about the blended family! Let's put everything in the past; the fight and everything else. I never meant to spoil your party it was my friend's idea. It was juvenile and stupid; I hope you can forgive me. No more drama. I know that there's nothing between Rodney and I. He's moved on and is happy with you. I just want him to be there for his son."

"Bitch are you high or something? Put the past

behind us? Forgive you? Blended family? Are you serious?" Rhonda snapped.

"Actually I am serious! I know it's going to take some time but our children will be siblings and I really want us to get along."

"Yeah well you should have thought of that before you put our business in the streets!"

"Well Rodney... I'll see you tomorrow when you pick the baby up." Kenya replied ignoring Rhonda.

"Tomorrow? Oh no ma'am! We will be picking up baby? You need to be concentrating on who's going to pick you up off of this floor! Girl you better be glad I'm at work or I'd be picking up something and bash your skull in until I can see your thoughts! Rodney you better check this rat!"

"Baby girl...calm down... ain't no need for all of that! I don't want Rodney. I just want him to be a father to our son." Kenya replied agitating Rhonda even more.

"First of all...tell that shit to somebody who's going to believe it because I'm not the one! Secondly...we ain't friends... so don't be calling me no damn baby girl! To you...I'm Mrs. Hughes! Last time I checked Rodney aint Will and I damn sure ain't Jada! So don't kick me blended family bullshit to me! Rodney you better get her ass out of here before I lose my mind and job. Coming up in here with that Rodney King, *"can't we all get along"* bullshit... Bitch please!"

"Kenya... I think you should leave. I'm going to get with **you** later." Kenya replied with an emphasis.

"Okay I'll go. I'll be in touch. Bye Rhonda...I mean Mrs. Hughes! It was nice seeing you again. I'm serious about us being friends."

"What-the-fuck-ever!"
Kenya excited the office and Rhonda flipped out.

"Rhonda calm down. We at work!"

"First she steals my man's sperm. Then she fucks up my birthday party! Now she's fucking with my job! She got the wrong mother fucking one! That bitch is lying through her buck teeth…but you know what? Whatever is going on will come out. What you do in the dark eventually come to light. God don't like ugly!"

"Ain't nothing goin' to come to light! Ain't nothing going on! Kenya has a man. Besides…I thought you said that you trust me." I questioned.

"Oh… now all of a sudden she's got a boyfriend. Boy, do I look stupid or something? Boyfriend my ass! You better stop playing with me. Same thing make you laugh, make you cry!"

Just think I'm marrying this woman on Thanksgiving Day. Supposedly, we have so much to be thankful for. What a joke! I feel like the biggest jerk of all times. I looked Rhonda dead in her face and I lied like a motha'. I lied like she was my judge on sentencing day. This situation is quickly getting out of hand. Kenya's timing is perfect for what she's trying to accomplish. I mean; Kenya's looking like a wet dream while Rhonda is looking like a nightmare! Sex is my weakness; I can't help it. I'm always thinking with the wrong head! Rhonda is seven and a half months pregnant; she won't give up off the loving. Something on her is always hurting. Her back! Her feet! Her head! Something! I'm tired of that shit; she can do something for a brother. Her neck and mouth shouldn't hurt because she ain't using those either! Kenya's giving it up like I have a stack of Free Sex coupons. What's a brother to do?

20

"That is not his baby!" I screamed at the lady guest on the Maury show. These talk shows make my pressure rise. I can't believe people do so much dumb shit then get on TV and talk about it; can you? That baby is black! The both of them are white as the driven snow. Watch this! Let me turn the TV up.

"In the case of 2 yr old Demonte...Charles you are not the father!" Maury announced.

Of course she jumped up and ran into the back crying like she was in shock. I told you! She needs to be shot. She knew damn well that wasn't his baby. Shit he knew it wasn't his baby! She even gave the baby a black name; Demonte. She's black! He's black! That child is as white as the driven snow. What white boy you know named Demonte! Some of the business they tell; I would take with me to my grave. You'd have to pry my mouth open with a crowbar and I still wouldn't say shit. These women let men take them through all kinds of shit. Not me! I refuse to play the role of anyone's fool. I don't want anybody that doesn't want me! Rodney can try me if he wants to. I forgave you once and that's my limit. The only reason I took him back is because of the baby. I want my baby to grow up with both parents but if he plays me again, all he's going to see is assholes and elbows as I hit the door. I wasn't going to let that bitch and her baby have him; my baby and I come first! You know what I'm saying? Okay!

I honestly believe Rodney loves me. But, I can't seem to shake the feeling the something's up. Women's intuition is a mother! I know something ain't right. He's been acting too attentive; like he's trying to cover his tracks. His mother thinks that he's just excited about the baby coming, yeah and every chick with a bone straight weave and a pair of flat irons got Indian in her family.

Rodney is up to no good. I ain't stupid! In time it will all come out. I'm just laying in the cut; waiting for the drama to unfold. I beat that bitch's ass once; this time is going to be a lot worse. All of this drama going on in my life, I need to write a book. I know it would be a bestseller. Let me go on Baisdenlive.com and get Michael Baisden's info. I'm so serious! I just might do that! Everybody else is writing books; why can't I?

Anyway, today is my baby shower. It's all about my baby and me! I should be exited but I'm not. I really don't feel like going anywhere. I'll just be glad when they get this baby out of me. I'm too, too miserable. I'm swollen like an Oompa Loompa and I always have to pee. Nobody should have to suffer like this. I'm not having any more kids; believe that! This baby will be an only child. Oh yeah, I forgot Rodney already has a kid.

Anyway! I'm in one of my rap moods. Feeling real gangsta! First, I popped in Will's, "Don't Start None". Then I had to hear Dread's "Marinate" while I got dressed. I'm feeling some type of way. Listening to Dread makes me think about my girl Tonya Williams. She would've been the first person at the shower with the biggest gift. I miss her spirit and her smile so much. I've got to stop talking about her before I start crying. So let's change the subject. What's your opinion on today's rap music? I myself feel that the rappers are just discussing their piece of reality. What do you think? Yeah, you're right. Shit! I don't have anything to wear. I swear that I don't want to go! My feet are swollen. I hate this! I'll be so glad when this is over; it's driving me nuts. The bigger I get; the more I hate Rodney. By the time I have this baby he'll be number three on my hit list; right below Kenya and Simone. Why can't he get fat? Have aches, pains, and hunger attacks? Run to the bathroom all day? Swell up? He ain't going through shit! That's still my baby though. Whew! These mood swings are rough.

"Willy! Are you ready yet?" Lexie yelled from downstairs

"In a minute."

Chris has nicknamed me Willy; after the movie. You know the one about the whale. Now every time they see me they start humming the melody to that song. Dum, Dadadadadum, dadadadadum. If they weren't my very best friends I might be offended. I know that no matter how I look they've got my back; so it's cool. Besides, I still look good! Forget them!

"Wassup girl! You ready for the party?" I asked.

"I'm almost scared after the first party. Hopefully...Rodney doesn't have any more baby mothers stashed away."

"I know what you're saying. I still have a bad taste in my mouth from that party myself. But we whipped some ass didn't we girl?"

"Oh yeah...they thought it was a game! C'mon momma ...waddle on out to the car. Did you forget anything? You hungry or something?" Lexie asked.

"I've got everything! But I do want to stop past Taco Bell. I have been craving tacos for two days".

"It's one on the way to your mother's house."

"Get to moving woman... get to moving!"

It's good to have friends that don't try to get all in your business. Some things are best left unsaid. I know that I'm a fool for Rodney; I don't need to continuously be reminded of it. Opinions are like assholes everybody's got one! Bitches always trying to tell you what to do with your man! That's why I love Lexie; she minds her business. Yes, Taco Bell! I jumped out of the car and rushed for the door; like I was really running for the border. I'm so hungry; I can eat this porcelain tile that makes up the counter.

"May I have a dozen supreme taco's please?"

"You sure can when I ask for your order."

"What…what did she say?" Lexie asked surprised.

"I heard her. Yes, she tried it!"

"Yes she did! Taco girl better act like she knows!" she laughed.

"Naw, she can keep right on acting like she don't and watch me snatch her ass over that counter. I'll drag that bitch by that $2.00 yak hair. I know her necks itching like a motha! Oh no see, she's fucking with the right one. Pregnant or not I'll stomp a mud holes in her ass. I'm not the one today…for real!"

"Can I take your order please?" she asked nicely.

It took everything I had for me not to leave that chick toothless. People are always trying you. She's acting like it's my fault she works here; like I filled out the application and put her name on it. You know what I'm saying? She's got me fucked up! I have a feeling that this is the beginning of a very long day. Ump humph! See, I told you! It just went from bad to worse! Look over there; see that silver Lexus that's parked right beside Lexie's car? That's Patrick! Lord, give me strength. I told you about Patrick right? I really don't feel like this shit right now; not him of all people!

Patrick is Simone's cousin and my X boyfriend. Dog! Dog! Dog! He dogged me like a hydrant; just pissed all on my emotions. I would go into detail but he isn't worth the air that would escape my lungs in order for me to tell you. Let's just say that he's less than zero. Take any ruggedly handsome, sexy, well-endowed, thuggish, upright walking K9 and multiply him by twenty; then your beginning to get Patrick. He ain't worth shit! Not even the toilet paper you wipe your ass with! I've never had a man to use me and have me convinced it was my fault that he was cheating. I broke my neck trying to please him in and out of bed. I even had ménage trios with some stripper bitch named "Juicy" in efforts to keep him happy. That was the worst night of my life. I'm not gay; nor have I ever been curious. I compromised every moral instilled in me for his no good ass. I kept my eyes closed the whole time. I will never forget it. My body was in overdrive from the oral pleasure I was receiving. When I finally opened my eyes; I saw her. I burst into tears and ran into the bathroom; locking the door behind me. I felt guilty and sinful for enjoying it. I have never had anyone please me like she did. After that night I never spoke to Patrick again. I was beyond stupid when it came to him. I've taken being a fool to a whole 'nother level. He had my brain fried like chicken. I never knew if I was coming or going. I haven't seen him since that night. Until now! He sees me. Shit! Here he comes!

"Hey Chocolate…how you doing wit' you're pretty self?"

"Wassup Patrick?" I grunted

"Simone told me that you were pregnant…you know that's supposed to be my baby?"

"I hear you." I snapped

"For real girl! You know I still love you, right?"

"Me and how many others?"

"Aw, c'mon now… why you going there on a brother? So look here…why don't you call me after you drop that load. Maybe we can hook up and do a little something, something. I know that bamma ain't hittin' it right! I know what you like and how you like it" Patrick replied licking his tongue out between a V he's made with his two fingers.

"Not in this life and definitely not in reincarnation."

"Why you faking? You know you miss me…you know you still love me! Once you love me its forever."

"Hold your breath and I'll see you at your funeral."

"Juicy asked about you." He teased.

"You good Sis?" Lexie questioned interrupting the uncomfortable conversation.

"I don't know….am I Patrick?"

"Most definitely! It was nice seeing you." Patrick replied as he retreated.

Patrick turned and beat feet the hell up out of there with the quickness. He must be smoking some good shit. What makes him think that I still want him? What makes him think he can still hit this? He acts like he has a lifetime membership. He is really feeling himself. What lies have they been telling him? I didn't want him when I had him. How can he assume that I'm not with my baby's father? All he did was reassure my feeling for Rodney. I've got a man; not a wannabe pimp. I've been too hasty in judging Rodney. I know he's not doing anything! I know he wants me; not Kenya. It's just these mood swings. Got a sister feeling bi-polar as hell! Rodney loves me and I love him; bottom line! I'm so glad I'm through dealing with trifling ass fools like Patrick. One thing for sure, Patrick ain't crazy. He sees who I'm with so he didn't go halfway as hard as he would have. Right now he's trying to figure out how I even know Lexie let alone have her refer to me as "Sis".

Finally here! I sincerely hope that this party moves quickly; so I can go home and get in my bed. I'm really in no mood to play the overjoyed expecting mother. Don't get me wrong; I'm happy about the baby. I'm just not sure I'm ready for all of the other things that come with it. You know what I mean? Okay; time to grin and bear it. What if they did me like they did Sharon? Remember that? Oh, you haven't heard? Well hears the dirt; no one showed up for her shower but me. I felt so bad for her. It was the most pitiful thing I'd ever seen. Now that I think about it; the whole thing is kind of funny. If I had any sense; I would have taken a hint from them and stayed home too. That's what she deserved anyway; to be alone. She was pregnant by her sister's husband. Child, it was a mess! I'll have to tell you about her scandalous ass at another time. The story requires more time than I have.

"Hey little momma! Hello, Lexie baby!"

"Hey Ma ... I mean Laila.." Lexie joked with my mom.

"Lexie…somebody should've told her about messing with the family. She thought it was a game." My mother laughed.

"Yeah…well I think she got the message."

"How's my baby?"

"I'm fine Ma."

"Surprise!" voiced shouted in unison.

People are everywhere. Crawling out from under lamps; like big roaches running from Raid. This is so nice. All of these people came for me; Rhonda Washington! Just now it really hit me. I'm about to bring another life into the world. God is actually going to trust me with another human life. I better get my act together now; right now! A lot of things are going to have to change. Immediately!

The best of Luther Vandross provided and R&B drum roll as I opened my presents. I love me some Lufa! I got two strollers! Diapers! A crib! Clothes! Lexie gave the baby a pink diamond cross. Baby ain't even here and got better jewelry than me. Want to hear something funny? Check this out Lee Lee gave me an envelope full of coupons and $20.00. Coupons? What was she smoking? That child puts the eap in cheap! If she couldn't get a gift why'd she come? Penny pinching ass! Just look at her! Now that doesn't make any sense! Now I know why she came! She came to eat! She's been posted up at the buffet table all afternoon. Damn, she's cheap and hungry; with her broke ass self!

When I got to Kiki's gift I started crying immediately. I miss her so much. She gave the baby a beautiful receiving blanket made of silk with family pictures woven into it. She made it by hand and Rodney's mother finished it. It's breathtaking. I wish she was here with me! Excuse me for a minute! I need a moment to myself.

Sorry about that; you know how it is! I had to get myself together. I told you my emotions are all over the place. I'm okay now. I was wrong earlier; this is a great party. Just what I needed! Laughter has snuck up on me and I'm actually having fun. We're all sitting around telling jokes and lies. They started doing the bump when mom's put the old Gap Band album on. It wasn't long before the men stories kicked in; we started reminiscing about our old relationships. The baby father horror stories are abundant. It feels good to get out with my girls. I'm about to piss on myself from laughing at Lexie. She's in the middle of the floor doing line dancing her tail off in her wheelchair. She has the nerve to dance better than half of the people up there with her. That's my girl. Go Lexie! Go Lexie!

My mother and Sandra are so happy; they're ecstatic. I'm surprised that they haven't fractured their jawbones long ago smiling. It feels good to be celebrating for a change. Between, Greg and I, in the hospital and Kiki getting killed, this hasn't exactly been what you'd call a good year. The doorbell rang. Momma told Lee Lee to get the door. She needs to do something, make herself useful. She ain't doing nothing but eating anyway; wit' her hungry ass! A hush fell over the room. What's wrong? I turned to see what was going on. Oh hell no! Guess who it is? She must think she's 'bout it 'bout it for real!

"Simone, I'm sorry but you're going to have to leave. You're not welcome in my house." My mom snapped.

"Yes, Ms. Washington, I know. I just came to give Rhonda her gift and then I'll leave." Simone explained.

"I don't want your gift. I don't want a damn thing from you!" I barked.

"Whose baby is that you're carrying? Is that my son's baby?" Ma Wheeler inquired.

236

"No ma'm." Simone whispered

"How you know that she ain't lying about that? She lies about everything else!"

"I'm sorry about what happened with Greg." Simone pleaded

"Let me beat her ass for you Ma Wheeler." My cousin Karen chirped in.

"Of my fifty three years on this earth I never thought I'd have the desire to take a person's life, until I met you." Ma Wheeler threatened.

"If you know what's good for you, you'll get on 'bout your business. Little tramp!"

"Nobody wants you here!"

"Jean get that gold-digging bitch out of here. I swear I'll kill her right now with my bare hands."

"Calm down Ms. Betty. Don't get yourself all worked up. You know you've got to watch your pressure. Here have a seat."

"Pressure my ass! If pressure burst a pipe you know what it'll do to me so you know what I'm going to do to her before I go. You better get that trash out of her before I kill her, pregnant or not!"

"Simone you're going to have to leave and I don't repeat myself." Lexie instructed

Simone immediately turned to leave the same way she came; with the present still in her hand. How dare she show up here? I know she feels like some shit. That's what she gets! Talk about bold! I promise you that I will never have another party. Every party I have gets ruined. If Simone wasn't pregnant, somebody in here would've beaten her ass; believe that. Betty probably would have thrown her out of the window. I wonder whose baby it is? I didn't even know she was pregnant. Why didn't you tell me? Oh, you didn't know either. Yeah well, she appears to be about five to six months. That would be right around the time Marvin came home; then again it could be Greg's.

I know for a fact she was still sleeping with Greg up until the morning she left him; they had sex the night before. Greg or Marvin? Marvin or Greg? Whose could it be? Knowing her that could be anybody's baby! Wit' her loose booty ass! She screwed half of the city and 3/4ths of the suburbs. Well, at least I know that's one baby that's not Rodney's. Ha! Ha! Ha! What? It's just a joke.

21

Ha! Ha, my ass! Bitch the joke is on you! Rhonda, Jean, and Betty; every last one of you bitches! The gift didn't cost me a dime. It was a box full of my shit! That's what she is so that's what I gave her! I got the better end of the deal. I'm with Marvin; the man I want to be with! Not who they think I should be with! This is my life! I don't give a fuck what you'll think! I can't stand you'll drunk on Saturday, in church on Sunday, fake religious, self-righteous bitches! Always talking about what they would and wouldn't do. Passing judgment on somebody like their shit don't stink; like I really give a fuck! I bet if they were in my shoes they'd do the same thing. It's not my fault that I didn't love Greg. He just wasn't my type. And let's not forget one important thing; what went on between Greg and me; is between Greg and me. I never lied to him. Never!

Okay, let me break it down to the least common denominator and make sure you understand. I don't need you trying to figure it out so I'm gonna let you know. I need a roughneck, street smart, arrogant type guy. A man's' man! A man with a voice! A man that takes control of the situation! Greg was just the opposite. He was a sucker. A yes man! "Yes baby…sure baby…anything you want baby." That shit got to be sickening. I ran all over him. He was no challenge for me; whatsoever. I know some people may say that he was just trying to make me happy and that might be true but to me he was a trick. A flunkie! He was workable! An ATM with legs! There was no excitement in our relationship. If I said piss, I guarantee he'd drop his pants. Who really wants a man like that? Do you? Yeah, that's what I thought. Like I said, Greg was a borderline bitch in my book. Like Toni Braxton says, *"He wasn't man enough for me"*.

Marvin on the other hand is everything a woman could possibly want in a man. I ain't gonna fake. He was a little upset with me when he found out about the things that I'd done while he was locked up. Child, he found out everything. When I say everything, I mean everything! Half of the people he found out about, I'd forgotten. Ooh, maybe I shouldn't say that. That didn't come out right. I can trust you right? Yeah, we peoples. I know you ain't going to tell my business. So where was I? Oh yeah, let's just say I was really busy. Marvin's starting to come around now since the pregnancy.

He's been home more and drinking less. Things are going to work out. I think he forgives me. He loves kids. This will be our second child. He's really concerned about being around for this baby and Minyon. He says he wants to be the father that he never had. He missed so many important events in Minyon's growing up that he's determined not to miss these. Little does he know; this baby may not be his? The week this baby was conceived according to my calculations, I'd been with Greg, Marvin, Keith, Man Man, and Rodney. Yeah Rodney! What? Forget you! Anyway, I'll just hold my breath and pray it's his. Tina broke my chain of thought.

"Ooh Simone girl, you did your thang. My hair looks fierce." My client Tina replied as she looked into the mirror.

"You like it?" I questioned already knowing the answer.

"Like? Girl this hairdo is going to help me get some coins. I'm gonna get big play. I can see the men lining up now. I'm working this hairdo. It shows off my eyes."

"Alright Ms. Thang, go 'head with your bad self." I sarcastically encouraged.

What I really want to say is; "*go head with that active imagination*". She sounds like a fool. Who's going to pay her? She's snaggletooth and the few teeth she does have look like sticks of butter. I think she has that stuff; what do you call it? Ump! Pyria of the gums or something

240

like that? Yeah that's it! Her breath can tweeze you're
eyebrows and her underarms smell like musty chitterlings.
Now you tell me, who's going to deal with that? I know
that she notices people spraying Lysol and lighting candles
when she comes into the shop.

"Girl, you know Rite-Aid is having a 2 for 1 sale on
everything; deodorant, toothpaste, mouthwash, douche's,
everything is on sale!" I strongly suggested

"Yeah, I heard. Everybody's been telling me about
the sale. I'm going down there."

"You going now?"

"No, but I am going to get down there. See you
Simone."

"Okay."

Working in this salon has convinced me that I've
earned the title of miracle worker. You wouldn't believe
what people ask for. For instance a girl with hair that's the
length of eyelashes will ask for finger waves. C'mon now,
let's be real. Sometimes, I just don't understand people.
Don't they know that everything ain't for everybody; know
what I'm saying? Just because they see a hairdo in the
video; they want it. Yeah right! Shit, those video chicks
paying top dollar for that hair. That shit is coming straight
off the head of a bald head Brazilian. These hookers that
roll up in here can barely afford a wig, let alone a lace front
one. If they know like I know they'd get paid when laid; so
they can keep themselves up to par. First get the money
right, then I'll get your look right.

This day is moving entirely to slow. I'm ready to
go. Tina was my last scheduled appointment and I'm not
taking any walk-ins. I'm out of here. I don't care who it is.
Tony didn't come in today. It's boring in here and I don't
have anyone to argue with. I need his goofy butt to make
me laugh. My feet are swelling anyway. I'm tired of being
cooped up in here. Yep, that's what I'm going to do; go
home. They better not even part their lips to ask me about

241

doing a walk-in. I wish they would!

"Tasha, I'm gone."

"Ump humph!"

"Oh yeah…don't schedule any appointments for me for Thursday or Friday."

"Why?"

"None of your business." I snapped.

"Well excuse me."

"There's no excuse for you…wit' your nosey ass self. Get a life and get out of mines."

"Look bitch, don't push it. Don't think that because you're pregnant I won't tap that chin!"

"Bitch please! Don't flatter yourself! You and I both know that you want no parts of this." Tasha replied.

"I most certainly do!"

"I tell you what; I have an appointment to schedule for you. One month after you drop that load, I'm going to take you up on that offer. You think it's a game, game over!"

"Oh bitch, we ain't got to wait. I keep something in my purse especially for bitches like you. Run up!"

"Okay that's enough! We have customers in here, squash it." Yelled Tahesha

"Alright Lil' Gansta Momma…keep jumping out there. You'll be sorry you did. Bet your last dollar I'm going to take you up on that offer!"

"I said that's enough." Tahesha warned.

Tasha sounds like a fool. How the hell is she going to try and threaten somebody? She's just mad because last year I slept with her fake ass baby daddy and he gave me their rent money. If she knows like I know; she'd get over it. I did! Trust me, he's not all that. If "*her man*" was into her or had any respect for their relationship, he wouldn't have been with me in the first place. Am I right? Don't hate the playa hate the game! Women are always trying to blame the other women for the problems they're having with their man. They had problems long before I came into the picture. I knew she was a little on the dingy side but she's just straight up dumb! Do you know she's still with his no good ass? And trust when I tell you, I wasn't the only one he cheated with. Every time he comes into the shop he brings me food and gives me money in her face. Yeah, that's what I said, in her face! Now you tell me where she's keeping her helmet because I know she rode the short bus to school. Her ass is SSSLLLOOOOWWW!

Why are women so obsessive and possessive over a man? They're people not property. You don't own another human being. People are going to do what they want to do! A man will change his woman before he changes his ways. Just because she wants a committed relationship doesn't mean he does. These types of thoughts irked me all the way home. I just don't understand. No matter how hard I try, I just don't get it. All I know is; it's not for me. You ain't gon' piss on my head and tell me it's raining. I will never make a fool of myself over Marvin or anybody else. Oh no, not the kid! I am not the one! Now don't get me wrong, I love me some Marvin but just because I love him doesn't mean I stopped loving myself. I refuse to let him or any other dude carry me! Momma ain't raise no fool. Messing around with you, I forgot to renew this rental car. What's today? Good it's not due until tomorrow. I've got to keep this joint for at least another two weeks. I got things to do and Marvin is always gone with my truck. I got so tired of arguing about it; I just got myself a rental. Now, what was I saying?

If I caught Marvin with someone else or even heard about it, I wouldn't blame her. He's the one that is wrong! Now if I knew the girl and she knew that I was with Marvin; that would be a different story. I'd bash her head in with the quickness. However, if I didn't know her it wouldn't be her fault. I don't know what Marvin could have been telling her. You know what I'm saying? And believe me when I tell you, she can have him. Ain't going to be no choosing her or me! He's going to have to choose her because I don't share! And I sure don't want sloppy seconds. I'm not the one! Simone does no crying, pleading or begging. Believe that!

There is no man on the face of this earth that's worth making a fool out of you! My mother would beat me down if she even thought I was playing myself for some dude. I love him and all that good shit but never will I let any man carry me. I can't fake he carried me the first round but I was young. I'm not the same woman! I've been with enough men that supposedly belong to another woman to know better. I know the shit they say and do. I not into keeping nobody that don't want to be kept. You feel me!

Oh my God! Nooooooooooooo! What happened? Lord please, let Marvin be okay! You see my truck? It's fucked up! The entire front on the driver's side is crushed like a soda can. This nigga ain't got no license in the country. Oh shit! I knew I should have taken my truck from him. I wonder if he's hurt? Did he hurt somebody else? This is not happening. I ran to my condo door. You hear that? Marvin's got the stereo blasting, *"We Both Grown"* by William Casanova. I know damn well he ain't partying with my truck looking like it's been in a demolition derby. I swear I hope he's alright; so I can kill him! All the mess I went through to get that truck and he comes straight home and fucks it up! Hell no! Sssh! Be quiet; I'm going to creep in on him. He's going to be so surprised. He's not expecting me for another four hours. I want to hear what the fuck happened to my truck! Being with him is bringing me down fast.

I turned my key trying to enter but I can't; the door won't move. With all the strength I have I pushed with all of my might and the door opened just a crack. *"What the hell?"* Now I see why the door wouldn't open. What is going on? The suitcases that are now overturned on the floor; had apparently been propped up against the door. Is Marvin going somewhere? Without me? Normally, I would call out his name but I'm so mad; I can't get it out. I hear something coming from the bedroom. What's that noise? You hear that? The music is so loud; I can't tell who it is or what they're saying. Maybe it's one of Marvin's friends who just got out of jail or something. Marvin must've offered him a place to stay. I speeded up my step kicked off my shoes, and wrapped my hair into a quick bun. First the jail dudes calling here; now they staying here. Oh hell no! Then on top of that my truck is all crunched up! Somebody is going to tell me something.

Approaching the door, I'm hearing what sounds like groans of pleasure. I know damn well this bastard ain't crazy for real. There better not be a bitch up in here! He better be beating his meat! I tried to turn the knob but the door is locked. I kicked the door but it didn't open! Ssshhh! You hear that? I began banging on the door kicking and screaming, "*Let me in*!" That's too many footsteps to be one pair of legs. I can definitely hear two sets of footsteps running around the room. I ran and got Marvin's Glock from the closet and went back to banging like the police. I know damn well this motherfucker ain't sleeping with another bitch in my house. He has lost his mother fucking mind.

"Marvin…Marvin…Marvin! Open this mother fucking door before I blow a hole in it! If it's a bitch in there, we're going to be on the news tonight." I cocked the gun to load the chamber.

Finally he snatched open the door. He's butt naked with a bed sheet wrapped around his waist; dripping in sweat. This room stinks of sex. What the fuck…! Condoms wrappers are spread all over the floor. My mind is moving 100 mph but I can't move. This is not happening! I know this mother fucker ain't crazy enough to bring a bitch in our home and fuck her in our bed. I'm going to jail tonight!

He's looking at me like I'm his parole officer or something. He's scared out of his mind.

"Baby what are you doing here?" He asked calmly.

"I live here that's what the fuck I'm doing here! The question is what the fuck are you doing? Who you got in my house and what the fuck happened to my truck? Move the fuck out my way!"

Pushing Marvin to the side, I bogarded my way into the bedroom. The gun is cocked and I'm ready to rumble; pregnant and all. Whoever it is still has to be here unless she can grow wings. There's no way for her to get out. One thing I know for sure is they can't jump out of the window. We live on the tenth floor of a high-rise; ain't nothing but plenty concrete waiting. First, I looked under the bed. Marvin keeps grabbing me trying to stop the search. Then, I went straight for the walk-in closet. I'm trying to open the door but the person inside is pulling against me. Damn, she's strong! But I'll betcha she ain't stronger than this bullet. I'm going to kill her strong ass. Bet on it!

"Bitch you better let go of this knob before I start putting holes in this motherfucker!"

I ain't never even fired this gun but she don't know that. Honestly, one part of me doesn't really want this door to open but another part of me has to see who she is. Yanking the door open, my heart fell to my feet and my mouth dropped open. I feel like I'm going to faint. It's someone I know. This situation is totally fucked up! Oh my God! How am I supposed to handle this? Standing before me naked is the one person I trusted. My co-defendant. My partner in crime! It's my mother! Yes, the woman that gave birth to me. No bullshit! Right before my eyes, titties swinging and all. What the fuck? Shit! Is this a joke? This is not happening. While Marvin was incarcerated not only did he acquire knowledge he apparently also acquired a taste for gray haired pussy and old bitches. This bamma is traveling the geriatric highway. My knees gave away; I collapsed fortunately the bed caught me. I feel nauseous.

"Oh my God! I think I'm gonna be sick!"

"Simone...cut all that soap opera shit out... you know you don't deserve him."

Crying uncontrollably, I rushed into the bathroom and threw up. Knowing that what I'd been putting in my mouth he'd been putting in my mother; threw me for a loop. Not to mention, my mother is a bigger whore than me. She's had so many dicks in her it's ridiculous. Last month she had Chlamydia. I grabbed a toothbrush and began scrubbing my teeth until my mouth was bleeding. Oh my God, has Marvin given me something. I flew to the phone to schedule a doctor's appointment. This is not happening. How am I supposed to handle this? I could handle it better if it was an outside woman. How do you compete with your mother? This motherfucker is sick! I don't know what to do. I sat on the couch crying. They both emerged from the room fully dressed.

"Simone, I've been trying to find a way to tell you that I'm leaving but I couldn't"

"Get out of my house! Get the fuck out now! Before I call the police! I should have you arrested for fucking senior citizens. I hate you! I hate you!"

I popped him in the nose with the barrel of the gun. He responded with a punch that sent a surge of pain across the left side of my face. I lunged toward my mother trying to smack her with the pistol on my way to the floor.

"I'm calling the police." I screamed

"Go head! ...

He grabbed the phone and handed me the receiver.

...here...I'll dial the number for you!"

"I hate you...I hate you both...get the hell out of my house!"

"You ain't got to tell me to leave...I was leaving

anyway! You see that my shit is packed!"

"How could you do this to me? To us? After all I've been through with you? You owe me!"

"Owe you? Bitch, I don't owe you nothing! If anything you're snitching ass owe me! If you would've kept your fucking mouth closed I never would've been locked up. Owe? You owe me 5 years. 1,825 days! It was your testimony that sent me to jail. It was you that took the stand, to snitch on me!"

"Baby, it wasn't like that…they said they would lock me up too! I was worried about Minyon…you said you forgave me! Can't we work this out? I love you? Why are you doing this? You don't want that kind of life. Please baby… I love you" I pleaded.

"You're incapable of loving anyone but yourself. I was bursting my ass and jeopardizing my freedom to provide for you."

"You're leaving me for my mother? C'mon now…you've got to be kidding! Ma what the hell is you doing? This is not happening!"

"Yeah… well whatever…everything was fine as long as I was giving your little dirty ass everything. When the shit got thick and I really needed you; you turned on me. You fake ass ride or die chick! You fell down trying to get on the stand and tell. I should've never come here. If it wasn't for my daughter…I wouldn't have had shit to do with your trifling ass."

"C'mon let's go!" My mother interrupted.

I lashed out and began to physically attack Marvin and my mother again. I was screaming, crying, and throwing wild punches. I zapped out! I was trying to fight my mother and Marvin at the same time. Someone is going to pay for this pain I feel! How could they do this to me? What did I do wrong? Shit, I was afraid of going to jail! **He's** the one who told me to take the deal in exchange for immunity; now he's going to hold it against me. What's wrong with him? Don't I keep him satisfied? Why does he want her? I can't believe I gave up everything to end up like this. As quick as you could snap your fingers; I changed. I started begging and pleading with Marvin to stay. We can't end like this! It can't be over! I've given up a wonderful man who worshiped the ground I walk on; for this. I recited promises of change over and over. I promised I'd be whatever he needed. He just looked at me like I was stupid. Lord, please don't let him leave me.

"Marvin, let me make it up to you. I can be whatever you want."

"You're making a fool out of yourself." My mother sarcastically added kicking my hand free from Marvin's ankle.

"Stay out of this! Go get in the car!" Marvin warned.

My mother fell in line like a trained soldier. As watched in disbelief as she grabbed his overturned bags from the floor and exited.

"Please don't go! What about our daughter? The new baby? What about me? Please Marvin don't go! I love you!" I pleaded.

"You don't love anybody but you're damn self! Now you're with the one you love! Yourself!"

" I'm going to kill myself and the baby!"

"No you're not!" Marvin snapped.
He picked up the rest of his stuff still wrapped in the bed sheet and began to turn the knob. I put the pistol to my head hoping it would stop him in his tracks.

"Marvin! Don't go!" I yelled.
He didn't even look back. The door slammed behind him. Who am I fooling? He knew that I wouldn't do it. Just like he said I love myself too much!

22

What about you? That's the question that jumped into my mind listening to Simone screaming and hollering something about Marvin. Between the vomiting and crying, I can't understand what she's talking about. All I can make out is that Marvin did something and her mother had betrayed her. Like I really give a fuck! Shit, she betrayed me! What goes around comes around. I know one thing; she's giving me a mother-fucking headache; calling me with this bullshit! I've got my own problems. The other line is clicking. I told her to hold on; I don't even think she heard me. So what! I clicked over anyway. I hope she gets tired of waiting and hangs up. How is she going to call me crying about the same dude that she left me for? Whatever he did, that's what she gets! Karma is a bitch!

"Wassup...for real? I'm on my way."

That was Rodney calling. Rhonda's in labor! I clicked back over to Simone and told her I'd call her back. She's still screaming, hollering, and carrying on. It's something about Marvin and her mother; I hung up on her. Fuck her! On the real the only reason I even talk to her is because there's a possibility that the baby she's carrying is mines. If the baby is mine; I'm taking her ass straight to court for custody. That whore will never spend another dime of mine. She's going to be paying me child support when I'm finished with her scandalous ass. Ain't no court in the world going to find her to be a fit mother. No way, no how! No child deserves to have a mother like her! Besides, there's no room in her heart to love anyone else; she's too busy loving herself. Her trifling ass would probably give me the baby anyway. She's too busy tricking for breast feeding and babysitting.

Driving to the hospital I'm starting to get nervous

for Rodney. I've only had this feeling one time before.
That was when my cousin Anthony and his wife Lady T
had their daughter, Toni. She was so cute and little. I
remember I was scared to hold her. She's a grown woman
now; driving cars and working. Anthony and I, walked
holes in the waiting room floor! That fool passed out in the
delivery room. It was crazy! Time sure flies. This time is
going to be even more hilarious because Rodney has no
patience at all. He catches an attitude waiting in line at the
drive thru. My man is going to act a fool; I just know it.
This will be the first baby he's ever seen being born. I got
him passing out. I've to get my camcorder for this one.

In my opinion Rodney and Rhonda can have
everything if he just remains honest with her but I know
that's not going to happen. Rodney's the type of person
that gets bored quickly. Once things start to become
routine and too comfortable, he starts to fuck up. That's
why they've been going through it lately. He knows she
loves him and he is using it to his advantage. He can't help
himself. He believes that she'll always forgive him; now
that she's forgiven him once. I hope he doesn't end up
dogging Rhonda but I know he's going to mess up.
She's a beautiful sister. I wish I had someone like her in
my life. I always end up with the gold-digging bitches.
Why is it that dudes like Rodney always gets the good
women? Where have they been looking? I consider myself
a good man and I'm not the only one out here. Brothers like
me always get the short end of the stick. Women are
always hollering they can't find a good man. That's some
bullshit invented by some woman with a long list of shit
that she wants from a man. They want a fairy tale prince
not a human being. He's got to look like this, drive that,
and make this much with no kids. Where the hell are you
going to find somebody like that nowadays? The real deal
is that when they get a good man, they don't know what to
do with him. They'd rather have a nigga that'll dog them,

cheat on them, and beat their ass. Now the dudes that act like that; they'll love his dirty draws. Why is that? The more abuse the better. Maybe, I should just treat the next female like shit and she'll love me? What you think?

Walking into the delivery waiting room feels like I've just rolled up in the club. Everyone's here! Coco is issuing cigars from the three cartons he's toting. The mood is festive, to say the least. People are celebrating and smiling. Rodney, on the other hand, is a nervous wreck. He stands up. He sits down. He paces. Walking in circles like a dog chasing his tail. He's going crazy. When the nurse came to take him to the scrub room he broke out like a crack-head with a stolen stash running down the corridor. The nurse laughed and commented on the proud soon-to-be father. Proud ain't the word!

As they are wheeling Rhonda into the delivery room you can hear her miles away. She's screaming at the top of her lungs and calling Rodney every name in the book; except a child of God. We all laughed as we listened to Rodney's apologies. He sounds pitiful. The last thing we heard was Rhonda hollering *"Get this baby out of me!"* Twenty minutes later Rodney burst through the delivery room doors; jumping up and down like he was on a trampoline. Screaming at the top of his lungs, it's a girl! I got a little girl! I'm a daddy! This has to be the proudest moment of his life because normally he wouldn't say any shit like that. Between, you and me, I can't help but feel a little jealous. I wish it was me! Had Simone not acted like an ass; it would've been. I can't wait until my seed is born.

"Congratulations…about time you did something right!"

"Way to go brother!"

"I'm a grandma." Sandra screamed.

"Hey, don't forget about me. My daughter had something to do with this too, remember?" Jean reminded.

"Rodney, what are you'll going to name the baby?"

"Kinesha Mercedes Hughes" Rodney replied.

"You named her after Kiki?" Coco asked with tears forming in his eyes.

"Yeah bro, we loved Kiki...she was a strong black woman. This way she'll always be with us."

Rodney and Coco began to hug. I know Coo is feeling some type of way right now. We all miss Kiki; but I know it's nothing compared to how he feels. I hope I never know that feeling! Simone's leaving was bad but I can get over that. Death stays in your heart forever! I'm sorry; I drifted off into thought for a minute. What was I saying? Oh yeah, this is truly going down in history as an event I'll never forget. Then as if someone fired a starter pistol, everyone dashed for the elevator to the recovery room. Rhonda's out for the count! She looks whipped! Baby girl, looks like she just finished a thirty round bout with the heavyweight champ; she's through booking. You'd think we'd never seen a baby before. We almost trampled each other getting to the nursery. The hospital staff keeps warning us to be quiet. They're threatening to throw us out. The expression on Jeans' face says it all. They can try and put us out of here and we'll be on the six o'clock news.

This is one beautiful baby. She has a head full of curly jet-black hair. One dimple in her right cheek; just like Rodney. I wish she'd open up her eyes. She's so beautiful! I'm glad she's not an ugly baby; you know what I'm saying? It's hard to play that off. Rodney must've done something right in his life. With parents like Rodney and Rhonda the baby was destined to be cute. Rhonda's gorgeous and Rodney thinks he's the best looking thing since income tax return checks.

"Oh, she's so precious."

"She's going to be a little heartbreaker."

"Rodney man, you gon' have to beat those little boys off with a stick."

"A big stick." Coco added

"Ha man!"

"Jean, we've got to go shopping."

"Sandra… I beat you to the punch."

"My niece can never have too much."

"You hear these crazy people Kinesha? They're going to spoil you rotten."

"To the core!" Coco added.

"She's going to be a doctor." Jean added.

"No she's going to be a lawyer." Sandra suggested.

"You'll so crazy."

"She's so beautiful. Look how tiny she is. Rodney, I feel sorry for you." I added.

"Why do you say that?" Rodney asked.

"Little boys are going to be camped outside your door." I joked.

"No they ain't, Kinesha ain't dating 'til she's forty. Matter of fact, she's not even coming outside until she's thirty nine and a half." Rodney proclaimed.

"Boy, you sound like a fool."

"G, I want you to do something for me?"

"Anything…wassup?" I asked.

"Rhonda asked Lexie to be her Godmother and I want you to be my daughters' God-father."

"I'd be honored." I replied.

Talk about a surprise; he caught me off guard with that one. I had no idea he was going to ask me that. Now I feel as though I have a daughter too! Damn! He trusts me enough to put his child's life in my hand if something happens to him. I knew we were tight but that was unexpected. Yeah, that's what I'm talking about! I'm going to make sure that I'm always there for her. I promise you, she will never want for anything!

"Visiting hours are over. I'm sorry but I'm going to have to ask you to leave." The nurse requested.

"Keep an eye on my baby and my lady. Rhonda, baby, I'll be back in a little while." Rodney ordered.

"Don't let anything happen to them. I'm holding you responsible."

"Yeah, cause we'd hate to have to blow this mother up!"

"She's in great hands. I'll personally watch her, I promise!" The nurse replied laughing.

"She's beautiful ain't she?"

"Yes sir she is. Congratulations! Is this your first child?"

"No, I have a son."

"I'm quite sure you'll be the perfect family. May God continue to bless you."

"Thank you."

"Now, I'm sorry but you really must leave now so that the mother and baby can get some rest."

"Okay...okay! Can I just hold her one more time before I leave?" Rodney pleaded

"Sure but you're going to have to make it quick."

Watching Rodney hold Kinesha was like watching him show off priceless art. As we left the nursery everyone had these ear-to-ear smiles stuck on our faces. We look like we're in some kind of toothpaste commercial.

"Party time!"

"Cigars...cigars!" Coco chanted

"Meet me at my house." Jean requested.

"Alright."

"Okay."

Everyone piled into separate cars. Parade style we drove to Jeans' house. The sounds of Charlie Wilson ride shotgun with me. I can't help but think about Simone and the baby she's carrying. I wonder if that's my baby. You think that's my baby? I wonder what she was trying to tell me earlier. Oh shit, you think something happened to the baby? I got to call her back and find out what's going on with her. Everything about her ass if foul!

Once inside Jean's house the party is on! Turnup!

255

Everyone's smoking cigars; even Sandra and my mother.
You should see them. Dancing! Popping bottle after bottle
of Moet! Jean is sipping on that Smirnoff kind of heavily. I
feel her though! Finally something to celebrate! The last
couple of months have been rough but we survived. After
telling the delivery story 100 times and laughing at Rodney,
they broke out the oldies but goodies. Between cheers and
tears we started dancing. I often wish that I'd grown up
when my parents did; life was much simpler then. Black
people were united. Strong families! Strong leaders!
Strong everything!

    I know everyone is thinking the same thing. You
can't help but remember Kiki at a time like this; she was
the life of the party. I miss her so much. The saddest part
of the whole thing is that we found out she was pregnant
when she got killed. Life can be cruel than a mother fucker.
You feel me? She or Coco didn't even know yet. Man, on
man; they were about to have it all. They would have made
it. I still feel responsible for that shit! I wish they never
took me out that night. She would still be here today!
That's it no more drinking for me. Every time I drink I
think of her; her death starts fucking with me.

    Even though we all have to go to work in the
morning, we partied until the break of dawn; like we don't
have jobs. Lexie left early; she said hanging with us would
put her in the poor house. As much money as she has I
know she ain't trying to end up there! Everyone was too
drunk to drive so we crashed. After a couple of hours and
two cups of coffee; I've sobered up enough to drive. Its
6:30 in the morning. It's a good thing my first appointment
isn't until two o'clock; I'm going to go home and catch me
some more Z's. Rodney had mumbled something earlier
about going to see Kenya to celebrate. I thought he was
joking; I guess he wasn't. He disappeared in the middle of
the night. I hope she ain't got him getting high again.
When he's on that shit he doesn't give a fuck about nothing

or nobody; just them drugs! I wish he never met Kenya.
Man, you should see her; I hate that bitch almost as much
as Simone! Excuse my language. I don't' usually refer to
women like that; but her and Simone's asses are
exceptions.

I don't even want to go to work today; I thought to
myself as I drove to Annapolis for my two o'clock
appointment. I have been real lazy lately. I think it's just
leftover embarrassment from what I did. Pride is a
motherfucker! I still can't believe I did that bamma ass shit!
I went out like a cold-blooded pussy-whipped punk on that
one. We here; time to handle business. It was an easy sale.
They already wanted the house so I didn't have to work
that hard. Counting my newly earned commission is giving
me some energy. I drove up Wisconsin Avenue and picked
up some gifts for my godchild. Speaking of gifts, Simone
hasn't called me back yet. I guess whatever she was
talking about couldn't have been that important. If she
wanted something she'd worry me to death. I ran back and
forth to the hospital like everyone else. She had some
minor complications during the delivery so they kept her
and extra day. She's coming home tomorrow. Tonight
Rodney's coming over to watch the Redskins game with
me. I'm going to holler at him about this Kenya shit too! I
want to know what's really going on! I think she's got him
getting high again. That's my partner so I can look at him
and tell! We went through this shit once already. He's here.

As soon as he crossed the door seal we cracked
open some Ciroc. The delivery dude arrived with the pizza
and wings. After a couple of shots, Rodney lunched out. He
started talking some crazy shit!

"Greg man…you know what?" Rodney started.
"What?"
"I've been thinking…I love Rhonda but I don't
want to be with her. I'm not in love with her!"
"Say what? Man, you drunk…lay your ass down."

"Naw dawg...I'm serious. This is some real shit I'm telling you! For real! I'm not ready for the husband and family thing right now!"

"Yeah right!"

"What? You don't believe me or something?"

"Juice man...have you been smoking that shit."

"Sike! I'm just bullshitting! You know that Rhonda is my baby!"

For a minute he had me going. I mean, he just came out the blue with that shit. He got that druggie look though! It wasn't long before Rodney passed out on the floor and I ain't about to pick his ass up either. He'll be sleeping on the floor tonight. And they call me crazy? Shit! If he even entertained the thought of choosing Kenya over Rhonda, he's the one that needs to be in the mental ward. We both fell off into a drunken slumber in the living room. The furthest I made it was to the couch.

When I woke up the next morning Rodney was gone. I don't even know when he left. I hope he came to his senses. He needs to stay away from Kenya. He was definitely high! Now that she's got that baby, she's got her hooks in him. It's already one o'clock. I wonder what time Rhonda's getting home. I think I'm going to go by and drop off the stuff that I'd bought for Kinesha. Rodney is probably already picked her up by now. She was supposed to be released at noon. I jumped in the shower and got dressed. As I was on my way out the door the phone started ringing. I started not to answer it but for some reason I did. I thought it may be Simone calling back. I answered to someone crying on the other end. It sounds like Rhonda.

"Hello...hello...Rhonda, is that you?"

"Yes." She whimpered.

"What's wrong? Why do you sound like that?"

"I've been calling Rodney's' cell phone all morning. At first it would just ring. Then it was turned off and went straight to voicemail. He knew he was supposed to pick me up at noon. I got scared thinking that something has happened to him so I tried calling on his cell phone again.

"Did he answer or call back yet?"

"Yeah…he called back to tell me that he doesn't love me anymore and he's not picking me up. I'm too embarrassed to call my mother and I don't want to see anyone who slightly resembles Rodney. Lexie's has gone out of town. I have no one else to call. Will you please come and get us?" Rhonda pleaded.

"Sure baby! I'll be right there."

I take it that Juice wasn't joking last night. He was dead serious. This is some cold shit! How could he kick her to the curb like that? I wouldn't treat a dog like that. He could've at least picked her up. I flew to the hospital and picked up a shattered, badly hurt version of what was once a strong woman. Baby girl is going through it! She's trying to put on a brave front for the nurses but everyone can see she's faking. She's fighting back tears with all her might. With her "*It's a girl*" balloons and two bags, she eased into the car and covered her face with Kinesha's blanket trying to muffle her cries. I want to comfort her but I don't know what to say; so we rode in silence. Rhonda's rocking, crying and holding onto Kinesha's diaper bag for dear life. This is the saddest shit I've ever seen. How could he do her like this?

Never in my life have I seen anything like this. Rhonda's so heartbroken she can't even walk. Between the pain from the delivery and the pain in her heart; she's weak. Rodney has packed his clothes and left. She came home to an empty house; just like I did. All of his shit is gone! We stood in the doorway with our mouths hanging open in disbelief. This was like dejavu for me. I know exactly how she feels right now. Next thing I know; her knees buckled and she collapsed onto the floor. Heartbreak folded her body up into the fetal position as she washed the floor with her tears. I sat the baby down and scooped Rhonda into my arms. I carried her upstairs and gently laid her on the bare mattress and box spring Rodney had left behind on the floor. I laid Kinesha on the mattress beside her mom and I laid on the cold hardwood floor in disbelief. Rodney didn't even leave the girl a blanket. I have no experience at all with babies but I spent the rest of the night taking care of Kinesha to the best of my ability. Rhonda had cried herself to sleep.

As soon as the sun rose, I called Jean and she came over. When Jean got arrived I couldn't even look her in the face. I feel like I've done something wrong. Damn! Later, I went back to check up on Rhonda but she was gone. So I figured she'd be at Jeans. I went over there looking for her. Her mother said she'd gone away to get herself together. She went to visit her friend Kim who just moved to Atlanta for a little while. I walked away from Jean's porch heartbroken and wondering if I'll ever see Rhonda or Kinesha again. I don't know if I'll see her; but when I see Rodney I'm going fuck his ass up. Then I'm going to drag his ass to rehab. I know exactly how she feels and I wouldn't wish that feeling on my worst enemy. I know that Rodney is a better man than this! I guess I gave him too much underserved credit. I feel like a co-defendant to his fucked up emotional crime. How could he treat Kenya like a queen and Rhonda like shit? This right here lets me know for fact that he's back on that shit! That's the only thing that would make him do some foul shit like this. Cocaine is a helluva drug! I hope I see her again.

To Be Continued!

UP NEXT

What do you do when your best friend and man both leave you for dead? Find out what happen's to Rhonda's cousin Karen! Will she survive?

Using Lies As Alibi's

O. G. Smiley

turns up the heat!!!!

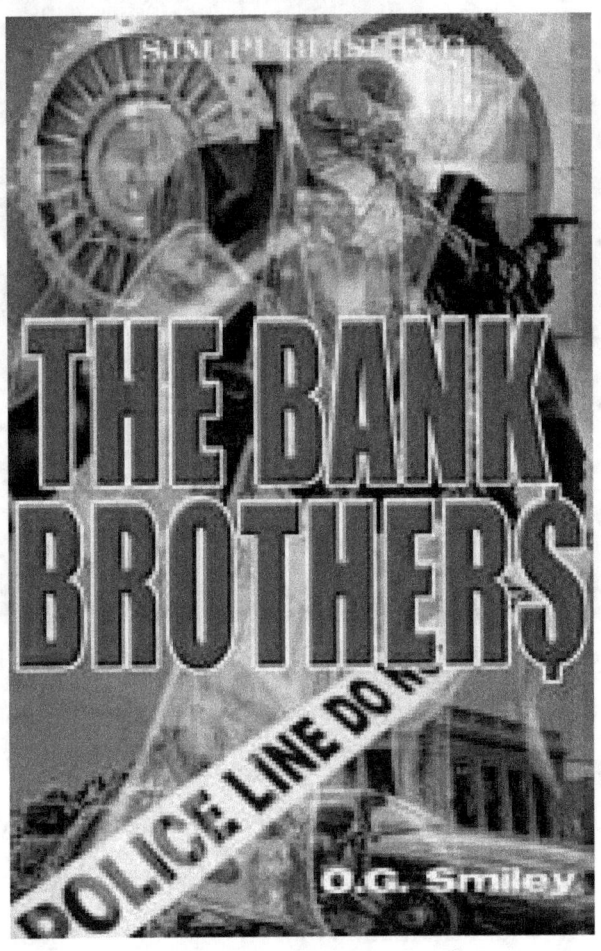

It's going to be a very hot summer!

Upscale LIVE Magazine is a free bi-monthly online magazine available in all social media formats. It is our goal to shine the spotlight on the movers and shakers making a difference! We salute you! Contact us: livemagonline@gmail.com www.sjmlivemedia.com

Are you a mover or shaker? SJM Publishing wants to hear from you! Maybe you can be spotlighted in our bi-monthly online magazine Upscale Live. You must be accomplished in your field to be eligible for interviews and covers. We do have a section for those on the grind. Like us on Facebook and email your information to livemagonline@gmail.com for potential article. You never know who you're standing right next to. Check out past issues to see what I mean.

Meet Queen Benjamin! She's as beautiful as she is deadly!

Check out SJM's new webisode mini-series in April.

It will leave you begging for more!

SJM on the web!

Keep up with SJM

Like us on Facebook

SJM Publishing – Willi Will – Fatboy Crank

for William Casanova

Follow me @SJMSilk

on Twitter and IG

Follow William Casanova

On Twitter @ Fatboycrank

Follow Will @ Williweed

On Twitter and IG

THANK

YOU

FOR

YOUR

SUPPORT!!!!

www.sjm-publishing.com